White Hill

Devon De'Ath

Copyright © 2021 Devon De'Ath

All rights reserved.

ISBN-13: 979-8-71101-504-8

This is a work of fiction. Names, characters, businesses, places, events, locales and incidents are either the products of the author's imagination or used in a fictitious manner. Any resemblance to actual persons, living or dead, or actual events is purely coincidental.

DEDICATION

In loving memory of Martin Harding :

Kind friend and former colleague with a wonderful dry wit.

A talented mechanic with a great love of cars. You are missed.

CONTENTS

1	Many Roads	7
2	Bare Cupboards	29
3	Charlie	47
4	Ultimum Religio	69
5	Conflicting Passions	87
6	Flawed Communications	108
7	A Storm of Spirits	128
8	Woodland Meetings	147
9	Seeking Answers	170
10	Consultation	190
11	Louise	213
12	The Vessel	236
13	Her Cup Runneth Over	259
14	Unexpected Visitors	283
15	On the Offensive	305
16	Julliberrie Down	319
17	The Path	342

1
Many Roads

Harry Andrea had stayed off the sauce all night. And what a night: a hectic social playing bass at a private New Year's Eve bash, way out in the sticks. He hauled his solid instrument flight case into the rear of a battered blue Mercedes C-Class; the apple of some stock broker's eye, a quarter of a century ago.

"Good gig, Haralambos." Terry Wyatt tucked a piccolo snare drum alongside assorted percussion pieces filling his red Volvo estate.

Harry raised an eyebrow at the use of his Greek Cypriot first name. A second-generation immigrant to the UK, he'd adopted the anglicised alternative 'Harry' as a moniker since his late teens. Even his own father, a stick-in-the-mud Greek traditionalist, accepted the change over time. But Terry and the other band members liked to roll out 'Haralambos' whenever they were in a buoyant mood. Harry closed the boot lid, then pulled a packet of fags from his jacket pocket. He inserted a cigarette between lips chilled by the frosty night air, then cupped a lighter in front and took a long drag.

Terry secured his own vehicle and watched Harry blow out a cloud of smoke. "I can do that without the benefit of shoving a death stick in my gob, mate." He zipped his coat higher and exhaled a stream of hot air which condensed into vapour. "Bloomin' brass monkeys out here after the atmosphere in that barn."

Harry took another drag. He held the smoke captive in his mouth before expelling it in a well-defined ring. "I could have murdered a drink. It's the only downside to gigging when you've got to drive yourself home afterwards."

Terry twisted an idle foot into the gravel. "Is that what your extra bass slapping and popping was about? You wanted a drink? Shit, I thought you were going to compete with Paul for solos. Either that or drop your guitar, take a stage dive and go crowd surfing."

Harry grinned and patted one hand against a portly stomach. "With my frame? Our clients wouldn't appreciate calling an ambulance for squashed guests."

Terry pulled out his car keys. "Are you heading back to West Malling tonight?"

Harry dropped his cigarette and crushed it into the driveway with his shoe; a mirror of the drummer's previous unconscious action. "Nah. Olive sent me a text asking if I'd like to stay over. Time to see in what's left of the New Year with a err…"

"Bang?" Terry smirked.

Harry shrugged. "Your words, not mine."

Terry opened the Volvo driver's door. "You two have been together for a couple of months now. Where does she live again?"

"Bodsham. Near 'The Timber Batts.' You remember."

"That's right. You met her after that Halloween gig we played there. Great ale house. I must take Carly back for a meal. Well, have a safe journey."

"Cheers, Terry." Harry slid into his car and inserted the ignition key. After three attempts by the starter motor, the German executive ride caught and turned over. The engine revved hard at pressure from Harry's frustrated right foot against the accelerator pedal. A faint whiff of burnt oil teased his flaring nostrils. Harry clicked his seatbelt home and muttered to himself. "I must get that head gasket checked before it blows." His stare fell upon the odometer reading of 235,000 miles. "The whole bloody top end needs attention by now." He crunched the gears into reverse and backed in an arc as Terry tooted the Volvo's horn and disappeared down the drive. Harry flashed his headlights, then rolled forward to follow until they reached a lane near Throwley Forstal. Here the drivers parted ways. Their band member peers had left ten minutes earlier. Harry turned his windshield fan up to high, then cranked the temperature control into the red. He leaned across and retrieved a chamois leather from the glove box to clear a patch of misting, chilled glass above the steering wheel. High hedgerows flashed past on either side. He signalled right onto the southbound A251, fishtailing the vehicle on a patch of ice during an enthusiastic pull away. Now Harry's thoughts turned to Olive. A feisty, freckled brunette with massive brown eyes, she'd turned his head more than any other woman. Not that the list was long. Harry avoided the clichéd, stereotypical promiscuity of gigging musicians in favour of lasting connection and true intimacy, wherever he could find it. He was a no-nonsense beefcake with a marshmallow heart. A well-concealed pussycat in tough guy clothing.

The fat-chimneyed 'Halfway House' pub appeared across a roundabout at the village of Challock. Harry drove straight past. *I'll cut through the woods. I can climb straight up through Wye and Hastingleigh once I've crossed the valley. No sense driving into Ashford.* He flicked the indicator stalk to signal left, then turned at a sign which read *'Wye.'* An interest marker for *'Stour Valley Arts'* hung below it. Twenty yards in, intermittent white central divider lines disappeared as the side road narrowed. Trees arched over the thoroughfare in long, organic tunnels. A warning sign for crossing deer caused Harry to glance left and right into the edges of thick, mixed conifer and broad leafed woodland. At 588 hectares, King's Wood (often referred to by locals as 'Challock' in recognition of its closest hamlet) proved a popular beauty and recreation spot by day, and shagging venue by night. Harry grinned to himself as the main, uneven forest car park drifted past his passenger window. Three vehicles with interior lights on and misted glass bounced and jostled in rhythmic motions at various spots. Harry wondered how many would receive a knock on their windows from passing police patrols. The raging hormones of Kent's next generation of teenagers, interrupted by the long and disappointing arm of the law. The sight of those cars getting a gentle suspension workout turned his thoughts to Olive once more. *I hope she doesn't fall asleep before I arrive.*

The road descended the North Downs in a snaking ribbon of high-banked curves. Harry shifted into a lower gear. A fawn leapt through the bushes to his right as he rounded a sharp left-hander. He squinted after it, then looked straight ahead and shrieked. "Shit!"

A woman clad in white stood before him, hemmed in by the lane's natural earthen barriers. There was nowhere to swerve the Mercedes. All Harry could do was jam on his anchors. Mesmerising, flashing eyes stared straight at him. Pallid lips curled into an eerie smile as the motor's bonnet made contact with the figure in a bone-crunching impact. Her still-smiling face slammed into the windshield before she rolled off the car. Brakes squealed in protest to accompany the C-Class lurching to a halt.

Harry's skull pressed back into the headrest. A deafening rush of blood throbbed in his ears while he fought for breath and the nerve to get out and investigate. *Pull yourself together, Harry. If she's still alive, that woman will need the paramedics.* He reached for his mobile phone, clicked on the vehicle's hazard lights, and then released the driver's door. With stilted movements he rose into an icy, moisture-heavy blackness enshrouding the unlit rural lane. The phone's screen lit up a dim circle around him. Harry used it like a torch while he crouched to peer beneath the car. The road lay thick with frost. It glittered in crisp reflection, but remained empty. Harry worked his way around the rear, sweeping the phone from side to side. With every heartless motion, he feared the uncovering of a lifeless foot or hand. Or worse still, those eyes gazing up at him in a piercing, empty death stare. But his search proved fruitless. Harry's breath puffed in fast-paced clouds of agitated steam. "Where can she have gone?" He spoke the words aloud for comfort on that silent, wooded hill. *Did I hit that woman hard enough to toss her body clear of the banks?* He scratched his head. The drone of an approaching engine climbed towards him from The Great Stour Valley. Harry stepped behind the Mercedes' boot for his own protection, lest he suffer the same fate as his unfortunate victim. When a ŠKODA patrol vehicle from Kent Police rounded the bend, he didn't know whether to feel relieved or worried. Roof strobes illuminated the narrow lane with pulses of blue, before he even had time to step in front of its occupants.

The police car drew up alongside, its driver's window lowering. A female officer craned her head out. "Good evening, Sir. Have you broken down?"

Harry gulped. "No. Thank goodness you're here. I struck a woman with my car. She was standing in the middle of the road when I rounded the bend. I wasn't driving fast, but had no way of avoiding her. She rolled over my bonnet. I can't find her anywhere."

The female officer exchanged glances with a man beside her, then jerked her head past Harry towards the wooded bank. "We'll pull up behind you and search the bushes."

Ten minutes later, after a brief examination of the undergrowth, both police officers hopped down into the lane. Each clicked off a powerful torch.

"There's no sign of her anywhere." The female officer checked no other vehicles were approaching from either direction, while her colleague walked to the front of Harry's car.

He painted the badge with his torch beam. "If you'd struck someone hard enough for them to clear the bonnet, I would expect damage to the front of your car."

Harry shuffled over to join him. "I haven't even checked it." He blinked at the aged but otherwise undamaged bumper and radiator grille. "How is that possible?"

The male officer stepped closer to study Harry's eyes, then sniffed. "Can you provide a brief description of your movements this evening, Sir? The basics will suffice: Where you've come from; what you were doing; where you were headed."

Harry cleared his throat. "Of course. I played bass guitar at a New Year's gig near Throwley Forstal. After it finished, I was due to stay at my girlfriend's place in Bodsham." Harry waved a loose hand in a southerly direction.

"I see. Did you drink anything at the gig?"

"No. I'd like to have sampled one or two, but never do that before driving. Breathalyse me if you want."

"Are you taking any medication: prescription or otherwise?"

Harry frowned. "I'm no druggie. Look, I know I'm a musician, but please hear me out. I'm not into all that nonsense. I'm telling you, I struck a woman. What I experienced before your arrival wasn't the product of my imagination, alcohol or drugs."

The female officer approached. "Can you describe her?"

Harry rubbed a stubbly chin. "Not well. It all happened so fast. She was wearing a white dress. Age… mid-thirties. I'd peg her around two or three years younger than myself." Hairs rose on the back of his neck, causing Harry to cringe.

"What is it?" the female officer asked.

"Her face. I know it sounds weird, but she was standing there smiling at me when I collided with her."

The police exchanged another hurried glance, then slipped away to stand out of earshot beside their patrol car.

Harry strained to listen. All he caught was snatches of the man asking, "EBA?" to which his colleague shook her head and added, "He's not tanked. You know what this is, Dean. The whole 'smiling' thing, undamaged car, the lot. How long have you worked this area?"

Harry stamped his feet against the tarmac to keep warm, awaiting the verdict from his would-be rescuers.

"Harry? Oh my God, what happened? Did the party last longer than expected?" A bleary-eyed Olive flung her arms around Harry's shoulders from the welcome warmth of an opened cottage door. "I was worried you'd had an accident or broken down."

Harry held her close. He found it impossible to conceal a trembling in his arms.

Olive stepped back to touch one of his wrists. "You're shaking. Come out of the cold and tell me what's going on."

Twenty minutes and a good stiff drink later, Harry sat on Olive's sofa having laid out the story of his shocking encounter. He set down an empty tumbler of brandy and cuddled Olive. "That's not the worst of it."

"Go on." Olive rubbed his leg. "That woman must have gone somewhere. What did the police say to you after their private chat?"

Harry took a breath. "That's what left me so unsettled. They told me this isn't the first time a motorist has struck someone at that spot, only to discover no body and their vehicle undamaged. The victim always locks eyes with the driver. She smiles right before the collision, too."

Olive stiffened. "Whoa. Are you saying the Police suggested you hit a ghost?"

"They did more than suggest it, though both

refrained from using the actual term. Deliberately, if you ask me. I suppose it harms their impartiality to categorise an unexplained event in concrete terms. Either way, my encounter wasn't new to them. They'd heard it all before."

"Flippin' heck. No wonder you were shaken. I'm gonna be terrified to go anywhere near that spot after dark, now. It's that lane down from Challock through the woods towards Wye?"

"Yeah. White Hill, they called it."

Even if he'd retained enough energy for romantic mattress shenanigans, by the time the couple tumbled into bed Harry's libido had evaporated. Images of that smiling woman's face distracted him. Her visage remained after his eyes closed. He spooned up behind Olive, amazed at his need for her warmth and closeness to instil a sense of security. Harry Andrea promised himself he'd never take the lane over White Hill again.

* * *

Nick Preston could best be described as sturdy. A whisker over six feet tall, this broad-shouldered man sported a muscular neck and short, shocking ginger hair clinging fast with tenacious, limpet-like determination to a diamond-shaped head. Watery blue, deep-set eyes scanned the world with a smouldering intensity and combined with a resolute jaw to give nothing away. Thin lips rising into a minor upturn around the edges could be smirking, indifferent, amused or masking a temper on the boil. It was impossible for the uninitiated to tell. Even his wife missed Nick's subtle emotional cues occasionally and misread him.

On this winter's morning, three days into the New Year, his aforementioned wife, Alana, followed half a dozen paces behind through the churchyard gates of St Mary Magdalene & St Denys, Midhurst.

Alana Preston's visual aspect offered a stark contrast to her husband. A mouth half open in a brilliant white smile, revealing the top row of teeth, echoed laughter, positivity and playful joy in her aquamarine eyes. Alana's side-parted, shoulder-length blonde hair and dark roots flowed around a teardrop head to settle above attractive womanly curves. A mere inch shorter than Nick and five years younger than his four decades on this earth, the pair still turned heads regularly. Today her shoulders sloped forward and that ivory smile remained tucked behind strained lips. The distance between the couple suggested nothing of romance or connection; rather the opposite.

Midhurst derived its name from the Old English for 'Middle Wooded Hill.' A man-made jewel of the West Sussex landscape, this ancient, quaint market town skirted the River Rother in a quiet spot twelve miles north of the cathedral city of Chichester. Ninety-four listed Tudor, Georgian and Victorian buildings tumbled over one another amidst narrow streets laid down long before the idea of the motor car entered any human imagination. If the man and woman who halted beside a clean headstone ever derived any pleasure from their hometown's aesthetic beauty, it passed unnoticed at that moment.

Nick squatted to wipe dove poop from the granite marker. His fingers rested in a reverent pause above the engraved lettering:

'Grant Preston - who departed this life, aged six. Suffer little children, and forbid them not, to come unto me: for of such is the kingdom of heaven.'

Alana slowed her already hesitant pace to a virtual crawl. She inhaled a shallow breath before speaking. "Grant would have loved the town's December street party this year."

Nick didn't respond or turn to face her. His watery blue eyes remained fixed on the lettering.

Alana tried again. "We must bring some fresh flowers with us, once the frosty nights end."

Nick gripped the stone and bowed his head. "Will that do anything for him?" His voice cut cold and hard as the granite of their son's memorial.

Alana flushed. "Damn it, Nick, he was my boy too. I carried him; I gave birth to him. He was my pride and joy." Tears brimmed her ducts, threatening an impending overflow. "How much longer will you punish me over this? It's been eighteen months."

"I'm surprised you weren't too busy with your phone to notice." Nick winced as the last word rasped from a crooked mouth. Alana didn't deserve that. He turned and rose.

Alana put her face in her hands and sobbed. "Why are you doing this? Destroying our marriage won't bring Grant back. Don't you think I torment myself enough with 'what ifs' about the event? What if I hadn't used my mobile? What if that speeding driver hadn't cut through a side street to avoid traffic? Jesus, what if I'd not been in shock and noted the vehicle details before it sped away?" She lowered her hands and stamped her foot. "You haven't cornered the market on needing closure. Grant was my only child and I want him back."

Nick sighed and lifted his face to the church spire. "I left my meeting on top of the world that day. It must have been around the time Grant was hit. The campaign came together; my clients signed on the dotted line. All I needed to cap it off was a slap-up lunch with my wife and son." He scratched the back of his neck. "I can't get past this, Alana. I realise you never get over bereavement, but shouldn't things have eased by now?" He glanced back at the inscription. "I need some assurance he's okay. It can't end like this. When I hugged him after our football kick-about in the garden that morning, I told him we'd visit any shop in Chichester he wanted, to buy something nice. A special treat. I never got to keep my promise."

"You think I didn't want to fulfil my own promises to him? Why did I give up my career as a council project officer to become a playgroup assistant?"

Nick folded his arms. "Because the council were cutting back and offered you a golden handshake."

Alana's mouth dropped open. "You know I loved that job. I saw an opportunity to provide childcare for Grant in a way many mothers can't. Those early years are so important. Most parents miss the best of them. I was sad when he started school."

Nick gritted his teeth. "Early years are all we'll ever have, thanks to that fuckin' phone call."

Alana scowled. "And I suppose the hit-and-run driver had nothing to do with it? Grant loved to dash about everywhere. He was full of beans."

"All the more reason to keep hold of him near a road. Even a quiet backstreet."

Alana rubbed her reddened eyes. "It was an accident, Nick. A horrible injustice we'll never understand or be able to change. Do you think Grant would want his mummy and daddy fighting like this every five minutes? Remember how sensitive he became when we quarrelled."

Nick wanted to say: *'Is that what you tell yourself to ease the guilt?'* Even in his state of constant heartbreak, he couldn't pummel his wife with an accusation like that. He loved Alana. Why was he pushing her away? Nick squeezed his eyes shut. *The last eighteen months have taught me there's no God. How can there be? But if there's any decency to the universe, please let this stop. Do you hear that, Universe? Help me see Grant again. Help me know he's safe and happy. In the name of goodness, help me stop taking this out on Alana.*

No more words were spoken at the graveside and the morning ticked on.

* * *

Nick exited the coast-bound M20 at junction nine, then followed sat nav instructions for the A28 Canterbury Road through the outskirts of Ashford. His silver Honda CR-V whispered like a sewing machine; quiet to the point of mock sympathy with its driver's inner turmoil. Nick glanced at the front passenger seat. Empty. Emptier than the pit of his stomach. Emptier than ever before, due to uncertainty whether Alana would ever sit beside him again. The rear seats remained empty too; devoid of the bubbly six-year-old who'd kept his father's head on a swivel with shouts of, '*Look at that, Dad.*'

Relationship tensions hadn't eased after that New Year visit to Grant's resting place. Nick mulled the term 'resting place' over in his mind as he pulled up at a set of lights in Kennington. *It's not a resting place. It's the spot we buried his lifeless flesh and bones out of sight. Where is he? Where is my boy?*

Two angry blasts from a car horn behind informed Nick the lights had turned green during his anguished meditation. "Keep your hair on." He grimaced at the rear-view mirror, then slipped into gear. The CR-V pulled away in a northeasterly direction, past a sign indicating the way to Canterbury and Brenzett.

A temporary relocation to Kent offered a ray of hope into the prison cell of Nick's grief. The split with Alana had been amicable, if painful. After much wrangling, she'd agreed to a period of separation and remained at their Midhurst home. Nick found a one-bedroom cottage to rent in Chilham - a picturesque village of mainly period houses located five miles southwest of Canterbury as the crow flies. He could be home to West Sussex in a couple of hours, yet remained far enough away to ease the persistent sting of loss. A helpful distance from constant reminders of the happy life stolen from him. Stour Cottage presented an opportunity to get his head together. Would it be too late to patch things up with Alana afterwards? Could their relationship ever return to how it was before? How did people move on? Would either of them ever countenance trying for another child? How would their past overshadow any second attempt at building a new family? There were too many questions he couldn't answer.

Nick drummed his fingers on the steering wheel, noticing a right-hand turn off for the village of Wye. Opposite the junction on his left, a rural lane vanished upwards into a wooded escarpment after a short stretch of flat ground. Modest road furniture designated the unremarkable thoroughfare: *'White Hill.'* He carried straight along the A28 without a second thought. The Great Stour River wended its way through this broad-bottomed valley, with that wooded hill close by on his left and another distant bank of undulating downs beyond Wye to his right. Nick mentally recited the cottage particulars which he'd committed to memory with characteristic accuracy:

'Attractive Grade 2 listed character cottage in a quiet location near Chilham village centre. The cottage which can

be let furnished or part-furnished, comprises a modern fitted kitchen with white goods, dining room with French doors to a terrace, and a lounge with inglenook fireplace and wood burner. Upstairs a bathroom with shower over bath, large double bedroom featuring lots of wardrobe and storage space and a landing suitable for use as a study complete the accommodation. An additional £109 per month is payable to the Landlord for council tax, water bills, ground maintenance and broadband Internet provision. The Landlord will charge electricity in accordance with usage. There is electric heating and off-road parking.'

From the pictures, it appeared the 'cottage' was in fact one third of a larger, traditional Kent yeoman's house, subdivided to provide its owners an additional income. Nick took the furnished option. He wasn't setting up home for the long term, after all.

Rolling hills and the river drew nearer to the road, with the watercourse keeping it a close, constant companion. The CR-V hung a left down a narrow lane called Branch Road that cut diagonally across a river meadow. Nick nodded to himself as a small country sports centre and surgery whipped by on either side. Two pubs, a cafe, church, castle and market square summed Chilham up in a nutshell. Yet those additional amenities he'd passed, combined with a fire station (not to mention a primary school across the lane from his new residence), made the compact population centre better served than many. A mainline railway station sat across the A28 from the village, beside the River Stour flowing towards Canterbury. Timber-framed houses with latticed windows and long, sloping roofs of Kent Peg tiles clung to the settlement's low hillside. Clumps of higgledy-piggledy properties flowed down across the incline in various directions towards leveller ground. Chilham was a place with the dubious honour of being on the way to somewhere else. Despite significant historical importance - including a period as a camp for Julius Caesar during his invasion of Britannia - its geographic position allowed the world (and over-development) to pass the village by. This suited Nick fine. He was looking for peace, but with the convenience of easy travel should the need arise.

The Woolpack Inn sat at the fork of a quiet road into the even quieter village. The right-hand branch ascended to the market square and church. Its sudden gradient surprised Nick, prompting a downshift. At its crest, the steep lane - edged by chocolate box homes on either side - bent first right and then opened left onto the market square, around which huddled The White Horse pub and more Tudor architectural marvels on three sides. The fourth side lay occupied by two impressive wooden castle gates and associated stone gatehouses. Occasional, teasing glimpses of a Jacobean stately home could be stolen along its drive from the correct viewing angle. An original, twelfth century hexagonal Norman keep hunkered down a short distance beyond. At the opposite end of the square, the clock and bell tower of St Mary's church dwarfed the village's second pub. Lanes disappeared in different, downhill directions from each of the market square's four corners.

Nick bore round to the left and followed the southeasterly road down School Hill. Beyond and opposite the primary school, he reached the characterful building owned by his new landlords. He rolled the Honda into a parking space labelled '*Stour Cottage.*' The strains of winter birdsong and the aroma of fresh wood smoke applied instant balm to his nerves upon exiting the vehicle. "Perfect."

The main rear door of the larger house portion swung open.

"Mr Preston?" A portly woman in a floral apron waddled out to greet the new arrival. Rosy cheeks and grey hair in a tight bun suggested a homemaker to Nick. That boded well for attention to detail in his bolt hole abode.

"Please call me Nick. You must be Mrs Calendar?"

"Doreen." The woman offered her hand.

Nick delivered a warm shake of greeting. "This is a pleasant spot. Just what I'm looking for."

Doreen retrieved a key from her apron pocket and clocked the ring on his finger. "Will your wife be joining you?"

"There are no immediate plans in that regard. I didn't explain earlier, but we're working through a troublesome time following the loss of our young son." Nick flinched. *We? I'm the one who needs help.*

Doreen placed lithe but work-toughened fingers across her mouth. "I'm sorry. I had no idea."

Nick fidgeted. "We've agreed to a temporary break, to stave off terminal relationship disaster." At that moment he wanted to crawl under the nearest rock. *I never realised what a cop-out this all sounds. If Alana ever takes me back, I'll be gob-smacked.*

Doreen studied him a little closer. "Then I hope the serenity of Chilham brings a speedy recovery. Not that Brian - that's my husband - and I are looking to get rid of you soon."

Nick relaxed at a kind twinkle in her eye. "Thank you."

Doreen walked from the driveway back to the lane with him. "Here's the key. You have your own door there." She pointed to a thick, blackened oak portal, beside which hung a square lantern. "I'll let you explore and settle in alone, without my fussing about. The property is separate inside, with no connecting doors to our portion. You've a basket of logs by the burner. Help yourself to more from the garden store as required. Brian and I don't charge extra for that. We know a local woodsman."

"I noticed a lot of woodlands surrounding the village. Do you know any decent walks?" Nick asked.

"The most popular is The Pilgrims' Way. It passes through the village on its route from Winchester to Canterbury. You'll find a road junction down from the cottage leading to a lane called Mountain Street." Doreen grinned. "There are no mountains around here. It's only a name. If you follow that a mile past the castle grounds rear entrance and a row of cottages on the other side, you'll reach a track. After a straight stretch, it bends uphill into King's Wood above Godmersham. There are numerous trails to follow, once inside. The woods are maintained by the Forestry Commission and remain open to the public. Keep an eye out for forest operation signs when they're cutting, though. Should you still be with us during the spring, King's Wood enjoys carpets of Bluebells. They're breathtaking, if you time your visit well."

"Thank you, I'll keep that in mind." Nick took the keys from her.

Doreen hesitated. "I didn't ask your profession?"

"I'm a freelance campaign marketing consultant."

Doreen blinked.

Nick cracked a half smile, familiar with that typical response to his job title. "I work from home, except for rare face-to-face meetings." His mouth dried up at the memory of those work activities the day Grant died, resurfacing through mental association. "I assess marketing campaigns for corporate clients, before they commit significant funds to them."

Doreen tightened her hair bun. "I see. Well, our Internet speed is pretty good for a rural village. Your predecessor was a financial guru with three different computers running city market data. He never experienced problems. Nice chap."

"I'm sure it'll be fine." Nick faced uphill towards the market square. "I discovered both pubs on my way in. I read about a cafe, also?"

"The Copper Kettle. Straight up the hill; you can't miss it. A half-timbered affair opposite the castle gate. Not that my description narrows the field much in Chilham." She chuckled under her breath. "The cafe features a hanging metal sign of a kettle. They make nice fruit scones and serve a decent mushroom omelette."

"Great." Nick shivered from a chill breeze, while cold light dimmed in a grey winter's sky. "I'd better unpack and sort myself out."

"Knock if you need anything or questions arise. Have a pleasant stay." Doreen wandered back to her home, leaving Nick to admire the quirky old structure.

2
Bare Cupboards

Cold air teased the hairs on Nick's right arm, as he clamped the double bed duvet against his sleeping form. Frigid temperatures above the locked-in warmth of his downy covering jarred his senses into wakefulness. Grey light crept between a gap in full height curtains drawn across secondary double glazing. These newer panes of glass backed the listed, leaded light casement and its typical exposure to draughts. Nick yanked his arm beneath the duvet.

Crumbs, it's cold in here. He turned over to face a free-standing, plug-in electric radiator near a dressing table across the beige carpet. No glow illuminated its red indicator light. *I'm sure I checked the thermostat on that before I went to sleep.* Nick swung his feet from beneath the covering, only to recoil at icy air cutting them off above the ankles. *Shit, this place is like a fridge.* He hurried to the radiator and checked the thermostat dial, before adjusting it to the highest setting. No response from the indicator light. The radiator's metal remained cold to the touch. *The fuse must have blown overnight, unless there was a power cut?* Nick clicked a wall switch next to the door. The ceiling lamp snapped on without incident. *Gotta be a fuse. I'll warm myself up with a shower and get dressed, then change it. That's assuming there aren't problems in the bathroom.*

To Nick's relief, he was spared a cold shower. The over-bath power unit comforted his prickly skin with jets of steamy, relaxing water.

Downstairs, the radiators functioned without incident. Descending the tiny, right-angled staircase felt like trekking down from a mountain snow line into a tropical rain forest below. *Odd that all this heat didn't rise.* Nick rummaged in a utility cupboard beneath the turn in the stairs, where the Calendars had provided a vacuum cleaner and basic home maintenance essentials. He located a sandwich box sized Tupperware container labelled *'Fuses'* alongside assorted spare bulbs. A thin-bladed, short screwdriver with plastic orange handle lay next to a dustpan and brush. *That'll do.* He took the box and screwdriver back upstairs to the master bedroom. A couple of minutes later, he'd prised the old fuse out and inserted a replacement. *Now for the acid test.* He plugged the radiator back in and switched on the juice. The indicator lamp lit straight away. *That was painless. Thank goodness. I'd best wipe the condensation from those windows.* The under stairs' utility cupboard door banged, causing Nick to jump. *I thought I'd closed that? Must have left it ajar or off the catch.* He clambered up from kneeling on the carpet, then collected the box of fuses and screwdriver from the dressing table. As he reached the bend in the stairs, a muffled noise rose beneath his feet. Nick froze and gripped the railing.

What was that? He held his breath and listened. Everything remained quiet. When he reached the bottom step, the noise came again with greater clarity. It sounded like a boy laughing, as though at play. Nick whipped his head around. Another series of giggles seeped out from the under stairs cupboard. *How did a child get inside the cottage? Don't say the locks have broken too.* Nick put down the box and screwdriver, then crouched before the cupboard. *I don't want to shock the little scamp, even if he has been naughty and crept inside someone else's home. He sounds not much older than...* Nick couldn't complete his mental sentence, unspoken though it was. *Oh, what I'd give to play with my boy again.* He gripped the cupboard door handle and eased it back at a delicate rate. Daylight from a window behind him cast a widening splash of illumination across the interior of the utility space. There was nobody inside.

A knocking from the rear door into the kitchen shook Nick's petrified face into motion. He stirred himself and passed through the shaker-style, galley cooking space to where an ageing, fat-faced man adorned with wispy grey hair beamed through panelled glass segments. Nick unlocked the door and yanked it open.

"I hope I'm not disturbing you," the man spoke with a resonant, fruity timbre as well-rounded as his retirement softened belly. "Brian Calendar. I'm Doreen's husband. It seemed courteous to make an introduction."

Nick wiped the frown from his visage, still

perplexed by that disembodied laughing underneath the stairs. "Of course. I'm pleased to meet you. Nick Preston." Frosty air invaded the opened portal like some opportunistic burglar. It reminded Nick he'd put nothing warm inside his body since waking up to an icy bedroom. "Would you like a tea or coffee? I haven't made myself one yet."

"Splendid." Brian crossed the threshold without further deliberation.

"Please go through to the dining room." Nick ushered him past so he could close the back door to keep the heat in. "There's only tea bags and instant coffee for now, I'm afraid. I've yet to undertake a big shop."

"A black coffee would be nice." Brian lingered in the doorway between kitchen and dining room. "What did you do for dinner last night? A visit to one of our hostelries?"

Nick filled the kettle and shook his head. "No, I haven't checked out the pubs yet. No doubt I'll try one this evening. I fixed a pot of instant noodles before bed." He plugged the kettle in, then spooned coffee into a pair of white china mugs. Nick hesitated, still clutching the spoon. "My boy used to describe them as *nasty dried worms*."

Brian clutched the door frame. "Doreen told me about your loss. I'm sorry."

Nick shook his head. "It's been a year and a half. I should be in a better place by now. It's me who ought to apologise." He mentally kicked himself. "I'm turning into that boring old fart everyone walks on eggshells around." He straightened. "One who bleats about whatever he can't let go of. You know the score: a woman who got away; an employer who didn't value his opinion; a time where everything was perfect (even if nobody else remembers it that way). Nobody wants to be that guy."

Brian stroked a patch of his silken grey hair. "I understand your concerns. They're well motivated, if a tad cynical." He shifted on the spot. "If I'd lost my son, I wouldn't expect to get over it in eighteen months."

The kettle clicked. Nick waited for it to settle before pouring out the contents. "Do you and Doreen have children?"

"Two. A boy and girl. They're both married with families of their own, now." He watched Nick stir the mugs. "I understand the irreplaceable love a parent feels for their offspring. Which mother or father wouldn't do anything for them, if they're honest with themselves?"

Nick nodded. "We're not supposed to outlive them though, are we?"

"No. That's what I'm sorry for. Doreen and I have never lost a child."

"Thank you." Nick waved over the mugs. "Sugar?"

"No, that's okay. I always tell my wife I'm sweet enough. I'm not sure she believes me." Brian took the mug offered him and stepped back into the dining room.

The compact eating area comprised a laminate floored, dual aspect space the width of the cottage. A round table with four chairs stood before two patio doors onto the rear terrace. Fresh flowers hung over the edge of a tall glass vase in the table centre. A housewarming touch from the Calendars that Nick appreciated.

Brian pulled out a chair to sit down. "How was your first night at Stour Cottage?"

Nick joined him opposite. "Grand. A fuse blew in the bedroom radiator, so I endured a chilly awakening. I replaced it with a fresh one from the utility cupboard. I hope that's okay? I'm not used to renting."

Brian sipped his coffee. "Fine by me. If you're happy changing fuses and bulbs, fill your boots. But don't feel obliged to address maintenance issues yourself. I live next door and don't suffer from a busy schedule these days."

"Do you mind if I ask what you did for a living?"

Brian's chair creaked. "I was an insurance underwriter in the city."

Nick raised an eyebrow. "Wow. How was it?"

"Better before widespread computerisation. I preferred long business lunches and measured, face-to-face contact to all this virtual, everything must be done yesterday, hi-tech nonsense. Still, the world moves on. I miss how the job used to be, but not what it became."

Nick lifted his mug in salute. "Sounds idyllic, once upon a time. I was born a generation too late."

Brian grinned. "Doreen said you work in marketing?"

Nick sighed. "For my sins. I'm a freelancer. No guaranteed regular pay, but I have the liberty to do stuff like this relocation."

Brian cleared his throat. "Life has a way of putting things in our path at the right moment. I've no personal ideology, but that one notion I've found to be true. If we listen and respond, things come good. Situations can resolve themselves beyond our logical comprehension. Not always, but more times than not. It's hardly an exact science."

Nick's eyelids half shuttered, but a grateful light glistened in his pupils. "Brian, you're a philosopher. I get the message. Thank you."

Brian locked his hands together, then rested his chin on a steeple formed from both index fingers. "Now then, do you need any advice on where best to shop?"

"Is there a supermarket nearby? I don't have anything."

"We've a small local store for basics. Chartham, the next village along the Stour towards Canterbury, has a convenience outlet. It's a bigger place. Most of the older kids around here attend secondary school in Chartham. My two did, many moons ago. If you're after a proper supermarket, I'd suggest the one at Wincheap."

"Wincheap?" Nick drained his coffee.

"It's a district south of Canterbury, outside the medieval walls. You pass through it on your way into the city from here. If you need a big shop and don't fancy chancing traffic on the ring road, it's your best bet. Drive past Chartham until you enter Thanington Without. Take the first left after a bridge over the A2."

"You sound like my sat nav. I'll give it a go. Thanks, Brian." Nick paused. "It's a pleasant cottage. How old is this place?"

"It's Tudor, like many in Chilham. Over five hundred years old. Are you a history buff?"

"Not in any formal capacity, though it interests me." Nick cast a glance back towards the staircase, but thought better of quizzing Brian over any previous weird experiences in his home. *My emotions are so up the spout, I could have imagined that child.*

Brian continued. "If you want to read up on local history, Canterbury Library is superb. Our vicar, Andrew Stallard, is also something of an authority on the area. He'll be at the Winter Fair tomorrow."

"Winter Fair?"

"Andrew introduced the celebration two years ago. Church and castle join forces to host a community event in the castle grounds during late January. It cheers people up on dark and grotty days. There's mulled wine and cider, home-baked stews and cakes, warming winter games for fun; a whole ramshackle spectacle of rustic rambunctiousness."

Laughter lines stretched around Nick's eyes. *"Ramshackle spectacle of rustic rambunctiousness?* That was a statement and a half. Are you a poet?"

Brian pushed back his chair to stand. "Only for pleasure. A good job too, with lines like that one, hey?"

"It was lyrical. Does this fair have an admission charge?"

"There's a modest entrance fee. Nobody makes a profit from the event. Doreen and I will be there."

"I may look in on it. Thanks again, Brian."

Brian moved back towards the kitchen. He deposited

his empty mug in the sink, then glanced over his shoulder. "If you suffer more grief from that radiator, let me know. I'll have an electrician check it out or source a replacement for you. Have a good day, Nick."

"You too. Thanks for dropping by." Nick saw him out, then retrieved a notepad and Biro he'd found in a drawer near the sink to begin a shopping list.

* * *

Nick staggered a short distance from The Woolpack Inn along the lower left fork of Hambrook Lane towards Stour Cottage in lazy zig-zags. He'd made a less than illustrious nighttime impression on patrons at the pub, having over-imbibed. It was an uncharacteristic episode of using alcohol as a crutch. Vague hopes diners there weren't locals, came and went in his befuddled brain. Odd flashback snatches of scenes where he started crying, then shouting at the top of his lungs, caused him to groan. The tarmac road surface glittered with frost like a treasure trap of dangerous jewels. Nick tripped over a series of whitewashed verge stones; an attractive feature to dissuade motorists from parking on flat patches of grass outside residences. A sudden difference in temperature from the hot bar aggravated copious booze sloshing in his gut. He doubled over and heaved a puddle of vomit into the roadside.

"Yuck." Nick straightened, then wiped his mouth on a jacket sleeve.

A car pulled off Bagham Road at the pub behind

him. Its twinkling halogen lights caused Nick to turn, flinch, and raise his hands in a protective gesture. He wobbled while waiting for it to pass, then stepped out into the lane again. The sole of his left shoe lost purchase on the slippery tarmac, dropping him with a jarring impact onto his side.

Nick lay on the damp, cold thoroughfare, catching his breath for a moment. He lifted his eyes to the crystal clear, inky heavens. "What am I doing? I feel so lost."

Another car rounded the bend ahead, travelling towards him this time. Nick wobbled aloft and stepped aside once more. When the coast was clear, he continued his meandering walk home. The act of being sick had cleared his muddled mind a fraction. Now a dazed confusion gave way to pangs of depression and misery.

It took him eight attempts to insert his key in the lock at Stour Cottage. He was lucid enough to realise he shouldn't wake his landlords in such a state, but might be left without a choice. At the last moment, the key found its slot. The latch released for him to tumble into the cottage hallway. He reached the kitchen and fumbled in a cupboard amongst the mugs. His clumsy, intoxicated hands knocked one clear. It shattered on the floor. "Crap." Nick left the mess and focused on retrieving another without inducing a similar fate. His brow evidenced the concentration of a bomb disposal expert at the most crucial moment. This time the mug reached the worktop, undamaged. He fixed himself a tar-like cup of strong, black coffee. As he finished stirring his caffeinated sludge, a bang shook the house from the stairs. Head throbbing, Nick moved from doorway to doorway. He pressed against each frame for support until he reached the source of the disturbance. The compact, under stairs utility door stood unfastened from its catch. Nick slaked his woolly tongue with what little saliva his mouth would produce. "Hello?"

The hallway remained silent.

He turned and clutched his forehead with a stiff hand. "What am I doing? There's nobody there." He put one foot forward, but never transferred his full weight onto it before freezing on the spot. Tones of a male child giggling from the cupboard, tensed his stomach muscles. The swiftness with which he swivelled and tugged open the utility storage area's door surprised Nick. Once again, the space remained unoccupied. He shut the cupboard with an enraged bang that his skull regretted. "Alcohol and grief don't make good bedfellows, Preston. You should know that." He retreated to the dining room and sat at the round table to sip his brain-bending coffee.

"Daddy Baddy, Daddy Baddy." The voice he'd longed to hear even one more time for the last eighteen months, jolted Nick upright like a puppet with strings pulled taut. The phrase Grant invented to tease his father after Alana scolded Nick for making a mess in the kitchen, was unmistakable. Again, its source was the hallway. Nick pushed himself onto shaky pins and stumbled towards the door. Thundering young feet tore past and hurried up the stairs. Nick reached the spot in time to catch a flash of dark red hair vanish around the corner. He gave chase. There was nowhere to run upstairs; no route of egress. Yet the landing, bathroom and master bedroom remained empty and free of obvious disturbances. Nick scrunched his face. Silent tears stained his cheeks. He allowed himself to topple forward onto the mattress and drifted into aching unconsciousness. Heartbreaking images of the last time he saw his boy alive, plagued his slumber.

Grant Preston's hair colour came straight from his father, albeit two shades darker. Its thickness, surging into a quiff above his blocky head, spoke more of Alana. Pale of complexion with his mother's eye colouring (though possessed of Nick's intense gaze), Grant was your typical child settling into his second year at primary school in a world of possibilities. A boy full of fun, yet with his father's propensity toward internalising emotions; Grant was a playful, deep thinker, despite his meagre accumulation of years.

Nick stood opposite him in the lush grass of their Midhurst back garden. Early morning sunlight warmed father and son as they passed a football back and forth.

Grant tensed, then gave the ball a solid kick. It sailed over Nick's crouched form, now imitating a waiting goalie. Grant jumped on the spot. "He shoots. He scores."

Nick grinned while retrieving the ball. "Nice one." He checked his watch. "I'm gonna have to get moving,

Son."

Grant's face fell to accompany his lowering shoulders.

Nick flicked the boy's chin upward with a gentle finger. "I'll see you and Mum for lunch after the meeting. Don't forget my promise."

Grant reached up and hugged his father. "I love you, Dad."

"I love you too."

Back at Stour Cottage, Nick stirred where he lay face down across the master bedroom mattress. He awoke whispering that last phrase aloud. "I love you too." His words faded into the room's wonky, characterful walls.

"Can we go shopping now?" Grant's voice from the landing, whipped Nick's countenance around. There the boy stood in the open bedroom doorway.

Nick rolled off the mattress onto the carpet, all vigour stolen from his muscles. "Grant?" He reached a trembling hand towards the child. "Can it be?" Alcohol levels subsided in his blood. Nick pulled the hand back to slap his own face. "No, of course it can't." All breathless wonder vanished from his voice now. When he rubbed his eyes, the vision of his departed son disappeared. Physical and emotional strength evaporated from his exhausted form. Lacking sufficient energy or will to pull himself back onto the mattress, Nick flopped his face into the carpet and lay out for the count.

* * *

Nick wasn't sure what time he awoke the next morning. The beige carpet left an impression on his face it would take a decent shower to shift. His head tingled with the fragility of a porcelain doll. "What were you thinking?" He crawled towards the bathroom to secure the invigorating power of water under pressure on his aching limbs. "Man, oh man, Grant looked so real last night. I could almost have reached out to touch him." A stabbing in his skull caused Nick to screw his eyes up. "There's got to be a better way to connect with him than booze. I need to face reality, not chase fantasies at the bottom of a pint glass." Minus the familiar presence of Alana or any other listener, he continued his vocalised monologue while shaving and getting dressed. "What about that cupboard under the stairs? Fair play while I was three sheets to the wind yesterday. But, the first time I heard that laugh before Brian called, I hadn't touched a drop." A sting of aftershave made his eyes water. "You're hearing what you want to hear; seeing what you want to see." Nick leaned closer to his facial reflection in the mirror. "It won't bring him back, Preston. Eventually you've got to face the truth and move on."

Downstairs, his half-drunk mug of coffee still stood on the dining room table. Cold and almost viscous, the odious sludge wrinkled his nose while he transported it to the kitchen. Fragments of the first broken mug lay strewn across the kitchen floor. *I'd better purchase a replacement for the Calendars once I find something similar.* Still tender of stomach, Nick opted for two slices of dry toast to start the day.

Parked cars filled Chilham market square after lunch, when Nick ambled up School Hill to the castle gates. A crowd of attendees lined up before a rough table to purchase tickets for the Winter Fair. A nearby folk music trio kept the hearty atmosphere stoked with positive energy. Strains of a violin, tin whistle and acoustic guitar hung in the clear air. Physical discomfort and vulnerability from his hangover had subsided, but it relieved Nick the group didn't include a percussionist. He couldn't handle drums or anything beating louder than his head today. He pulled a leather purse from his pocket, then passed a fiver to a bespectacled woman tearing red paper tickets off a roll.

"There we go." She handed him his access token.

"Thank you." Nick stuffed the ticket in his pocket and sauntered through the gates.

Inside, exquisite formal landscape gardens - attributed to Capability Brown - stretched away from one side of the castle, downhill to an ornamental lake. Stalls of provisions and crafts decorated with cheery bunting, stuck out at odd angles here and there. The largest crowd formed around a hotplate serving the mulled wine and cider Brian had mentioned.

"There he is." A familiar, fruity voice caused Nick to turn.

"Hi, Brian. How are you?"

Brian waddled closer, holding tight to a steaming cup of cider. "Fair to middling." He fixed Nick with a disarming stare. "So you enjoyed a few at The Woolpack last night?"

Nick winced. "I wouldn't go all the way to 'enjoyed,' though it's a great place. Oh God, have I already garnered a sketchy reputation in the village?"

Brian grinned. "Don't worry about that. A neighbour of ours was there. That's how I found out. I told him you were our new tenant and had been going through a tough time. He's no gossip. Most other locals were at The White Horse yesterday."

Nick puffed. "That's a relief. I'm amazed I wasn't arrested. If memory serves, I made a fool of myself. I'll be more restrained when I try the other place."

Brian lifted his cup. "Speaking of which, would you like a measure of this stuff? It's not half bad."

Nick shook his head. "I'd better not."

Brian inclined his face. "Hair of the Dog?"

"This dog is shaggy enough for today, thanks."

Brian almost spat his drink out in amusement during the next sip. "I like that. Can I introduce you to anyone?"

"I think I'll blend into the background. Folk wouldn't be catching me at my best. Oh, I'm afraid I broke a mug when I got home last night. I'll replace it, of course."

Brian shrugged. "Doreen and I aren't too precious about the contents, within reason. We don't count the silver to check every knife and fork after a tenant leaves. Don't go to any special trouble."

Nick indicated a pottery stand featuring glazed earthenware mugs painted with an outline image of the market square. Each bore the village's name. "How about if I add a Chilham mug to the crockery? It's not a match for the broken item, but it's local."

"Nellie Welstead makes those. She'd be glad of your business."

Nick pulled out his purse again. "Sorted." He made a beeline for the pottery stall to complete his purchase. Nellie Welstead's offer to wrap the mug in tissue paper for safety presented a perfect excuse. Now he could avoid the vigorous sports rowdy locals hectored people to take part in. His constitution wasn't up to that while hungover. Instead, he watched a group of teenage boys tackling one another with a dribbled football. Nick's eyes glazed over at imaginings of the larks he and Grant might have enjoyed throughout his son's older years. He moved away and bought himself a cup of hot chocolate. The winter warmer steamed into a dusky sky accompanying plummeting afternoon temperatures.

Between the pressing bodies, Nick caught odd glimpses of a dog collar milling about. He took careful steps to blend in and move aside whenever the vicar came near. The last thing he needed was a lot of probing questions directed at the village newcomer, regardless of how well intentioned.

Crows cawed amidst the fading light. After a brief pause for a bite to eat, the folk musicians accompanied the rosy-cheeked reverie of good cheer again. In the midst of the throng, Nick Preston wondered if he would find sufficient distraction on this sojourn to heal his open wound. His thoughts turned to Alana. Part of him wanted to load up the car and return to West Sussex without delay. It was a pointless desire. Without some change in his mood or spirit, Nick knew he'd be back to sparring with his wife within the week over a loss he felt unable to release. He stared across The Great Stour Valley at a well-defined hill. Its distinct character rose above the river towards Chartham and Canterbury beyond. *Either I kick this turmoil while I'm here, or there'll be no going back for Alana and I.* He grimaced. *Who am I kidding? There'll be no going back for my sanity!* He slouched, then worked his way through the mass of winter celebrants. Wrapped mug tucked under one arm, Nick left the castle grounds and strolled downhill to Stour Cottage.

3
Charlie

Charlie Brockman would have made the perfect model for a TV advertisement about retirement finance, orthopaedic mattresses, or hearing aids. A round head - bald on top - with archetypal tufts of fine, gossamer white hair above the ears, fit the bill. Deceptively spry, he still loved to walk in King's Wood. He and his wife, June, had done so regularly, ever since they settled in Chilham as a young couple during the mid-60s. Childless but very much in love, Charlie and June were a common sight on Mountain Street, strolling hand in hand to and from The Pilgrims' Way. Many a local cosy cottage and Tudor architectural wonder had tiles replaced by Charlie during his career as a self-employed roofer.

He coughed and cleared his throat while passing Stour Cottage. Nick Preston stepped out of the garden woodshed, clutching an armful of logs for the lounge burner. He watched the seventy-eight-year-old fellow puff uphill with remarkable stamina and a proud, erect posture.

"Dear Charlie Brockman," Brian Calendar followed from the shed with some logs of his own.

"Do you know him well?" Nick asked.

"And his late wife, June. They're from the next property down the hill. June succumbed to stomach cancer at Christmas." He gritted his teeth. "A lot of pain. I suppose it's a small mercy she progressed from diagnosis to death in less than eight weeks."

"Poor old boy. Is he out for an evening walk? It's getting dark."

"Only to The White Horse, where he's a regular." Brian nudged the woodshed door closed behind them with one foot.

Nick straightened. "I haven't tried that yet. Perhaps I'll follow along to see if he's a man in search of company."

Brian nodded. "He's a sociable sort. Everyone knows him at the pub." He set off across the garden to his back door. "Have a pleasant time."

Nestled in the quiet northwestern corner of the hilltop market square, The White Horse stood beside the main pathway to St Mary's Church. A lane skirting the churchyard swept down and away from the pub, leaving it in a position of prominence, distinct from many other buildings squashed together in a huddle. Smoke curled from high chimneys. Its fragrant aroma drew Nick closer. He quickened his strides across the open space, hands jammed into his pockets for warmth.

"There you go, Charlie. Get your laughing gear around that." The barmaid handed Charlie Brockman a pint of mild and bitter.

Nick closed the front door, his attention drawn to leaping tongues of flame from crackling logs in a large, welcoming inglenook fireplace. Horse brasses adorned a broad, blackened rustic beam supporting it. Two faded maps of the area from different time periods flanked a framed, panoramic watercolour print of the square. Decorative tankards hung at angles by their handles on hooks hammered into copious thick ceiling beams. A spark leapt from a fresh split in the logs, to extinguish in an instant on the flagstone floor.

Charlie was welcomed into a crowded corner of people from Nick's age upward. Nick squeezed past a young couple in the obvious first flush of love, lingering near the door. He made his way to the bar.

"What can I get you?" the barmaid asked.

"A pint of bitter, please." Nick directed his attention to the corner crowd as he spoke. The pub bustled, making it difficult to filter out and isolate the content of Charlie's animated discussion. Nick paid for his beer, then moved to a seat at a small round table near the fire. He didn't feel comfortable approaching the group uninvited.

"I tell you it was my June. We were childhood sweethearts. I know what my wife looks like." Charlie stamped an adamant foot against the stone floor.

Nick frowned and hunched over his drink for a closer listen.

A burly, boisterous man in his early fifties shook his

head. "We all miss June, Charlie. But think about what you're saying." His voice rang with careless resonance to carry across the barroom.

"Where was this?" A woman with a kind face, Nick assumed to be the burly man's long-suffering wife, rubbed the old man's shoulder with an affectionate hand.

"Up at King's Wood, where we always walked. She was standing on the path, midway along our favourite route. The same one we took several times a week."

"Did she speak to you?" The woman fluttered soft lashes over moistening eyes.

"No. She beckoned me to follow her. When I drew near, she vanished into the woods. I was too tired to search further."

The burly fellow hung his head and rocked on his heels. "Charlie, old man..." He sighed. "June passed away. She's not in the woods. I know it's difficult to handle those feelings, but-"

"I realise June is dead, Kevin. I'm not a senile old fool." Charlie's cheeks turned crimson.

Kevin's brow furrowed. "So what are you saying? You think June is a ghost, running around up there?"

"Kevin," the woman chided his caustic and cynical response. She nudged Charlie. "Sorry, Charlie."

"Why couldn't she be a ghost?" Charlie stuck his nose in the air.

Kevin shook his head and snorted. "There's no such thing."

Kevin's wife swallowed and attempted to calm the waters again. "Nobody knows that for certain, honey.

Many people have had explanation defying encounters."

A much younger man clad in a thick sweater lifted his pint glass at Kevin. "She's right. I can't claim personal knowledge, but when I grew up in Ardenham my kid brother's friends had a run-in with a ghost. A girl called Maria. She was famous for stalking the woods near our primary school. A group of boys camped there once. They weren't the same afterwards."

"Poppycock," Kevin jeered. "Your kid brother was yanking your chain and having a laugh, Ollie."

"I assure you he wasn't. Something scared those lads shitless."

Kevin gulped down some beer, then deposited his empty on the end of the bar. "Their own juvenile imaginations and a loud fox shrieking in the night, no doubt."

Charlie's eyes moved from Kevin to the barmaid. "Try telling Jenny there's no such thing as ghosts."

Jenny the barmaid looked up from wiping a glass. She shook back an errant strand of her short, straw blonde hair while clutching the receptacle to her fulsome chest. "What now?"

Charlie's face paled. "How many times have you seen the spectre of a monk sitting by the fire, right there?" He jerked a thumb across his shoulder towards Nick.

Nick jumped in his seat and scanned the other chairs beside the fireplace, half expecting to find a ghostly robed figure swigging from a tankard.

Jenny shrugged. "Enough."

Kevin guffawed. "You're not serious? Oh, come on, Jenny. Everyone knows that story is a gimmick to pull in punters."

Jenny scowled. "No, it isn't. They found a skeleton under the floorboards once, years before my time. Anyway, I've seen the monk. So have half a dozen regulars."

Kevin folded his arms. "Well, I've never seen it." He caught a surge of fire flashing in his wife's eyes, then softened his tone. "I'm sorry, Charlie. That vision of June must have seemed real to you. People often speak of encountering loved ones, right after they've passed away. If you ask me, it's a coping mechanism. A way for the heart and mind to adjust. It's natural and there's nothing wrong with it. Healthy, even. I didn't mean to come down you so hard." He rubbed his nose. "My cousin wasted his best years and a lot of money chasing the supernatural. He ended up a broken bum. It riles me when I hear people insisting it's all true."

Charlie finished his drink, face sombre. "I know what I saw with my own eyes."

Kevin's wife pursed her lips. "Can I get you another, Charlie?"

"No, thank you. I'm tired. Time to go home." He pulled his coat on.

Kevin grunted. "Don't be like that. I said I was sorry."

Charlie lifted a hand to the group as he wheeled about. "Have a good evening, everyone."

Kevin's wife thumped her husband's shoulder.

"Sometimes I could ring your bloody neck. You're a tactless bastard once you've had a couple, Kevin Pickford."

Nick chugged his beer down while the woman continued her tirade.

Charlie passed the bar.

"You off already, Charlie?" Jenny called over her shoulder while filling a measure of scotch from an optic.

Charlie nodded, glancing at her for a moment with sad eyes.

Jenny's expression showed great affection and sympathy. "You take care on that hill, walking home. It's frosty out."

Nick put down his glass and got up to follow the widower outside.

Jenny noticed his departure and offered an indifferent "Thanks," to the stranger in her establishment.

Charlie was already halfway across the market square when his intrigued pursuer made it outside. Nick hurried along behind, almost losing his footing despite a head clear as a bell this time. He coughed to alert the man to his presence, before calling out. "Mr Brockman?"

Charlie slowed to a halt. He performed a stiff twist for a better look at the approaching figure. Mild concern crinkled his facial muscles in the moonlight.

Nick held up a friendly hand. "Don't be alarmed. My

name is Nick Preston. I'm Doreen and Brian Calendar's latest tenant at Stour Cottage."

Any hint of discomfort evaporated from the old man's features. "You're a new neighbour?"

"That's right." Nick extended a hand in greeting.

Charlie shook it. "How did you know my name?"

"Brian pointed you out on your way past, this evening."

"Ah. Brian and Doreen are good people. My late wife, June, always reminded me how lucky we were to enjoy such great neighbours." He pulled out a handkerchief and blew his nose.

"Brian told me what happened to her. I'm sorry."

"Thank you, Mr Preston." Charlie folded the material square with meticulous care before re-inserting it into his pocket. "Did you overhear our rowdy discussion in there?"

"I did. It caught my interest as I suffered a bereavement myself sometime ago."

"Your wife?" Charlie tilted his head.

"Son. He was only six. It's been eighteen months, but in the last few days I could have sworn I heard and saw him." Nick grimaced. "Okay, on one occasion I'd had far too much to drink. But there was another time before that... It could be nothing. All I'm saying is: whether your friend back there was right about the vision being a coping mechanism or not, I know how real and painful that feels."

"Thank you again, Mr Preston. I'm sorry about your boy. It must be hard to lose a child. June and I never had kids of our own, though we wanted them. She was a primary school teacher here in the village, once upon a time. We bought our home across from the school, right after we married."

"And you've lived there ever since?" Nick smiled.

"We have. Or rather, we did. Is your wife not with you this evening?"

Numbed by icy weather seeping through his jeans and chilling his legs, Nick started walking with Charlie at his side. "No, I left her at our home in Midhurst. We've had some problems. I came here to sort myself out before it's too late for us."

Charlie squinted to suggest he didn't understand the logic behind that statement.

Nick rubbed the back of his neck. "Yeah, it sounds crazy to me too, when I say it out loud. Alana, my wife, was with our boy when a car struck and killed him. She got distracted while Grant ran out into the road."

Charlie muttered. "Do you blame her?"

Nick sighed as they started down School Hill. "I don't want to; don't even mean to. I suppose it's the way he was taken and how I never got to say goodbye. The hurt won't go away, and the two of us end up rowing all the time. We never used to fight. No more than regular couples, anyway. I imagine you and June got along like a house on fire?"

Charlie grinned. "Did we, heck. June and I loved a good barney to clear the air. We always settled them afterwards on our walks up to the woods. Somehow nature reminded us what was important. We arrived back like a pair of young lovers again. Similar to that couple in the pub doorway who couldn't take their eyes off each other."

"Is that the woods on that odd shaped hill?" Nick nodded at the curious outline he'd noticed from the castle grounds during the fair.

"No. That's Julliberrie Down across the river. It's a famous Neolithic and Roman long barrow. June and I walked up in King's Wood, further back along The Pilgrims' Way."

"At the end of Mountain Street?"

"That's it. Have you been?"

"No. Doreen mentioned it."

Charlie's eyes fixed. "It's a beautiful place. The Canterbury pilgrims, made famous by Chaucer, used to travel that path from Winchester. Part way into the woods along the trail, there's an amazing view of Canterbury Cathedral in the distance. It would have been their first glimpse of it."

"I'll have to check it out. All that walking must have kept you both in good shape?"

Charlie's face lowered. "For all the good it did us in the end."

Nick screwed up his nose. "I'm sorry, I-"

"No, Mr Preston. Don't mind me. June and I had a long and wonderful life together. I'm…"

"Suffering? How could you not be?" Nick paused outside Stour Cottage.

"Yes." Charlie shook his hand again. "It was a pleasure making your acquaintance. I appreciate you walking home with me. These lanes are treacherous in the frost. Living on a hill is great, unless you have to go anywhere in the ice, snow or rain."

"Take care." Nick stood at the gate until the old man disappeared inside his own front door. He pulled out his keys, feeling them press cold against his palm. "Loss is a bitch and no mistake. What is this life all about?" He stretched, then opened up and went inside.

* * *

"Bungle? Bungle, where are you?" Fifteen-year-old Amy Williamson's feet squelched to a halt on a muddy forest track. She flicked an empty dog lead against one thigh and peered through the heavy morning mist. *Where can that dog have scampered off to now?* "Bungle?" Thick, moist air deadened and muffled her voice. A faint barking made her turn aside. "Yuck." Her wellington boots sunk into bog-like, water-filled rivulets in the track caused by felling machinery or a Forestry Commission ranger truck. Their murky contents sucked and gurgled like a sink plunger with every difficult step she took. Each time she pulled a foot free, her balance suffered. Bungle barked again. "That's it, don't come back to your owner. Make her come to you, why don't you?" Amy chided the absent hound as though he were an inconsiderate peer. Casting scorn upon the invisible dog, obscured by a fog bank, set her mind at ease. Life as a farmer's daughter on White Hill had its rewards. Views across The Great Stour Valley to Wye from her bedroom were a joy. She loved her idyllic country life. But taking the family Airedale for his morning constitutional in the woods in weather like this, always filled her with dread. She never walked the lane at night and steered clear of the trees after dark or when bad daytime weather closed in. But Bungle needed his exercise. She was the one who'd promised to care for him, the day she'd begged her parents for a dog. Amy once caught the flash of a woman in white on the lane from her window, three years prior. She'd witnessed no other phantoms, but knew all the stories. In her mind, days like this might see ghosts reach out to grab her from the fog with cold, lifeless, skeletal hands in an iron grip. She gulped and pushed through thin, snapping twigs of undergrowth that scratched against her clothing. The Airedale's silhouette filtered through low winter cloud on the wooded hilltop.

"What is it, boy?" Amy reached out to steady herself against a tree trunk as Bungle's outline sharpened.

The dog whined, turned to look at her, and then barked once more.

"What have you found?" Amy pressed in closer.

Beyond a moss carpeted log lay a bulky object. The dog padded clear, exposing the fixed, terrified visage of a round-headed old man sporting gossamer strands of white hair. He lay on his back, skull pressed into a mulch of decayed leaves, face staring open-mouthed at the interlocking tree canopies.

Amy shrieked, causing Bungle to erupt in a confused but protective series of barks. She clutched her chest, against which her heart hammered a mile a minute. "No."

* * *

Nick glanced towards Taylors Hill from the village fire station on its western edge. He'd taken a stroll down there to walk circuits around the overflow car park, away from prying eyes. It seemed a better option than prowling the market square in full view of twitching curtains. *Less than a month in the village, and one of the first acquaintances I make winds up dead. Not a brilliant start. So much for escaping grief.* He paced close to some bushes beside a low, brick built public convenience. He'd already availed himself of the facilities and observed its interior graffiti artwork of erect male members and the slogan '*Kerry sucks. Call me for a go,*' followed by a telephone number. Some poor girl would endure unwanted communications from any card carrying pervert who noted down the text, scrawled by whichever vandal wished her grief.

Nick changed direction to observe occasional traffic on the hedge-lined Challock bound A252. He pondered the manner in which Brian Calendar had informed him of Charlie Brockman's demise. At first he'd thought his landlord was popping round for a chat. That, or to tell him something important about the cottage he hadn't mentioned. Instead, Nick was struck by the report a dog walker discovered Charlie's lifeless body, deep into King's Wood near The Pilgrims' Way. Nothing could have prepared him for such news. He'd only met the man three days before his death, yet taken an instant shine to his honest good nature. In reality, Nick could have excused himself from attending the funeral after such a brief encounter. But that felt wrong. The lovely old boy had no-one left in the world - except the Calendars and a few surviving villagers of the same generation - to witness his final journey. Nick mused that the ceremony might take his focus off Grant. Could it put his own concerns into better perspective? He clutched at that hopeful straw, unable to assemble a cohesive or definitive answer. *For a man of little faith, I'm relying on belief in something these days.*

A sprinkle of light rain tickled his face. He'd told the Calendars he would make his own way to the service and that they needn't call on him. That was true enough, if not the entire picture. Nick remained uneasy about connecting with locals or forming new bonds. The daft notion a new social circle could all wind up like Charlie Brockman, reassured him of a choice well made. It was a convenient, if ridiculous and self-deluding excuse he avoided examining in depth. Yet, Nick yearned to unburden himself. Twice more in the last twenty-four hours he'd heard, seen, or felt what he believed to be Grant's presence. Charlie's companionable stroll back from the pub brought with it a sense of solidarity. Here was a man who'd suffered loss, yet encountered his beloved again afterwards. How close to his own experiences could you get? What were the chances of meeting someone else like that? Nick had hoped for further chats with the retired roofer. Now they would never speak again.

He set off up Taylors Hill. The welcoming aroma of ground coffee filled his nostrils. Nick noticed a metal sign for The Copper Kettle. He was toying with whether to pop in for a drink, when a shiny black hearse drew into the square from School Hill opposite, a coffin in the rear. Nick spied the church tower clock. *Crap, I was mooching around down there longer than I thought.* He hurried to reach the path beside the pub to St Mary's, before the funeral vehicle came to a halt.

Inside the expansive 13th Century church, Nick discovered a modest handful of attendees scattered across dark wooden pews either side of a striking blue aisle carpet. The Calendars occupied the front row on one side. Nick squeezed himself in at the rear for anonymity and as a mark of respect. It was a courtesy for the old boy in whose village he was only a recent visitor.

The crowd stood. Coffin bearers processed past, supporting Charlie's pine box. Nick watched them go. All the while he wondered about the man's last moments. *Did he see June again? Did she beckon him back into the woods where the devoted couple always walked? Could it be Charlie went looking for her without success, then succumbed to fatigue and exposure?* Nick scratched his chin. *He was a fit chap, despite his age. Still, the cold and damp gets in my own bones. Perhaps he waited in their favourite spot for his wife and refused to leave until it killed him?*

The church organist began a rendition of '*Abide with Me.*' Nick picked up a hymnal, then turned to the numbered entry indicated on a board beside the pulpit. He took a deep breath and sung out in efforts to fill the church with sound in lieu of a larger flock of mourners.

As the hymn rolled on, it surprised Nick to notice an unexpected vibrato wobbling many of the notes from his mouth. His focus wandered up to follow each vocalised song lyric towards high wooden beams in the roof of the clean, white stone interior. Flowers clung to the pews and adorned planters beside pillars supporting Gothic arches.

The last notes reverberated around the structure, and the Reverend Andrew Stallard motioned for them to sit.

Nick shut his eyes throughout most of the service. More words of hope in the face of tragic loss washed over his already saturated heart. Worrying thoughts of hopelessness and despair taunted his mind with subtle whispers inviting suicide. Nick shook them loose and flicked through the hymnal again, scanning random blocks of text as a distraction. He gritted his teeth. *If there is a hereafter and you're looking down, don't think ill of me for not paying attention, Charlie. I've endured too much of this stuff. Your vicar's words will do little for me now.*

Watching Charlie Brockman's coffin lowered into a joint plot his late wife had occupied for little more than a month, added a finality to proceedings.

Nick stepped away from the graveside to skirt the church tower. He took a long, pensive breath and passed an ancient yew tree. Beside it, a tall stone cross set in an octagonal base with lists of engraved names, constituted the village war memorial.

"Nick?" Doreen Calendar called after him.

Nick stopped and half turned.

Doreen drew closer. "There's a small buffet and drinks in The White Horse to celebrate Charlie's life. It would be nice if you could join us."

Nick was about to excuse himself before the tone of that second comment suggested a refusal would affront Doreen. "Thank you."

Brian emerged around the church tower base. "Is he coming?"

Doreen nodded.

"Jolly good." Brian continued walking in his lumbering gait.

"There you go." Jenny the barmaid handed Nick a freshly pulled pint.

Nick fished out his purse, hesitating at a raised hand from the publican.

"No charge." Her eyes twinkled.

Nick frowned. "How come?"

"After June died, Charlie put money behind the bar for anyone who showed up to his funeral. Your drink is on him."

A weight yanked at Nick's heartstrings. He put his purse away again and lifted the glass. "Then I'll savour every sip. Thank you."

Brian sidled up to Nick with a beer of his own. "Come and meet Andrew, Nick."

"Andrew?" Nick stepped away from the bar.

"Our vicar."

In the confines of The White Horse there was nowhere to run, even had Nick wanted to. This time he'd bite the bullet and hope this minister didn't ply him with platitudes that set his teeth on edge. Flooring a local man of the cloth in frustration wouldn't endear him to his landlords and new neighbours.

Doreen Calendar stood clutching a glass of sherry by the fire, chatting with Andrew Stallard.

A fit, muscular form decried Andrew Stallard's fifty-five years as a decade less than reality. So did a full head of forward-brushed brown hair bearing the faintest suggestion of grey. Shaved eyebrows capped thin-framed octagonal glasses perched on a broad nose. Not your average, middle-aged C of E vicar by appearance, Andrew might be confused with the livelier, 'Spring Harvest' Anglican crowd. Yet as a keen scholar and ardent student of history, his evident, grounded nature soon dismissed such speculations. Andrew was an ecclesiastical enigma, and he enjoyed the dichotomy that presented to life's labellers. He studied Nick with gentle, watchful eyes as the pair approached.

Brian cleared his throat. "Nick Preston, meet Andrew Stallard, our vicar."

Andrew passed a snifter of cognac from his right hand into his left, freeing himself to offer Nick a handshake.

Nick accepted and was surprised by the firmness of the man's grip. "I'm pleased to meet you."

"Likewise. I noticed you at the Winter Fair, but didn't get a chance to introduce myself."

Nick cringed. "Sorry about that." He held up his glass. "I'd over-imbibed the night before and wasn't my best self. Not something I make a habit of."

Andrew noticed Nick's eyes fall upon the dog collar around his neck. "It's none of my concern if you do."

Sensing the pair should have a moment alone, Doreen dragged her husband across the bar to chat with an elderly couple who'd also attended the service and burial.

Andrew motioned to a chair by the fire. Waves of heat from its flames restored circulation after a frosty morning committal.

Nick sat down with the vicar beside him. "I only met Charlie once, but we formed an instant connection. Such a shame he's gone."

Andrew swirled the spirit around his glass, warming its underside with his fingers. "On account of his claims about meeting June in the woods? Forgive me, but the Calendars apprised me of your situation. I hope they didn't overstep the mark?"

Nick batted the comment aside. "It's okay. At least I won't have to explain myself to someone else. Did Charlie tell you what he experienced?"

"Not in so many words."

"Were you at the pub that night when he blurted it out?"

"No, but word soon gets around a small village. Sometimes we vicars shut our ears. At others, we sift truth from gossip to identify actionable intelligence requiring our attention."

Nick raised an eyebrow and smirked. "You make it

sound like the Royal Corps of Signals."

Andrew roared. "I like that. Well, we're in a spiritual war, so why not?" He sipped his cognac, then eyed Nick. "Listen, I don't want you to feel the need to avoid me. Don't be uncomfortable in my presence. It sounds like you've been through hell. I wouldn't blame you if you've no time for God or religion. In my line, it's a sad fact of life after people suffer the tragic loss of a loved one. I won't preach or shower you with dogma. That's not my bag."

Nick nodded. "I appreciate that. So what's your background?"

Andrew stretched his feet forward to toast them against the radiating logs. A sweet aroma of onions escaped the pub kitchen. "I studied theology and history at university, before choosing this career. I'm unmarried; committed to this parish and learning lessons on life and spirituality from those who've gone before. People with much to teach us."

"Do you know a lot about the area?"

Andrew shrugged. "I love to read local histories and old texts. My favourite dream comprises visiting Chilham as it was in centuries past." His eyes wandered across the pub. "If these old buildings could talk, what stories they'd tell us."

"You seem pragmatic and open-minded for a man of the cloth. A touch poetic, too." Nick offered a salute with his glass. "That's a compliment, in case it didn't sound like one."

Andrew grinned. "Why be anything but? My approach sometimes conflicts with those of a more rigid, religious disposition. That can't be helped. Chilham and its environs have witnessed multiple beliefs among residents down through the centuries. My interpretation of God and religious faith inspires my own actions. But I count that interpretation neither absolute nor inviolable. It's personal." His brow creased. "No matter where you look today, somebody is always telling others what to say, think, or do. I put it to you that won't end well. No-one likes a dictator. We're adults, capable of making up our own minds and accepting responsibility for our own choices."

Nick finished his drink. "For what it's worth, if there were more like you, I'd give your beliefs a second look." His jaw tightened. "Under different circumstances."

Andrew placed his snifter on a side table. "On that note, I'd be remiss if I didn't tell you my door is always open. You're on a journey you want to navigate under your own steam, Nick. I get that. All I'm saying is: if you need a sounding board, fancy a drink and a chat, or even want to sit in the church alone with your thoughts undisturbed, then knock on the vicarage door, okay? I find most people already know the solution to their problems, without my input. All they need is someone to listen while they discover that for themselves. Humans are amazing creatures once you scratch beneath the surface."

Nick offered his hand this time as the pair stood. "I'm glad we met."

"Me too." Andrew shook it. "Look after yourself. Don't be anxious about asking for a leg up, should you need one."

Nick gave a thoughtful, silent nod, then made for the door.

4
Ultimum Religio

"This soup will warm me up, thanks." A near permanent, wide but close-mouthed smile soothed anyone who encountered Oliver Hall. At fifty-three with cropped white hair and a short but stocky frame, his penchant for jogging, power walking and cycling kept the middle-aged IT Manager in fine fettle. Driven yet warm; only the lazy caught the sharper side of his nature, reserved for those who didn't embrace life with gratitude and zeal. Oliver believed if you worked hard and pushed forward, everything would come together. At least, he used to believe it. In the last year, circumstances conspired to undermine the bedrock of his simple ethos.

He tore off a hunk of crusty bread and dipped it into a steaming bowl of tomato soup. Half a dozen people occupied various tables at The Tickled Trout, a fine Kentish inn beside a bridge over the River Stour in the village of Wye.

"My good lady and I have followed the progress of your sponsored walk on-line, ever since you left Winchester." Gary Timon, the landlord tapped a tea towel hanging across his left forearm. "Daylight is fading. Do you have accommodation booked this evening?"

Oliver finished a mouthful, then wiped tomato stains from one corner of his mouth. "I'm aiming to make Chilham before nightfall. A good night's rest, then a final push to Canterbury tomorrow. I added another Pilgrim's Passport stamp at Boughton Aluph church, before turning aside here for a bite."

One of Gary's regular patrons clocked the diner's backpack and walking poles resting beside his table. He called to the publican. "What's all that about, Gary?"

Gary touched Oliver's pack while addressing the customer. "This chap is undertaking a sponsored power walk of The Pilgrims' Way."

The man gawped. "What, *all* of it?"

Gary flicked his tea towel out like a banner. "The whole 133 Miles, Ian. He's raising money for charity."

Ian tutted. "I got that from the '*sponsored*' part. Which one?"

Oliver twisted in his seat. "The Crusader Stroke Trust. They helped my late wife, Pauline, after a stroke paralysed her. A second finished her. We wouldn't have managed the precious time in between, were it not for Crusaders."

Ian banged an approving hand on his table. "Well done, Sir. My sympathies. Is it too late to sponsor you?"

"Not at all. Thank you." Oliver tore off another hunk of bread.

Gary pulled out his food order pad. "I'll jot the website address down for you, Ian."

Oliver stepped out into the early dusk. Pink hues stained the sky with a pastel wash. The river flowed past the pub after tumbling down a weir beside a level crossing at the village train station. He shouldered his pack, heart touched by Gary Timon's refusal to accept payment for the vittles. *Pauline would have enjoyed that place.* He adjusted the height of his walking poles for comfort, then set off to wait for a passing train to clear the crossing. Memories of his wife re-surfaced, still beautiful at the end, if broken by her illness.

Pauline's stiff, rakish broom handle figure echoed a timid spirit which never believed she was good enough. Often this manifested as works of generosity and self-sacrifice the late forties youth centre coordinator lavished upon others. Pretty but shy with bright eyes and short, curly blonde hair; yoga helped Pauline calm a disposition otherwise tuned to a station of worry on permanent broadcast. The most regular recipient of the aforementioned generous deeds was her husband Oliver, whom she met when he volunteered to install a computer network at the charity where she worked. At the ages of thirty-two and thirty-eight, Pauline and Oliver knew each had found their soulmate. Three months on, they married; a relationship only The Grim Reaper could disrupt when he paid Pauline a visit fifteen years later.

Oliver zoomed the digital Ordnance Survey map on

his GPS for a closer scale inspection. *Okay. Back across the A28, then part way up the lane I came down earlier, before turning northeast towards Soakham Farm on the hillside.*

The crossing barriers opened and Oliver marched onward, getting back into his stride. Pauline had always done things for Oliver, but struggled when he returned her kindness with acts of his own. The realisation it took her death for him to break that cycle caused his heart to hang heavy. In the final analysis, this sponsored walk would benefit others rather than his wife.

When a gap in traffic presented itself, Oliver dashed across the fast-moving A28 to the relative quiet of a narrow country lane winding up the downs. He clocked its sign while steeling himself for the ascent. "White Hill, here we come."

An open, flat expanse gave way to a dark, tree-shrouded tunnel as the lane sloped upward. Oliver turned right, opposite the footpath he'd left before the break to visit Wye. Here the North Downs Way and Pilgrims' Way ran in tandem. Rough tarmac transitioned into an unmade track of water-filled potholes. Beyond Soakham Farm, the track narrowed further and turned upward to disappear in a woodland canopy-laden footpath. Oliver checked his headlamp batteries with a click of the switch. *I'll be needing this before I reach Chilham. Thank goodness the track is well worn and I have my GPS.* His breathing quickened and came in heavy puffs from the effort of his ascent. By the time the path levelled into a ridge line, Oliver had never felt so alone. Not one for flights of fancy, he rubbed his neck to flatten fine, agitated hairs. A moisture-heavy, chill mist settled over the footpath, snaking out between the trees on either side in defined, sinister tendrils. Like cotton wool in his ears, it dulled all sound but amplified his loneliness. Oliver bolstered his flagging spirit with an amusing, imaginary notion he might have stepped out of time. At any minute, the ancient Canterbury pilgrims could appear on the trail beside him. He snorted at the absurdity of such an idea.

From deep in the trees to his left, a sharp, panicked female scream sliced through the gloom.

Oliver froze. *What the hell was that?*

Another scream followed by another caused him to illuminate his headlamp and shine its beam into the dense forest. A fourth outburst ended in a tightening gurgle.

Oliver plunged into the undergrowth. Tree roots snagged his ankles and batted the walking poles back and forth. Oliver collapsed the telescopic aids and slid them into a sling strapped around his pack. The correct heading became evident from continued gurgling, although its vigour and volume faded with the last light of day. Oliver swung his head from side to side, causing the headlamp to sweep about like some manic lighthouse suffering an epileptic fit. Its beam reflected off the fog and splashed against rugged tree trunks closer at hand. Oliver's foot caught on some brambles and sent him sprawling face first onto the forest floor. The headlamp flickered and extinguished. He pushed his torso away from the spongy surface, groping around for something to provide leverage. His hand found a solid shape with an opening. He pressed his fingers inside in the blackness, disoriented without illumination or visual reference. Something firm scraped against his digits, ending in a wet, lolling sensation. Oliver panted and reached his free hand up to tap the side of his headlamp. It flickered again, then sprang to life. Light fell upon the face of a mid-thirties woman clad in a white dress. The hole his other hand rested in was her open mouth, stretched wide in terror. The firmness scraping his fingers came from her teeth and the wet sensation her tongue. Oliver recoiled with a yelp, unable to tear his gaze away from the lifeless eyes staring upward into darkness. Angry bruising appeared like a collar around her windpipe.

Up to his right, someone darted between trees, snapping twigs and unsettling fallen leaves. The disruption pulled Oliver's focus away. *That must be her murderer*. He reached for a nearby tree to clamber off the wet ground. When his eyes moved down again, the forest floor lay empty with no sign of the woman in white. Oliver's muscles tensed. "What is going on?" His words hung empty in the fading light. With no other obvious course of action, he gave chase into the rustling undergrowth, desperate for answers. A slender, feminine figure dashed through a broad depression with fewer obstructions. Oliver discarded his pack for extra agility. He'd never catch her otherwise, and the pack's material was bright enough to locate again with his torch. Passionate feet pounded the earth. His mind grappled with realisations the figure ahead could be some cold-blooded killer. A pale echo of his rugby-playing youth, he launched into a flying tackle and brought his quarry to the ground.

Saliva thick with adrenaline, he forced out a demand as he rolled the woman's body over. "You'd better have some answers for…" Oliver's face solidified into an unquantifiable expression of myriad emotions, frozen like a victim of Medusa's stare.

Shy, bright eyes shone out amidst the curly blonde hair of his wife's head. Oliver's shaking hands gripped her shoulders. His voice rasped in an agonised whisper. "Pauline?"

Pauline's mouth curled into a leering smile. Tiny fractures like dry, broken earth spread across her smooth complexion. Those blonde curls grew into a lion's mane of unkempt, tangled locks. She eyed Oliver and licked her lips with a blackening tongue. It halted mid stroke and lay still. Bright eyes collapsed inward. Her crumbling skull pressed down into a wood ant mound. The disturbed, biting insects swarmed from now empty eye sockets and a dislocated jaw turning to bone amidst dissolving flesh.

Oliver screamed. "Noo."

Pauline's ribcage disintegrated, expelling clouds of pungent green gas. Its foul stench forced entry into Oliver's nasal cavity. He retched and struggled, gasping for air amidst a rising wave of vomit. Acidic bile and lumps of partially digested crusty bread from The Tickled Trout sprayed across that face decaying before his eyes. Pain wracked his chest, its grip unforgiving. Oliver released Pauline's now disjointed, skeletal shoulders and pressed splayed fingers against the merciless agony of his over-pumping heart. He rolled over on his back beside the putrid remains decomposing like a time lapse film. His lungs strained for breath, but his body refused to respond. The weight of a millstone pressed against his chest, nullifying any attempt to receive life-giving oxygen. Shining straight upward, the headlamp illuminated nothing but swirling, ice cold vapour. A collapsing iris of darkness enfolded those clouds in his narrowing field of vision. Oliver lay still.

* * *

Nick placed two tins of baked beans, a loaf of bread and a pint of milk on the village shop counter. The headline of a local paper drew his gaze: *'Charity fundraiser suffers fatal heart attack on White Hill.'*

"That was a nasty business." A buxom, elderly woman, way past typical retirement age clasped her hands together beside the till.

"What was it all about?" Nick asked.

"Some gentleman in his early fifties was walking The Pilgrims' Way to raise money for charity. An outfit who cared for his wife after a stroke, before she passed away."

"Did he keel over?" Nick retrieved a copy of the paper to go with his shopping.

"Less than a day from his goal. So sad."

A tall, beanpole customer of similar vintage to the

shopkeeper stooped against a rustic, knotted walking stick. "That's not the half of it, May. Did you hear how he was found?"

May shook her head. "The paper didn't say, Larry."

Larry left the vegetables he was surveying and crossed the small shop floor. His frame surged with renewed vigour at being able to unburden his news. "Face up in a depression amidst the undergrowth. One of the forest rangers passed by and noticed an artificial light flickering amongst the trees. The dead bloke wore one of those headlamp gadgets walkers sometimes have. It was switched on."

May fidgeted. "The paper said he'd stopped for a bite to eat in Wye, before pressing on towards here around dusk. How did he wander off the path? Was he lost?"

Larry shook his head. "His pack was dumped a hundred yards away, beside a tree. Even that was a reasonable distance from the footpath. Someone or something lured him in there."

May folded her arms. "Pish and tosh. Not more of your wild stories, Larry?"

Larry's hirsute eyebrows butted together. He pointed a bony finger at the shopkeeper. "You've lived here almost as long as me. They found that chap on White Hill. White Hill, May. Think about it."

Nick cocked his head. "White Hill? Where have I encountered that name before?"

Larry looked him up and down. "You're the Calendars' new tenant, aren't you?"

"That's right."

Larry jerked a hooked nose towards the shop window. "White Hill lies along The Pilgrims' Way in King's Wood."

Nick glanced at May as she began ringing up his purchases. He continued addressing the thin old man. "I must have passed it on my way here. Is it significant the fellow suffered a heart attack on White Hill? Has that happened before?"

Larry banged his stick against the counter. "He perished close to where that dog walker stumbled on Charlie Brockman's corpse."

Nick squinted through glazed eyes. "It's a tragic coincidence."

"Coincidence?" Larry muttered, eyes downcast. "Never go alone." He staggered back to the vegetables, mumbling under his breath. All previous enthusiasm vanished from his movements.

May took a ten pound note Nick offered her. She bent forward to speak in guarded tones. "Don't bother yourself about him. We were all fed ghost stories about White Hill as kids. Some never grew out of them." Her eyes softened in time to notice Larry place a lettuce in his shopping basket. "When you've nought left in life, any excitement - however fanciful - is a welcome diversion." She handed Nick his change.

Nick put it away. "Thank you."

"How are you settling in at Stour Cottage?"

Nick didn't wish to linger for questioning. "It's a comfortable little home. Brian and Doreen are fine landlords. I couldn't be happier." Nick laughed inside. *I couldn't be happier? What a crock! Sure, I'm satisfied with my temporary domestic arrangements, but when will I ever be happy again?*

May sensed his mild agitation and eagerness to depart. She stepped back. "I hope we'll see you again soon." She left it at that and watched Nick leave.

Back at Stour Cottage, Nick stowed his shopping and sat down at the dining table with a cuppa and the paper. Its front-page article detailed the bare minimum facts of Oliver Hall's fate as described by May, the shopkeeper. None of Larry's gossip-fuelled embellishments were included. Nick clutched his mug in both hands. He considered the old man's assertions about Charlie Brockman being discovered near the same spot. *Charlie said he and June liked to walk in King's Wood. Oliver Hall was a fitness nut who keeled over. Not the first time that's happened. And after the strain of becoming a widower, too.* He left the article alone and continued flicking through the pages. At the obituaries he found an entry the Calendars had published for Charlie. "That was nice of them." His spoken words filled the smothering loneliness of that attractive but empty room. A breeze brushed past his neck. Nick glanced round for any sign the French doors might be loose, but they remained secure. Beyond by the woodshed, a short figure stood watching him, silhouetted by low winter sun. Nick rose and shielded his eyes without success at identifying what appeared to be a child. The sun passed behind a cloud and his watcher whirled and ran into the bushes. Nick fell forward against the glass panes of the double doors at the sight of dark ginger hair and a blue and white checked shirt he knew. It was the same shirt Grant wore the day he died. For one confused moment, Nick considered giving chase. *What am I going to find? A load of wet bushes and nothing more. It's an illusion, Preston. Another product of your mixed up mind and struggling heart.*

He trudged back to the dining table and closed the newspaper. *I've got to stop listening to ghost stories.*

The French doors rattled from a sudden impact.

Nick spun. A black and white football rolled away from the cottage, across the lawn. This time he grabbed his jacket from the hall, stuffed his feet into a pair of slip-on shoes and tugged open the kitchen door.

Outside, the lawn lay empty with no sign of the ball. Nick rummaged around in the grass and checked the bushes behind the woodshed. No footprints or signs of human passage disturbed the lush environment.

"Everything okay, Nick?" Brian Calendar looked up from loading some old paperwork into a metal incinerator.

Nick flushed. "Something struck the cottage. I thought it was a child's football."

Brian grinned. "Can't say I've seen any kids around here. They're all at school today."

Nick backpedalled. "It could have been a bird flying into the glass." He knew that was a lie and changed the subject. "I read your obituary for Charlie in the local paper."

Brian crouched to light the incinerator. "A trifle. One

small way for his name to live in posterity. They keep every edition of those papers as historical records. Doreen and I were glad to do it."

"Did you read about that charity walker they found near the same spot?"

Brian backed away as smoke rose from a pipe atop his waste disposal unit. "Yes. What a tragedy. He was raising money for an organisation that helped his wife, so the papers said."

Nick read Brian's body language. He appeared nonchalant. If he'd heard the rumours Larry spouted in the shop, there was no sign of him withholding items of interest. Nick thought better of delving into tales of the supernatural. It felt disrespectful, so soon after discussing the recently deceased.

"Are you working today?" Brian moved towards the house.

"I will be. I've a new campaign to review. My client hopes I'll streamline it for a better return on investment."

Brian squinted. "How much of that is science and how much would you benefit from a crystal ball?"

Nick's stiff frame slackened at the friendly jibe. "Show me one form of prediction - from weather to the stock market - where pure science and analytical experience are infallible. I lessen the odds and risk a little; nothing more."

"Sounds like my old career. Good luck with it."

"Cheers." Nick went back inside.

An hour after ploughing through pages of digital work documents, Nick pushed back his seat in the upstairs landing study area. No matter how hard he tried, reading each paragraph felt like an uphill struggle today. He closed the electronic folder on his laptop and launched a web browser. Fingers tapping away at the keyboard formed the words *'White Hill Kent'* in an on-screen search box. An immediate, highlighted map loaded above the results. The named side road from Challock down towards Wye appeared in red. He clicked the map for a full-screen view. So *I did pass it on the way here. I must have read a road sign without taking it in. That's a fair stretch along Mountain Street and through the woods. Charlie was a man on a mission the day he died, all right. Poor old guy. Still, I can understand that. I'd walk all the way back to Midhurst if I thought I could see Grant again.* He closed the browser and shut down his computer.

* * *

It wasn't Nick Preston's first visit to Canterbury. He'd made a flying overnight business trip to assist with a project at the city council, three years earlier. But he'd never wandered the streets like a tourist, nor needed to visit the ancient settlement's majestic library.

He parked his Honda close to the Marlowe Theatre and sauntered out onto the pedestrianised High Street. At its northwestern end, the curved medieval Westgate Towers from the old city wall stood resplendent before a block paved avenue of shops. Many of them seemed to look down at passersby with paternal vigilance, confident in five or more centuries under their belts.

A slight incline signalled a shallow, humpbacked bridge midway along the thoroughfare. Nick watched tourists enjoying a boat ride below. The current swept underwater weeds out like luminous green hair in a stiff breeze. *So that's The Great Stour again? The same river that runs close to Chilham.* He pushed away from a set of glossy black railings and continued beyond a junction with a side road called Best Lane.

The library stood an imposing Tudor Revival building, designed at the end of the nineteenth century by a local surveyor. Referred to as the *'Beaney House of Art and Knowledge,'* it also featured the central museum and art gallery. Nick took in its three main storeys plus basement. Intricate brickwork blended with exposed beams and ornate windows in a semi-Gothic appearance. The style reminded Nick of Cragside in Northumberland, albeit on a much smaller and urban-centric scale. He climbed a set of seven steps with white painted risers beneath a sign which declared: *'Royal Museum and Free Library. (Founded 1858).'* Carved gargoyles grinned down from a porch entrance roof on either side.

Nick had no cohesive reason for coming here. Nice though his new dwelling was, he wished to escape the cottage for a morning. His attention wandered whenever he sat down to attempt work. On the rare occasions he reached a state of professional flow, an interruption soon followed: a knock at the door, kids running up and down the lane before and after school, or the more worrying encounters he couldn't explain surrounding Grant. He could always rely on some disturbance or other. A full workday felt like a distant memory, ever since his arrival in Kent.

It was those inexplicable encounters with Grant that drew him here. Nothing like it had ever happened in West Sussex. *Why, of all places, should a location without links to Grant produce such striking manifestations?* At the back of his mind, Nick harboured concerns he was losing the plot. Moving away from Alana and living alone was a new experience. Now, no familiar daily activity filtered between him and his grief. No age-old routine masked or muffled his raw emotions breaking loose at Stour Cottage.

The Beaney's bright, modern interior took Nick by surprise. Swathes of overhead strip lighting reflected off white paint and plate glass interior walls. It presented a marked contrast to the building's intricate facade. He wondered how long ago this refit of clean lines and minimalist surfaces occurred. That fleeting question evaporated once his eyes focused on an index of library sections. He drifted between the rows for *'Religion & Spirituality,'* and *'The Supernatural & Occult.'* After forty minutes of intense browsing, Nick sat down at a table clutching a pile of books covering everything from Near-Death Experiences to Kent Ghosts and Folklore. He didn't expect to discover some magical paragraph of text to transform his situation. More than anything, he sought the solidarity he'd enjoyed the night he met Charlie Brockman. Any title featuring those who'd claimed similar experiences would help.

Most of all, recorded accounts of how people coped. That cynic at The White Horse, Kevin Pickford, was right: the bereaved often met and even spoke with their departed nearest and dearest, soon after death. In those assorted volumes he located numerous stories in a similar vein. Accounts of people hearing, glimpsing, or having other memory-specific sensory encounters with loved ones proved a common feature. Nick pored over an open book. *Could that be what's happening to me with Grant?*

By early afternoon his eyes grew tired. The trip had served its purpose in terms of encouragement and reassurance. As he suspected, none of those books provided concrete answers about how and why it all happened. Nothing bar parapsychologists spouting random theories he could have constructed himself. The last book in the pile detailed ghostly happenings and traditional stories around the county, sorted by area. Nick ran his index finger down the contents list for familiar names. He almost pushed it through the page when it highlighted '*White Hill - Challock.*' Pages flashed past until he reached a frustratingly sparse entry. It detailed various motorists who'd struck a woman on the lane after dark, only to discover no sign of a body afterwards. In every account, the victim smiled at the point of impact (a detail relayed with great relish by the book's author, who savoured the creepiness of it). Suggested explanations pointed to a woman in her thirties, strangled in the woods nearby during the 1990s. Other stories mentioned ghosts of murdered girls from the last two hundred years.

Details remained scarce, but focused on instances of spectral, screaming voices and the terrified living chased through King's Wood by some unseen pursuer.

Nick photocopied and paid for the pages of interest, then returned the titles and left the library. His stomach rumbled. *I've had no lunch.* At the corner of Best Lane he spied an attractive, independent Italian restaurant. *Why not? I won't have to cook later.*

While he waited upstairs in the restaurant for his Spaghetti Aragosta, Nick pulled out the photocopied pages again. He'd no idea why he wished to retain such information. *Larry in the shop seemed convinced Charlie and Oliver both died in suspicious circumstances. Does any of this have bearing on my situation and recovery from losing Grant? Unlikely. But it feels good to pursue an interest outside of the norm. Anything separate from work and my all-pervasive sadness.* An aroma of garlic and herbs hung in the air. Nick tucked the pages away in time to spy a pretty, beaming waitress bearing his steaming plate of lobster meat, tomatoes and pasta. He sat upright and smiled to himself. *I'll return to Alana two stone heavier and a committed spook investigator, if I don't watch out.*

5
Conflicting Passions

Buff for a mid-forties accountant, many thought Ian Wallis kept himself fit to counteract the effects of a sedentary job. In reality, he couldn't release teenage dreams of becoming a professional athlete, despite a tragic back injury that forever reduced them to ashes. Sometimes, Ian pushed himself too far in his day-to-day workout and wound up in bed - to the annoyance and scolding of his wife, Deborah. Toned, with back-combed, greying chestnut hair, a short beard and large round glasses, Ian presented a pigeonhole paradox to casual observers.

He secured the central locking on his black, 3 Series BMW and pulled his jacket collar high against the evening wind. Floodlights illuminated an eight lane running track at the Julie Rose Stadium in Ashford. Ian sidled into the stands to sit beneath a fixed white awning in ten white crests resembling meringue peaks. He jumped up again and clutched a railing as a sixteen-year-old athlete rounded a bend in the track and flashed past. The boy almost collapsed from efforts to catch his breath. At the finish line, his coach clicked a digital stopwatch and rubbed his face. A long stream of vapour escaped his mouth.

Ian descended steps and crossed the track to join them.

Upon registering his approaching observer, the boy's face reddened and fell. A keen young athlete with medium length brown hair, Barry Wallis wore a cheeky grin that brimmed over with confidence under normal circumstances. This combination of athleticism and approachability made him popular with girls at school. Yet, Barry never forgot nor abandoned his long-term childhood friends. Not even when he became the centre of female attention and they did not. He attempted to smile at his father. The result lacked commitment, like the laps he'd run moments before. "I'll get changed." He hobbled off.

"How's he doing, Mike?" Ian asked the coach.

Mike Brewer jotted the stopwatch reading down on a clipboard. "All over the place. I don't know what to tell you. Time was when Barry reached a new high each week. Now…?" He flicked his crew cut flattop. "His heart isn't in it."

Ian frowned. "You think he's become complacent? Does he need better rewards to celebrate milestones? What?"

Mike tucked the clipboard under one arm. "Has he got a new interest? A girl or some other hobby?"

Ian swayed. "No, I don't believe so. He dates girls, but isn't fixated on anyone I'm aware of. That's a worrying development. Is he off the pace by a lot?"

Mike placed the stopwatch neck cord over his head. "Today's times are behind where he was six months ago. It's disappointing. He's dropped from being my number one track star to not even a competitor."

Blood rose to Ian's cheeks. His jaw tightened. "I'll have a chat with him. Thanks, Mike."

"I hope you're a better motivator than I've turned out to be. My encouragement falls on deaf ears now, as far as Barry is concerned."

Ian stormed off to wait by the car.

Barry emerged from the changing rooms, a sports bag slung over one shoulder. He sipped spring water from a clear plastic bottle.

Kelly Mason opened the women's door opposite. The teenage girl's brown eyes lit up upon spying a peer she always exchanged flirtatious banter with each week. "Hey, Barry." She tidied short chestnut hair between hurried fingers.

Barry screwed the cap on his bottle, then stowed it in the bag. "Hey yourself, Kelly."

"What happened out there today? Aren't you feeling well?" Kelly drew nearer.

"I'm off my game. I have been for a while." Barry dumped his bag on a nearby bench.

"How come?" Kelly stood before him now.

Barry found her stare intoxicating, but his eyes scanned the floor. "I'm sick of my father driving me to achieve sporting greatness. I love running, but that's the point: I want to do it for pleasure, not to become a world competitor."

"Have you told him that?"

Barry sighed. "I've tried. Winning medals and living life as a professional athlete was his dream. It's not mine. I hate being pushed all the time."

"Doesn't your dad work in finance? What happened?"

"That's right. He suffered a spinal injury, years before I came along. It nixed his hopes."

Kelly adopted a demure posture, voice softening. "Do you know what you'd like to do?"

Barry flushed. "I want to be a car mechanic."

"That's a good job." Kelly made a lazy circle with the toe of one foot.

"Try telling my father that. I did once. He almost blew a gasket."

One corner of Kelly's mouth curled into a mischievous smile. "If you were a mechanic, you could fix a blown gasket."

Barry's shoulders lifted a fraction. He gazed into those beautiful, feminine eyes and caught Kelly moistening her lips. The pair had danced around this for months. Barry opted to seize the day. He placed a gentle hand in the small of Kelly's back and drew her close. Kelly melted into his embrace without resistance. Their lips met; tender at first, then with a hormone-fuelled hunger neither wished to resist. Barry pressed against her. His right hand descended from her back to squeeze peachy firm buttocks.

Kelly pulled her head away a touch, eyes glistening. She swallowed with a gentle, breathless gasp that turned into another cheeky smile. "You're naughty."

A sharp, frustrated man's voice echoed from the

changing area entrance. "Barry, I'm waiting to take you home. Your mother's dinner will be ruined if we don't hurry."

Barry released Kelly. A stirring in his intimate regions faded at the sight and sound of his pushy father.

Kelly's cheeks rouged. She collected her sports bag and avoided making eye contact with Ian Wallis.

Barry shouldered his gear again, then stormed past his father into the car park.

Indicator lights flashed and the BMW's doors unlocked. Barry dumped his holdall in the boot, then flopped into the front passenger seat.

Ian started the engine. The car pulled out of the stadium, turning right towards the A28. He waited until they were five minutes along the road before speaking again. "What's going on, Son?"

"How do you mean?"

"Mike said your times are all over the place. He can't motivate you."

"I enjoy running, Dad."

Ian's stiff posture slackened. His voice adopted a hitherto absent, positive tone. "Then what's the problem? Mike says you're not even a competitor now."

Barry stared out of his window. "I don't want to be a competitor."

Ian's face darkened again. "Why not? You have a gift. Gifts come with a responsibility not to squander them."

"I want to follow my passion."

"I thought running was your passion?"

"When it was fun," Barry muttered.

The volume ratcheted up in Ian's voice. "Oh, I see. You can't handle the challenge like a man. When something isn't fun anymore, you want to throw in the towel, is that it? You'll never amount to anything with an attitude like that. God knows how you'll earn a living."

"I'm not going to earn a living running round a track, Dad. I've never wanted to."

Ian's face strained. "But you could, Barry. You have it within you to become an all-star athlete."

"Don't you understand? Haven't you listened to a word I've said in the last month? It has to be in more than my body." Barry clutched his chest. "It's got to be in my heart."

Ian signalled left off the A28 opposite Wye, towards their home in Challock. He shifted down as the car started up White Hill. "And what has replaced it? That tart I caught you tongue wrestling with?"

Barry's eyes watered. "Kelly isn't a tart. That's the first time we've kissed."

"Imagine how proud you'd make her by winning a gold medal. She'd adore you for it." Ian gripped his son's leg.

Barry unhooked the clutching fingers. "I don't want her to adore me for winning a medal, Dad. Fuck, how insecure would that be?"

Ian shouted at his face. "Don't use language like th-"

He broke his tirade upon noticing Barry's eyes widen at something beyond the windshield. Ian's face snapped back to the road, and he stomped on the brake pedal. "No."

A mid-thirties woman in a flowing white dress stood smiling at them, mere feet from the car. The BMW's tyres squealed, but it was no use. Two impacts in different directions happened in unison. The bonnet struck the woman's body, launching her forwards over the front of the car. At the same moment Barry flew through the windshield in a shower of shattering safety glass. Ian's seatbelt locked tight; but during his earlier emotional upheaval, his teenage son had neglected to fasten his own. That sickening female grin slid over the roof out of view, while Barry's torpedo-like body collided with a tree and flopped onto the verge beside it.

Ian sat for a moment in shock, covered with broken glass. The stationary but still-running car's headlights illuminated Barry's motionless torso. "Oh, my God." Ian pressed his seatbelt release and tumbled out of the driver's door into the pitch-black lane. He staggered along the car, dumbstruck. The vehicle evidenced no bodywork damage from the collision. *Is that why the airbags didn't fire?* Ian glanced behind for signs of the pedestrian he'd struck, laying in the road. She was nowhere in sight. Torn between two possible fatalities, he hurried towards the visible body: that of his unmoving, helpless offspring. Ian's hands shook. He knelt at the roadside, pawing Barry's clothes. "Barry?" He swallowed hard. "Barry, can you hear me?" Barry's head flopped sideways on a broken neck as Ian rolled him over. Empty eyes reflected in the vehicle's headlights. The teenager's mouth dropped open without a sound. Ian cradled him close and rocked in a bout of heaving sobs. "No, Barry. Not my boy. Not my beautiful boy."

* * *

Ian Wallis spaced out in his executive, Challock home. He sat on Barry's bed surrounded by glossy posters of high performance cars.

Deborah Wallis lingered in the doorway, face downcast.

Ian lifted a junior athletic medal Barry won years before, from a stand beside the boy's alarm clock. He showed it to his wife, voice cracking. "More of this. That's all I wanted for Barry." He stood and dangled it before the motoring artwork, focus shifting. "But that's what Barry wanted." He put the medal down beside a partially constructed Tamiya radio-controlled car. It was the third his son had built in as many years. "He loved putting those things together, then installing and upgrading parts. I remember one day he was so excited about some oil filled shocks he'd bought at the hobby shop. I never listened." He sniffed. "He was my boy, and I never listened to him."

Deborah squeezed herself against the door frame, hugging the wall for comfort absent from her husband. She longed to hold her departed son. "He'd have made an excellent mechanic. It was his dream."

Ian pressed down the body of a 1/10 scale dune buggy. It sprang back on the same oil filled shocks he'd mentioned. "I should have checked he was wearing his seatbelt, Deb. I was the driver; it's my responsibility." He rubbed his eyes. "I was so obsessed with his poor track performance. It's all my fault."

A single tear trickled down Deborah's left cheek. She stared at Ian. "That won't bring him back. What about that woman in the road? Shouldn't she share the blame? Walking alone on a country lane after dark, with no light to warn oncoming traffic. Was she drunk?"

"I don't know. How could I? The police never recovered her body. They don't seem interested. Every time I phone the station for an update, there's a noncommittal response. I swear they aren't even looking. That woman couldn't have staggered off. I hit her square on at speed and she rolled over the roof."

"What about drugs? I've heard some varieties make people super strong or impervious to pain, for a while."

"The police Forensic Collision Investigation Unit said there was no evidence of a body or anything else striking the Beamer. The rozzers even breathalysed me, as though I were under the influence or making the whole story up."

"Are you certain there was a woman? You told me how upset you were."

Ian fumed. "Now you don't believe me either? A minute ago you were suggesting she shares blame for our boy's death."

Deborah wrung uncomfortable hands. "You know what you're like once the red mist descends, Ian. Something flashed in your headlights while you were flying around in a rage. You hit the brakes. Barry wasn't strapped in."

Ian clenched a fist and punched a bare patch of wall between posters. "I didn't imagine it, Deb. Bloody hell, the woman was smiling at us like some sick mental case. Barry saw her first. That's what made me look round."

Deborah sighed. "If you say so."

"I do say so." He pushed past her and stormed downstairs. "If Barry were here, he'd say so too. But he's not. He's not here because I didn't check his seatbelt." The front door opened and slammed shut.

Deborah slid down to rest on the carpet in a pitiful heap.

Ian opened the boot of his BMW. With only the windshield to replace, he'd already paid the insurance excess. Now the car appeared good as new. Several miles away at a mortuary in Ashford, the pallid, rigor mortis stiffened corpse of his son lay on a slab. No-one could fix *him*. Those lifeless eyes were shut now. Never again would they sparkle with enthusiasm. Never again would they capture the attention of the teenage girls with whom he was so popular. Barry's sports bag still lay inside where he'd stowed it at the Julie Rose Stadium. Ian bent to unzip it. He pulled out Barry's track top and pressed it against his face. The smell of his son's stale sweat still permeated the fabric. When Ian's dreams went up in smoke after his spinal injury, he felt like his world had ended. Then he met Deborah, fell in love and got married. The day she gave birth to a boy, felt like God giving him a second shot at a gold medal. Only now did he realise how much he'd vicariously lived his own life through his son. This second confounding revelation stung worse than the first. It carried with it a fresh awakening to the fact he'd *used* the precious young life entrusted to him, rather than treasuring it. When all was said and done, they'd never have driven up White Hill that fateful night were it not for Ian's insistence. At the very least, he'd have made sure Barry wore his seatbelt. He'd also have kept his eyes on the road.

Ian stowed the track top and fastened the bag again. His limp fingers trailed across sundry motoring items beside it: a petrol canister, a grey one litre plastic bottle of 15W-40 oil, a scuffed metal toolbox and an old tow rope. He gazed up into a harsh, gloomy winter sky and shut the boot lid.

The turnoff for King's Wood lay a mile down the A251 from the Wallis house. Cold evening drew in as Ian drove in silence beneath its cathedral arch of interconnecting canopies above the dark lane. He passed by the main woodland car park but kept going until the thoroughfare sloped downward near the crest of White Hill. A smaller, less well known car park lay further ahead on the left, not two-hundred yards from the spot Barry died. As expected at this time of day and during such dreary winter weather, Ian found it empty. He pulled in and brought the car to a halt.

Ian couldn't fathom how long he stood before the open boot again, touching, hugging and sniffing Barry's sports gear. Nothing mattered anymore. Life held no hopes for a brighter future or happier times ahead in his shattered world. He kissed the boy's shirt and folded it on top of the other holdall contents. Damp air descended. A lone car cruised down the hill and disappeared. Ian zipped the bag, then closed the boot. The looped tow rope swung free in his spare hand. He crossed the lane, listening for traffic. There stood the tree Barry struck during his ultimate moment of mortality. *Did I imagine that woman on the road? Was Deborah right? No, I'm sure she was there. Of course she was. No matter, now. It's all so pointless.* Half a dozen fragments of splintered bark were all that suggested something had collided with the tree. It stood unwavering, as it had for centuries. Ian touched the mild damage. *A poor arboreal eulogy for sixteen vibrant years of life.* He sat on the grass verge, reliving the moment where he'd clutched Barry to his chest. A doe leaped past, startled by his motionless presence. It skittered across the hill to vanish amidst rustling undergrowth opposite. Disturbed bracken stilled and silenced.

Ian reclined his back against the tree trunk, peering up through its branches. "I'm so sorry, Barry. I'd give anything to turn the clock back and change the way I treated you." He picked up the tow rope and knotted it between committed fingers. "Time to push the reset button."

* * *

A medium build figure, Jason Cooper's frame suggested neither athletic prowess nor yet physical weakness. He enjoyed walking; a helpful predisposition for a teenage lad not quite old enough to drive. Such was the rural existence of a Kent country boy who lived with his parents on a quiet back lane. Sandy hair crested his oblong head in a wave, clipped into a fade above the ears. A strong nose protruded between disarming lights twinkling from dark eyes. Jason would have made friends easily, were it not for minor social clumsiness. That and a penchant for drifting into whimsical worlds. What his life lacked in personal interaction, the richness of his imagination balanced out.

A passing rain shower caused Jason to double his pace along Mountain Street towards 'The Orchard,' a detached cottage near the outskirts of Chilham. Mud clung in clumps like a second pair of footwear to the soles of his walking boots.

"Look at the state of you." His mother, Helen Cooper, rolled out pastry in the kitchen while Jason sat on the rear step banging his boots together.

Raymond Cooper strode into the room, newspaper scrunched in one hand. "Is there any shortbread to go with my tea, love?" he asked his wife, then noticed Jason's cloud of flying mud fragments. "Honestly, Jason, why do you insist on walking in the woods when it's a quagmire up there?"

Helen put down her rolling pin, then retrieved a biscuit barrel from a nearby over-counter cupboard. "Leave him be, Ray. It's good for a growing boy to exercise."

Raymond shook his head. "Mooching about in King's Wood on his own? It wouldn't be so bad if he had a girlfriend to take along. For Chrissake, he's sixteen. I'd already been dating two years by the time I was his age."

Helen gave his shoulder a playful punch. "Don't swear. Jason will find a nice girl in his own time."

Raymond frowned. "By the time he gets around to it, he'll have no idea what to do. He can't (or won't) approach one now. I wish we'd never indulged his love of fantasy and the supernatural. Just once I'd like to stumble upon a girlie magazine in his room amidst all those volumes on dragons, witches and goblins." A thoughtful expression crossed his face. "Do teenage guys still use girlie magazines, or is everything online these days?"

"How should I know?" Helen almost laughed.

Raymond turned to Jason. "Girls, Son. They're those curvy people with higher pitched voices, longer hair, bumpy chests and different plumbing than you. Please investigate the concept."

Jason kept quiet and arranged his footwear next to the bristled kitchen doormat.

Raymond watched him for a moment, then rubbed his chin with the free hand. "With his circle of friends, Helen, I'm amazed he can't find someone. It's such a shame Barry Wallis was killed. He was popular with the girls. They'd known each other since they were six. I was hoping Barry would hook him up."

Helen posted a shortbread biscuit into her husband's mouth. "Use that to keep quiet." She cast a sympathetic, sidelong glance at her son. "Don't you think Jason is suffering enough over recent events? Try to lay off the girlfriend topic for a change and give him some space, would you?"

Raymond bit into the biscuit, pulled it free of his mouth, then kissed his wife on the cheek. "You're right. I'll be in the lounge if you need anything." He strode off.

"Did you find any Adders today?" Helen asked as Jason entered the kitchen proper and Raymond disappeared.

"Not at this time of year, Mum."

"Oh. Of course, I suppose you wouldn't in winter." Helen held out the biscuit barrel to him. "Shortbread?"

"No, that's okay. Thanks." A digital recording of a trumpet fanfare blared from his waist area. Jason lifted his pullover to reveal a smartphone tucked into a belt clip pouch. He tore open its Velcro fastener and answered the call. "Hello?"

A harried voice shouted in his ear. "Jason? It's Adam. Can you talk?"

Jason pulled the phone away from his head to avoid auditory pain. "Hang on, Adam. I'll run up to my room."

Helen put the biscuit barrel away without looking round. "Say hello for me."

"I will, Mum." Jason took the cottage stairs two at a time on his ascent, turning at a half landing which overlooked their small orchard to the rear. His room faced onto Mountain Street at the front of the property. A row of bookshelves groaned under the weight of colourful fantasy role playing game manuals, epic sword and sorcery novels, and a burgeoning library on ghosts, the supernatural and occult. Jason flopped down onto the bottom bunk of his bed. No mattress adorned the top. Instead, he used it as a storage area for additional books resting on a baseboard. He lay on his side, gazing at a line of metal fantasy miniatures he'd painted the week before. They stood in dramatic poses, weapons raised along a narrow shelf beside his nightstand. "What's up, Adam?" he spoke into the phone again.

"Did you hear about Barry's dad?"

"No. What about him?"

Adam took a breath to calm himself. "The police found him hanging from that tree where Barry died. Jonathan said it appears to be suicide. He used a tow rope from their car."

Colour drained from Jason's cheeks. "Oh, no. What must Barry's mum be going through?"

"Yeah. The word is: Mr Wallis blamed himself for what happened."

Jason rolled onto his back. "Barry told me his dad wouldn't listen to him about scaling back the athletics.

He'd been slowing down at the track on purpose, in hopes his coach might complain."

Adam groaned. "Barry's dad was always tough on him. How are you bearing up? You knew him longer than any of us. Through your old man, wasn't it?"

"Yeah. Ian Wallis managed Dad's business accounts for years. Man, he'll be upset when he hears about this." Jason thought for a moment. "I'm okay. I took a walk in the woods this morning."

"When don't you?"

"Funny. True, though. My mind wandered while I stomped around the same old paths on autopilot. Barry and I had so many great memories. It never surprised me he wanted to become a car mechanic. When we were seven, we dug our own road network in a patch of earth behind my house. Somewhere to push our Matchbox cars around."

A mellower tonal quality filtered into Adam's voice. "When was the last time you raced his Tamiyas?"

"Two months ago. He let me use his dune buggy with the upgraded motor. A radio-controlled beast. It moved like the clappers. Great fun."

"I bet he still beat you?"

"Yep. Hands down." Jason wiped the corner of one eye with his finger.

Adam chuckled. "Loser."

Jason sighed. "Don't start. Dad gave me the girlfriend lecture again when I got in."

"He wants you to dip your nib in some feminine ink, like any healthy teenager of legal age." Adam's voice brimmed with newfound excitement. "Speaking of which, I got my fingers down the front of Samantha's knickers last night. Right inside the waistband."

Jason bit his lip. "That's nice for you. Do I want to hear this?"

"Of course you do; you're one of my best mates. So, we were snogging on the sofa, when her hand strayed south of the border. I don't think she meant to, but I wasn't going to pass up the chance to reciprocate. Man, her patch was so silky. I tell you, Jason, she was puffy and wet down there. It's only a matter of time. Samantha's going to be the one; I know she is."

Jason gritted his teeth. His speech lacked any hint of enthusiasm. "Delightful. Any other news?"

Adam shouted in his ear again. "Shit. In all the commotion over Barry's dad, I almost forgot: Nathan got laid."

Jason sat upright and clonked his forehead on the underside of the upper bunk. "What? I didn't think he was seeing anyone."

"He isn't. Claudia Jones phoned him out of the blue. She came right out and said, '*So, do you want to do it?*' Nathan was never one to pass up a good thing, so he went with her."

Jason touched an instant bruise on his left temple from the impact. "Chlamydia Claudia? She's two years above us at school."

"Are you saying you wouldn't? Crap, she's hot as hell and hornier than a convention of rams. Eighteen. Oh God, it must have felt incredible. Nathan said she blew his mind. Some other things, too. I'm still trying to extract all the juicy details from him."

Jason huffed and spoke in a tired voice. "Enjoy your interrogation."

Adam grunted. "I don't understand you sometimes, mate. We're sixteen now; the age of consent. How come you're not out there trying to sow your oats? Don't tell me you're still stuck on Louise Squires?"

Jason winced. "I collided with her in the school hallway the other day. She was waiting for Karen outside the loo."

"A-n-d?" Adam stretched out the word, hoping for any sign of glowing embers in his friend's otherwise cold, affective life.

"She smiled at me and I said hello."

"You're not going to tell me that's it?" He hesitated. "You are, aren't you?"

"I tripped over my words," Jason stuttered. "I couldn't think of anything else to say. There was an awkward silence, and then Karen reappeared. Louise's smile turned into a frown. At least, I think it did. Perhaps she doesn't like me after all, and I'm a hopeless fool."

Adam laughed. "Maybe she'd have liked you to say more than 'hello,' rather than clamming up like a plonker? But you're right, mate: you *are* a hopeless fool."

"Thanks."

"Don't mention it." Adam's sarcastic voice melted into warmth. "Are you sure you're okay?"

Jason swung his legs around to sit on the side of the bed. "Compared to what? I miss Barry, Adam. We all do."

Adam took a pronounced breath. "You may be the world's worst, oblivious pussy tease, but no guy ever had a more loyal friend."

Jason's eyes watered, but he said nothing.

Adam reinforced his statement. "I mean it. Barry thought so, too. I still can't believe he's gone; snuffed out in an instant." He sighed. "Life is short. It's the reason we tease you about girls sometimes, you know? We don't want you to miss out. One day we'll all have adult responsibilities, Jason. Barry, Nathan, Jonathan and I kinda felt like you'd skipped the fun years and gone straight to that point. From childhood to mid-life without the juicy bits in between."

Jason cracked a half smile. "Please don't clarify it further. You started out with a decent compliment."

Adam delivered a pig-like grunt of amusement. "Okay. Are you going to tell your dad about Ian Wallis?"

"I suppose I'd better. That'll be tough. Mum says hello, by the way."

"Give her my regards. I'll be thinking of you." He chuckled. "Well, you and Samantha's engorged pussy, anyway."

Jason laughed aloud this time. "Oh, go away. You're a pain in the arse."

"Keep your chin up, Jason."

Jason hesitated to clear the air from their banter. "I will. Thanks for letting me know, Adam."

"Later, buddy. Bye."

"Bye." Jason hung up. He put down his phone and reached for a fantasy novel lying next to his bed. Its cover featured an ornate bastard sword rammed into a hill before a white castle. Jason opened the book and tugged out a photograph he used for a mark. It depicted a pretty, teenage girl with pouting lips and centre-parted, chest length fair hair. Beneath it he'd written the word '*Louise,*' with the letter '*o*' formed into a heart shape. He studied it for a moment, then placed the picture back inside the book with care and set it down again.

6
Flawed Communications

"Thanks for having us round, Jason." Nathan Bishop wandered over to Jason Cooper's bedroom window and gazed down into the deserted country lane.

"We haven't all hung out here since our last campaign." Jonathan Chapman sank into a beanbag on the carpet. He studied Jason's painted fantasy miniatures. "That must be six months ago."

"I had some ideas for a new series of adventures." Jason picked up a hardback role playing rulebook from the makeshift top bunk bookshelf.

Adam Little dumped himself on Jason's bed. "Some of us have been busy with 'campaigns' of our own in the real world." He stared at Nathan. "Old 'Basher Bishop' stopped bashing himself and plundered Claudia's treasure chest. He's levelled up from those experience points ahead of us." He grinned. "You're not supposed to leave the rest of the adventuring party behind, old man. Companions share the booty."

Jonathan folded his arms and rocked on the beanbag. "If you give Claudia your phone number, Adam, she'll more than likely share her 'booty' with you. Right, Nathan?"

Nathan shrugged. "There's a rumour she's working her way through the two lower years. I've no idea if it's true, but I don't regret what happened. She's a beautiful girl." He flushed. "It was nice to get that whole deal done and dusted."

Jason put his book down. "If we can talk Samantha into sleeping with Adam, maybe we'll get something other than raging hormones from him."

Adam frowned. His eyes strayed to the fantasy novel beside Jason's bed. Before its owner could object, he swiped it up and opened at the bookmark. "Here we go." He held up the photograph.

Jonathan scrabbled forwards for a better look. "Louise Squires? You're consistent, Jason."

Adam blew mocking kisses at the picture. "And consistently does nothing about it. I swear if he came home to find Louise spread naked on the mattress here, begging for him to take her, he'd run up the woods in a blind panic."

"Leave him alone, Adam." Nathan crossed the room and pulled the photograph from Adam's grasp. He handed it to Jason. "She's a nice girl, buddy. Claire Cummings told me Louise is seeing an older guy from Canterbury. Nobody we know. Sorry if that's hard for you to hear, but it might help."

Jason thumbed the picture, hollowed out by the news.

Adam's eyes twinkled. "Am I the only one who thinks 'Claire Cummings' sounds like a porn star?"

Nathan gave him a playful slap around the head. "Do us all a favour: dial back the smut and drag your mind out of the gutter for five minutes."

Jonathan watched the exchange with scrutinising interest. "It's bravado. Empty noise. Adam is trying to deal with his emotions over Barry, like the rest of us."

Adam's jovial smile turned downward. "When his coffin disappeared through those curtains at the crematorium yesterday…"

Nathan looked down at his friend as he stood over him. One hand of comfort rested on Adam's shoulder. "I know. That's when the penny dropped for me we'd never see or hear from him again."

Jonathan climbed off the beanbag to study Jason's library of paranormal books. "What if we could?"

"What if we could what?" Nathan turned.

"What if we could hear from him again?" Jonathan pulled out a volume called *'Voices from Beyond - True life accounts of post-death communication.'*

Adam lifted his head, which had sunk to fix on the carpet. "What are you suggesting?" He eyed the book cover. "A séance? Don't you need a medium for that to work?"

"How about a Ouija board?" Jonathan flicked through the pages.

Jason grunted. "You shouldn't mess with stuff like that."

Jonathan flashed the cover at him. "So why collect all these books?"

"Those subjects interest me," Jason replied. "There's a difference between learning about something and meddling in it. Anyway, we don't have a Ouija board."

"We don't need one." Jonathan snapped the book

shut and returned it to the shelf.

"Huh?" Adam frowned.

Jonathan dropped back onto the beanbag. "My cousin, Patrick, took part in a Ouija session with some friends. They wrote letters and numbers, plus the words '*Yes*,' '*No*,' and '*Goodbye*' on a large roll of artist's paper or card. Then they spread it on a table and used an overturned glass as a planchette. That's the item you focus communication with."

"Go on." Adam hunched over.

"At first the group moved the glass around with their fingers. Patrick said when it continued under its own steam, he almost crapped himself. But by that time he was too fascinated to run anywhere."

"What happened?" Jason asked.

"They contacted the spirit of a young girl who'd died six months earlier. Patrick's mum ran an antique shop. A fortnight prior, she'd acquired a pretty side table at auction, which she couldn't bring herself to sell. Instead, she brought it home. According to Patrick, the spirit told them it had been her bedside furniture when she passed away."

Nathan bit his lip. "That's freaky. Are you winding us up?"

"No." Jonathan's tone became adamant. "Patrick was dead serious." He winced. "No pun intended."

"So you're saying we can contact Barry?" Adam asked.

"Do we have anything to lose by trying?"

Nathan studied Jason. "You know more about this stuff than the rest of us. What do you think?"

Jason gripped the bedpost. "Some believe it's real. There are also any number of stories about people who've invited dark things into their lives with Ouija boards. Not the deceased loved ones they wanted."

Nathan nodded. "This isn't a game. I'd like to speak with Barry, but not like that. Besides, what if he's moved on?"

"To where?" Adam asked.

"To wherever most people go after they die," Nathan replied. "You don't think they're all milling around down here, do you?"

Jonathan picked up one of Jason's tabletop miniature figures. "You mean watching you become a notch in Claudia Jones' belt, Adam trying to talk Samantha out of her virginity, and Jason beating off to an old photograph of Louise Squires? You may recall that little girl Patrick communicated with had been dead for six months. He told me that sometimes spirits hang around for a while."

"So?" Nathan frowned.

"So, then they flit off to wherever you're suggesting."

Adam pounded his right knee with a fist. "In other words: the sooner we try contacting Barry, the more chance we have of it working?"

Jonathan flexed his fingers. "That's what I'm thinking. Barry's death was sudden and unexpected. Patrick said people in those situations can take a while to realise they're no longer among the living."

Adam rose off the mattress. "Not only could we say goodbye to Barry, we might even help him. You know:

assist our friend to cross over."

Nathan lifted both palms. "Wait a second. Barry was my mate too, but let's think this thing through with rational heads for a moment."

Adam scowled. "Do you want to help him or not?"

Nathan blinked. "Hey, it's not that simple."

"Isn't it?" Jonathan also got up. "I'm going to try. Penny wants me round to babysit for little Edward as usual, next week. I'll bring the paper and use her dining room for the session. But there's a better chance of success with multiple participants."

Adam grabbed his arm. "Count me in. Caution be buggered, I want to speak with Barry." He looked from Nathan to Jason. "Well? What about you two? The five of us have been inseparable since we were eleven. Or six, when it comes to you and Barry, Jason. Are you going to dig deep for a set of balls and chance your arm to connect with him? If he's stuck here, don't you want to help our friend find peace?"

Jason swallowed hard. His voice grew faint. "I suppose."

Adam slapped his shoulder. "That's what I'm talking about. How about you, Nathan? Are you in or out?"

Nathan sighed. "I still say this is a bad idea. Okay, I'm there. God knows what scrapes you three will wind up in without me to bail you out."

"Egotistical bastard." Adam offered Nathan his hand.

The pair shook.

* * *

Jason walked out of Canterbury West train station with Nathan and Adam at his side. "There's something I didn't mention the other day while Jonathan was talking. Several studies suggest Ouija boards don't communicate with anything but our own subconscious minds."

Adam regarded a passing car with pumping bass pouring from its stereo. "What about that glass or *plank* thing moving on its own?"

"Planchette," Jason corrected.

"Yeah, whatever. That can't be subconscious, can it?"

Jason rubbed his hands together for warmth. "Jonathan's cousin may have embellished that part. Most people move the planchette around themselves."

Nathan turned into the quiet residential street where Jonathan's older sister and her husband lived. "How do those studies explain it?"

Jason coughed. "There's something known as the 'Ideomotor Effect' scientists first researched during the mid-nineteenth century."

"Why then?" Nathan asked.

"Because interest in Ouija boards surged after catastrophic loss of life during the American Civil War. Many bereaved people sought comfort and a chance to bid their loved ones goodbye."

"Like with us and Barry," Adam muttered. "Okay, Jason, what is this 'Ideomotor Effect' all about?"

"It's unconscious, involuntary physical movement. The brain signals the body to move without us registering those communications or noticing our responses. They fly under the radar, neurologically speaking."

Adam grinned at Nathan. "I always speak neurologically. How about you?"

Nathan rolled his eyes. "Just because he knows more than us. This is interesting stuff." He nudged Jason. "Go on."

"Many scientists believe when one or more people ask questions of a Ouija board, that forms unconscious mental pictures in the mind or minds of the participants. The body responds by moving the planchette to spell out answers relating to those pictures."

Adam folded his arms. "Yeah, but hold on. What if a group of people all form unique pictures?"

"Then you'd get a load of gibberish, which sometimes happens during Ouija sessions. They did a literal blind test by covering participants' eyes. Unable to see the letters, numbers and so on, all that came back was a nonsense jumble. The same principle applies to dowsing or divining rods; or so some say. They claim the effect causes us to move them towards a desired outcome, without realising."

Adam tossed a carefree hand through his hair. "My 'divining rod' points at Samantha's crotch without fault, whenever it's wet down there."

Nathan cuffed him. "That's what Jason is saying, after a fashion. It subconsciously points at a desired outcome."

Adam groaned. "Oh man, is that a desired

outcome." He punched Nathan's shoulder. "Stop thumping me, you big lout."

Nathan nodded at a three bedroom semi. "There it is; number twelve."

Adam stopped and stared into Jason's eyes with a sad face. "You think we're going to communicate with someone we believe is Barry, but instead we'll be talking to ourselves? Deluded by answers our minds want to hear, as though it were really him?"

Jason's shoulders slumped. "It's possible."

Nathan opened the front gate and sauntered down the garden path. "If that's all there is to it, I feel better about this insanity. Does it matter if we walk away believing Barry has told us he's happy and in a good place? That's what we all want to hear."

Adam rang the doorbell. "Yeah, but from his lips - or whatever you use once they incinerate your body." He noticed Jason's sad eyes. "Sorry, mate. I've got a big mouth sometimes."

Nathan caught the sound of someone approaching from the hallway. "It's not the size of your gob that's the problem, Adam. It's the lack of a filter."

Jonathan Chapman opened the front door. "Hey guys. Are you ready for this?"

Adam crossed the threshold with a determined expression. "I was born ready."

Nathan made a swift face-palm. "God save us all from your action movie hero obsession." He followed inside with Jason bringing up the rear. "What time will Penny be home from work?"

"Not until after eleven." Jonathan closed the door.

"Edward is fast asleep in bed, dreaming a four-year-old's dreams."

Nathan took off his jacket. "They'll be more family friendly than Adam's."

Adam followed suit with a mischievous grin. "If there were a board of dream censors, I'd never be allowed to sleep again."

Jonathan hung up their jackets, then reached for Jason's. "Penny's husband is away, as usual. He only comes home from work at weekends, these days."

Jason looked around the living room. "That must be hard on their son."

Jonathan pointed through a doorway at the back of the room. "Penny makes sure she's home, most of the time Edward is awake. That's one reason she got a part-time, late evening job to boost their income. Neil is a good father. He spends every moment he can with his boy, Friday night through Monday morning."

Adam walked towards the door Jonathan had indicated. "It also provides you with regular cash. No need to hunt down some crappy weekend job, like others in our class. How did your Ouija artwork turn out?"

"See for yourself." Jonathan followed them into the dining room.

Full-length curtains were drawn across patio doors in a compact but comfortable dining space, capable of seating four. A serving hatch from the kitchen occupied one wall and a flat-pack DIY dresser its opposite. Spread out across a square dining table, lay a large piece of thick, white craft paper. Jonathan had unrolled it and used a dictionary to hold one end flat, with the table's usual, centrepiece fruit bowl securing the other.

Adam admired the layout of words, letters and numbers in blue marker pen. Jonathan had added crescent moons and stars around the outside in red pen for artistic effect. "What's with the witchy symbols?"

Jonathan shrugged. "I don't know. They seemed appropriate; like it needed something extra." He reached across to the dresser and opened one of its doors. "I thought we could use an overturned dessert bowl for a planchette. Easier for us all to touch at the same time. Penny and Neil own a pile of smoky glass ones. They're clear enough to read the letters through."

Nathan sat down at the table with his back to the patio doors. "You've given this some thought."

Adam positioned himself opposite. "Are we supposed to do this by candlelight?"

"We could. It might help us focus. Penny keeps a bulk bag of tea lights under the kitchen sink. I'll fetch a few and kill the lamp while you get settled." Jonathan disappeared into the kitchen.

Jason took a seat at the dresser end of the table.

Adam tapped his fingers on the decorated paper. "Do you want to tell Jonathan about that Ideomotor malarkey?"

"Do you think I should?" Jason replied.

Adam thought for a moment. "How about we do a blind test of our own?"

"What do you suggest?" Nathan asked.

"Have Jason question Barry about something the rest

of us wouldn't know the answer to. A specific piece of information. If we're all holding the planchette and the answer is gibberish, well and good. Otherwise... well, our minds can't form pictures or responses about something we don't know."

Nathan looked at Jason. "It's not an unreasonable idea. What do you think? Can you pick a question like that?"

"Okay, we'll try it." Jason clamped stiff fingers together.

Jonathan returned bearing a tray with four flickering tea lights. He set it down on the dresser and killed the overhead lamp.

Adam shut his eyes and whirled both arms about in arcane gestures. "Knock once for yes, Spirits." He clobbered the underside of the table with his knee, then gasped. "They're here."

Jonathan sat at the opposite end of the table from Jason. "If this is going to work, we need to be serious." He placed a glass dessert bowl face down on the paper in the middle of the table. "Let's start by taking some slow breaths. Patrick said if you inhale through your nose and exhale through your mouth, it stills the mind and makes you receptive."

Nathan shot Jason a knowing side-glance regarding their earlier discussion.

Jason joined Jonathan in placing his fingers on the planchette. Nathan did the same, with Adam last of all.

The friends watched Jonathan breathe, then followed his lead. With one motion, they moved the dessert bowl around.

After an interminable minute, Jonathan spoke in a calm, measured voice. "Barry Wallis. Barry, we are calling you forth. It's Jonathan, Adam, Nathan and Jason, your friends. Will you answer us?"

The group continued moving the bowl.

Jonathan went on. "Are you here, Barry?"

The bowl moved over the word, '*YES.*'

Hairs stood up on Adam's neck. He jolted, removing his finger from the planchette.

Jonathan inclined his head towards the bowl and Adam touched it again.

"How do we know it's him?" Nathan asked.

"Let me try." Adam licked his lips, a tremor in his voice. "Where were you killed, Barry?"

The planchette moved from letter to letter. '*W-H-I-T-E-H-I-L-L.*'

"Jesus," Jonathan exclaimed under his breath. "It works. Patrick was bang on."

Nathan spoke. "What make of radio-controlled car kits did you build, Barry?"

The planchette slid towards the letters again. '*T-A-M-I-Y-A.*'

Adam gasped with a rising pulse. "This is freaky. Freaky, but cool."

Nathan caught Jason's eye. "Have you got something you want to ask Barry, Jason?"

Jason drew in a deep breath. "Why did I cry, the day we dug that road for our toy cars in my back garden?"

The planchette circled twice, before forming three distinct words between swirls of the tabletop. '*L-O-S-T,*' '*F-A-V-O-U-R-I-T-E,*' '*C-A-R.*'

Adam leaned closer to Jason. "Is that right?"

He didn't need a verbal answer. The truth shone in Jason's worried eyes.

"So it *IS* him." Adam grew emboldened. "Barry. How can I get inside Samantha's knickers?"

Nathan scowled, then kicked him in the shins under the table. "Show some respect."

The bowl moved again. 'J-U-S-T,' 'F-U-C-K,' 'H-E-R.'

Physical leg pain morphed into a confident smile, bulging Adam's cheeks.

Jason released the bowl. "That's not Barry."

Nathan also let go. "I agree. Barry liked girls, but he didn't treat them like meat. He was cheeky, forward and confident, but always a gentleman." He fixed Adam with a fierce expression. "You know it too. He would never say that. Not even in a private chat between us guys."

Adam and Jonathan stopped moving the bowl and let go.

Jonathan sat back. "I concur. It could have been anyone. Maybe a drifting spirit, still caught in this world and longing to touch the living."

Adam regarded him. "But one that knew stuff about Barry. Even a personal story from his and Jason's childhood." He addressed Jason. "Not a product of our collective subconscious, right?"

Jonathan's brow creased at the opposite end of the table. "How's that?"

The bowl moved on its own.

"Fuck." All four boys pushed their chairs away.

The makeshift planchette drifted from letter to letter.

'*D-I-E,*' '*F-L-E-S-H-B-A-G-S.*' It circled in an accelerating loop of the tabletop.

Nathan looked from Jason to Jonathan with panicked eyes. "What do we do? How do we make it stop?"

Jonathan froze, head offering a tiny series of lost shakes.

The bowl shot off the table at Adam, who dived aside. It hit the dining room wall and shattered into a tinkling pile of fragments. The dresser tea lights blew out, plunging the boys into darkness. Upstairs, young Edward woke up crying.

Jonathan fumbled past Adam to reach for the light switch. The overhead lamp flickered on, then its bulb exploded. He tugged open the door to allow light in from the living room. "I'd best see to Edward."

Ten minutes later, when Jonathan came back downstairs, he found his friends sitting on the three-piece suite. "He had a nightmare."

Adam held up a trembling hand. "He's not the only one. Look at this."

Nathan grimaced. "We're all shaken, Adam." He addressed Jonathan. "Did Patrick experience anything like that?"

Jonathan's complexion paled. "No. But he said if the glass - or whatever you use - gets turned over, it grants a spirit access into the room and your lives."

"Oh, great." Adam put his head in his hands. "Ours broke against the wall. What does that mean?"

Nathan stood. "It means we should never have

dabbled."

Jonathan tensed his hands. "I'm sorry, guys. This is my fault."

Jason joined Nathan. "You didn't make us do it. We came of our own free will. If we're lucky, it'll be nothing more than a scary, isolated incident."

"I hope you're right," Jonathan muttered.

Adam stared into space. "For a moment I thought it was him, you know? I thought we'd have a final laugh with Barry. A chance to bid him farewell. One last goodbye his accident never afforded us."

Nathan helped his dazed chum off the sofa. "Barry is in a better place. I'm sure of it." He glanced at Jonathan. "Don't beat yourself up over this. Do you want a hand tidying up?"

Jonathan stared towards the dining room doorway. "Don't worry, I know where Penny and Neil keep the replacement bulbs. I'll clean the mess and tell my sister the light blew while I was eating some ice cream. I dropped the bowl from shock and it shattered. She'll be okay."

Jason retrieved their jackets from the hallway. "We've time to make the next train."

* * *

Nathan Bishop secured a tray of golden engagement rings in the safe at 'Hammond & Son Jewellers,' off the Butter Market in Canterbury.

Morgan Hammond closed its cumbersome door with a clank, then mopped his brow with a pristine handkerchief. He examined Nathan through beady but kind eyes behind large, round glasses perched on a triangular nose. "Your confidence with the customers is growing, Nathan. I'm glad I took you on as Saturday staff. You've a pleasant way about you."

"Thank you, Mr Hammond."

"What time is your train home?" The mid-fifties jeweller put his handkerchief away.

"I'm off to visit a friend, first. There's no hurry if you need additional help closing up."

Morgan pulled an antique pocket watch from his Paisley waistcoat. He flipped open the cover, then shut it with a click. "That's okay. Enjoy the rest of your weekend."

"You too, Mr Hammond." Nathan retrieved his jacket from a staff wardrobe behind the counter.

Everything about Hammond & Son spoke of quality and attention to detail. Morgan didn't like the idea of assorted - sometimes colourful - coats detracting from that image, hence his purchase of a fine, antique mahogany storage unit.

Nathan closed the wardrobe door and zipped himself into the padded, waterproof parka. The shop bell jangled as he left. He cast a wave back through the window at his particular but pleasant employer, then picked up a brisk pace through the early evening streets.

A commotion rang out ahead. Blue flashing lights reflected off tightly packed, historical buildings curving away round Sun Street. Nathan wished to avoid any potential hassle, so hung a right through the crenellated grandeur of Christchurch Gate into the cathedral precincts.

I'll cut through the cloisters and King's School, then come out at Northgate.

Flakes of snow settled on his nose. Nathan lifted his head to watch a flurry of white circling in a black sky above twin towers beside the cathedral's western door. He skirted the iconic house of worship into dark cloisters fronting its chapter house.

I can't wait for the clocks to go forward. Lighter evenings are better.

His attention wandered left to a grass quadrangle of assorted tombs. A high-pitched whirring brought him to a halt outside the chapter house door.

Is someone making repairs after dark?

He listened. The whirring sounded again. It sped up along the cloister passageway he'd traversed moments before.

That's a small, electric motor. Like one of Bar-.

His train of thought ceased as a radio-controlled beach buggy rounded the corner to stop three feet away, facing him.

Nathan took an uneasy breath. "Hello?" His voice boomed off the dark walls. He found enough courage to step towards the car. As he bent forwards, the motor spun up again, and the buggy reversed in an arc. A flash of moonlight glinted on a custom registration decal Nathan recognised in a tremulous heartbeat: 'WALLIS 1.'

If this is Adam playing some kind of sick joke, I'll break his fuckin' nose. That's not funny.

He chased the car. The buggy rounded the corner again, five seconds before its pursuer. Nathan clung to the stonework. The radio-controlled vehicle had vanished from sight and sound. At the far cloister entrance, a silhouette stood watching him.

"Hello?" Nathan called out.

A fresh flurry of snowflakes blew in from the grass quadrangle to sting his eyes. Nathan rubbed them clear and looked back. The passageway lay empty. His jugular throbbed.

I'm getting out of here.

He pivoted and hurried back past the chapter house, before joining another passage leading towards the historic grounds of The King's School. Something tripped his ankle in the darkness. Nathan tumbled forward into cold flagstones, then picked himself up in a hurry. A blow struck him in the lower back, its intensity knocking Nathan against the wall.

"Who's there?" He spun with clenched fists, ready to deliver a forceful blow to his concealed assailant.

A teenage boy's voice seeped from the velvet blackness. "Why did you summon me?"

Nathan unclenched one of his hands to clutch his aching heart. "Barry? My God, how can it be?"

A compact, jagged stone arced from the shadows and grazed Nathan's left temple.

The disembodied voice deepened in pitch and grew in volume. It adopted an unearthly, intimidating timbre. "Why did you summon me?"

Nathan pushed away from the wall and hurled himself towards an archway beneath a nearby medieval gatehouse. Beyond lay an open, tree-lined green surrounded by the ancient buildings of The King's School. He cut diagonally across the grass towards an exquisite external Norman staircase. Beside it, a short mews led into wide double wooden doors set in a flint wall opening onto Northgate.

A security guard stepped out of a hut to yell at Nathan. "Oi! What's the hurry? Should you be in here at this time of night?"

Nathan stumbled past and lost traction on a patch of settling snow. He skidded in time to screeching brakes from a blue Ford Focus. It rounded the corner towards King Street near the classic, four storey Tudor bookshop with its famous wonky door. The front of the car clipped Nathan's right knee. He sprawled face-down in the road, grateful this motorist enjoyed quick reflexes. Fierce pain ran down Nathan's right leg from his knee joint. He winced and gripped it.

"Are you all right?" A frantic young woman dashed from the car to crouch at his side.

Nathan fought against a rising yelp of pain. "I think I've broken something."

The security guard emerged from the double doorway. "Is he okay?"

"Call an ambulance," the driver shouted.

7

A Storm of Spirits

"Is Samantha coming round this afternoon?" Celia Little set down a platter of roast potatoes on the family dining table. "You could have invited her for Sunday lunch."

Adam scooped some roasties onto his plate alongside wafer-thin slices of steaming beef. "She might turn up. I didn't think about lunch."

"You don't sound too enthusiastic about her." Adam's father, Tony Little, poured himself a glass of claret from a decanter. "Did you two have a fight?"

"No, nothing like that."

Adam's twelve-year-old sister, Susan, grinned with an evil glint in her eyes. "It's because you won't let him take her up to his room." She made a loud chewing noise. "Adam can't touch her naughty bits on the sofa, while we're all sitting there."

Adam scowled at her.

Tony poured gravy over his food. "That's quite enough, young lady."

"Don't talk with your mouth full, Suzie." Celia took a seat after serving her family. She smiled at her son. "Samantha seems a nice girl. Her mother, Grace, is a pillar of the church."

Adam focused on his food to disguise his internal amusement. *Her daughter could snog for England.*

Susan cut open her potatoes for the steam to escape. "It's not like he had a huge choice of girlfriends in Chartham. Not if he wanted a local one."

Celia laughed. "The village isn't that small, darling. We're four times the size of Chilham, in population terms. Things must be tough for Jason Cooper."

Tony sipped his wine and thought for a moment. "He's only one stop on the train from here. A couple of minutes. Anyone would think we lived in the Alaskan wilderness, listening to you talk."

Celia changed the subject. "I didn't ask about your visit to Jonathan's sister's house last week. It's nice you boys are all pulling together after Barry's accident. Such a tragic loss; he was a lovely lad. What did you get up to?"

Adam swallowed hard. "We sat around and talked, batted some questions back and forth, and then his nephew woke up crying. Jason, Nathan and I left soon after."

"Jonathan has a knack with that child." Celia left it there and tucked into her food.

Once his parents dozed off in separate chairs after lunch - and while Susan watched a film on TV - Adam opted for a stroll around the village. Snow had fallen overnight, with the promise of more on the way. He performed a circuit over the river past Chartham's old paper mill, leaving fresh tracks in new powder. His mind still swam with questions and memories concerning their Ouija session.

If that wasn't Barry, how did it know such personal details? We can't have conjured those answers like Jason's scientific explanation. And what about that bowl moving under its own steam, then hitting the wall?

So absorbing was this mental discourse, it surprised him to find his house up ahead again in short order. An e-mail alert vibrated the phone in his pocket. He retrieved the device and read the contact name *'Nathan Bishop.'* It was a multi-recipient message addressed to the entire group. The digital envelope opened, causing Adam's eyes to widen at its contents:

'Guys,

I hope everyone is okay.

You may not believe this, but I swear it's the truth. After I finished at my Saturday job, I cut through the cathedral to visit Dominic Cox. Dom is selling his old laptop and made me an excellent offer. I was heading over for a look.

In the cloisters, I heard an electric motor. God strike me down if I'm telling a lie, but one of Barry's cars whizzed around the corner. I know it was his, because that custom 'WALLIS 1' decal was fixed to the rear. It roared off and vanished, but someone stood watching me. I was spooked and hurried on. Then a foot or leg tripped me in the darkness. I heard Barry say, 'Why did you summon me?' A stone hit my forehead, and he repeated himself in a voice like nothing on this earth. Man, it was eerie. I lit out of there like shit off a shovel and got struck by a car in Northgate. My right leg suffered a partial fracture below the knee. Painful, but not too serious. I spent several hours at Kent & Canterbury Hospital.

What did we unleash when that bowl shattered? The whole experience shook me up.

Have you guys encountered anything odd? Let me hear you're all right, so I can relax.

Stay safe.

Nathan.'

Adam put his phone away.

A sultry, feminine voice shook him free of his stupor. "You didn't invite me round for lunch."

Samantha stood on the lane before him, hands stuffed in her pockets. She shook back a thick mop of fair hair.

"Hey." Adam recovered his senses. "Sorry, I was caught up reading a message from Nathan." He kissed her on the cheek.

"Is everything okay?"

"He got struck by a car and wound up in hospital last night. He's out now."

"Where was this?"

"Canterbury."

"How did it happen?" Samantha pulled him into a

tight embrace, eyes large and unblinking.

Adam gulped as she flicked her tongue in his ear, then kissed his neck. Despite her question, Samantha appeared to have other things on her mind. "Careless, I guess." He rubbed her spine, then locked mouths and allowed his obvious arousal to press against her jeans.

After a minute of intensive face eating, Samantha fixed him with a determined stare. "I've decided today is the day."

Adam's heart skipped a beat. "The day for what?"

One corner of Samantha's mouth curled upwards. "You know."

"Do I?"

Her eyes flashed downward. "Your body seems to."

"I don't believe it." Adam attempted to disguise the frustration in his voice. "When my folks and sister were out a fortnight ago; when we… fumbled; that would have been the perfect moment. Now everyone is at home. You know I can't take you upstairs. Crap, we can't go to your place either. I bet the vicar is coming round for tea."

Samantha nuzzled his cheek and whispered in his ear. "What about your garden?"

"My garden? In winter snow? We'll catch frostbite."

"Didn't you tell me your dad keeps an electric heater running in that large shed of his?"

Adam's mind grappled for a logistical solution. It was true, his father's shed was lined and wired up to the mains as an occasional hobby room. He kept it at a constant temperature and the windows faced away from their house towards the river. Peace and privacy in a dry, warm environment were assured. "It won't be that comfortable inside, furniture wise. There's nothing much to sit on."

Samantha bit his earlobe, adding more lead to Adam's pencil. "Then we'll stand."

Ducks passing on the Stour beyond the shed windows added a surreal tone to Adam's unexpected stroke of luck. Samantha bent over his father's workbench facing the glass, jeans and panties heaped around her ankles. She groaned and whimpered in delightful outbursts, stimulating herself as her overjoyed but inexperienced boyfriend held fast to her hips. Adam fought to control his breathing, and with it an insistent urge to explode inside the mind-blowing velvet vice massaging his manhood.

Samantha went rigid, then panted. "That's it. Give it to me." Her voice became husky. "Don't stop."

Adam rejoiced in wilful obedience, driving with such ferocity he feared to become the only sixteen-year-old he knew requiring a hip replacement. He couldn't believe the speed with which his girlfriend had progressed from teasing timidity to rapacious randiness.

"Ooh, yeah." Samantha's head bobbed. "Faster." Her now guttural tones morphed from feminine to masculine; the epitome of a startling voice box Adam knew of old. "Faster like you're racing one of my cars, Adam."

Samantha tossed her shoulder-length fair hair aside

and winked at him. Her facial muscles distorted into the visage of Barry Wallis, like a boy in drag.

Adam pulled out in horror, arousal dissipating like melting snowflakes.

Samantha jerked her head and laughed first with a deep and then shrill pitch.

Adam fell against a rack of garden tools, which toppled with a clatter. His heart thrummed. He reached for the door and hobbled up the garden, screaming like his kid sister having a tantrum during her younger years.

"What on earth?" Celia Little peered across the kitchen sink, in the middle of soaping a metal carving platter.

Tony wiped the inside of his wine glass with a tea towel. He joined his wife at the kitchen window.

Adam slipped in the snow and toppled, courtesy of his lowered trousers and y-fronts. His voice heaved in a panicked shriek.

Susan entered the kitchen in time to see him fall. "Oh my goodness. Why is my perverted brother rolling around in the snow with his willy out?"

"Go back into the lounge." Tony pointed a stern finger behind him while Celia donned a coat and shoes. She yanked open the back door and rushed to their son's aid.

With his mother's help, Adam stood. He staggered beside her into the kitchen, clothing now pulled aloft for modesty.

Celia sat him down at their round breakfast table. "What happened?"

Adam shivered, unable to conjure either the terrifying truth or some clever, alternative deception to explain his compromising situation. In that moment, he had no words to offer.

Tony glanced down the garden. "He's left the shed door open. I'd better secure it before all the heat escapes. See if you can pry some sense out of him, Celia."

Tony found the shed empty. He straightened the fallen tools, then locked the door.

Back inside the house, Adam sat in a wide-eyed stupor.

Celia winced at her husband and shook her head.

The doorbell rang.

"Please can you get that, Suzie?" Celia called.

"Okay, Mum." Susan hurried into the hallway. The door opened, and she called over her shoulder with a vindictive lilt. "It's Samantha for Adam. Shall I tell her what happened?"

* * *

Jonathan Chapman sat on the sofa at his sister's house, mobile phone clamped to one ear. On a rug before the fireplace, young Edward crawled around pushing toy cars and making engine noises.

Adam Little's voice gabbed a mile a minute from the phone speaker. The startling content of his vocal torrent caused Jonathan to drop the device, then scoop it up again. Was it his imagination, or had a chill crept in from somewhere?

"Adam, slow down. Are you certain it all happened that way?"

The speaker almost exploded from Adam's end, emotive force laced with intermittent expletives erupting into the room.

Jonathan screwed up his eyes and waited for a second of silence to jump in. "Okay, okay. I'm not calling you a liar. I got Nathan's e-mail, too." He rubbed his eyes. "Jesus, this is beyond belief. And then Samantha arrived on your doorstep? So who was in the shed?" He listened. "Your dad found it empty. Shit. How did you explain everything to your folks?"

A stilted jumble of phrases followed.

Jonathan squinted at the ceiling. "You refused to answer their questions? I don't blame you. They must think you're on drugs to behave like that. What did Samantha say?" He listened again. "Uh-huh. I'm not surprised you had your Mum send her home. But you're going to face her, eventually. What will you tell her?"

The line remained quiet.

Jonathan broke the stalemate. "Have you spoken with Jason? Now school is closed because of the snow, I haven't seen him. He was closest to Barry out of all of us. If you and Nathan both suffered these encounters, he must be due a visit too." Jonathan peered over the top of the sofa, half expecting some bogeyman to leap from the shadows. "Me? No, everything has stayed quiet so far. Edward is playing with his cars. I'll put him to bed soon. Penny was fine about the dessert bowl last week."

A drawn-out sigh huffed in his ear from the phone.

Jonathan echoed one of his own. "Okay, thanks for telling me. I hope nothing else happens. Get some rest, Adam. Try to throw yourself into exam study if you can. I've found it helps take my mind off everything. Bye." He hung up.

Edward dragged a car transporter lorry across the rug, then lowered its ramp. He giggled to himself with contentment, lost in the game.

Jonathan put his phone down and sat forward on the edge of the sofa cushion. "Let's pack your cars away, Edward. I promised Mummy I'd have you in bed by now. You've had an extra twenty minutes of play."

Edward hung his head and moaned.

Jonathan grinned. "I know how annoying it is when you're enjoying a good game. You can drive them some more tomorrow. Your cars will still be here." Jonathan got down on his hands and knees to help the child pile his metal toys into a rectangular, open plastic container. "That's it. Put each down with care. Don't drop them on top of one another or you'll chip the paint."

"I love my cars." Edward cooed like the infantile equivalent of a lovesick paramour. His voice deepened as though from a miraculous, sudden onset of puberty. "I always loved my cars."

Jonathan focused on the transporter, head down. He couldn't bring himself to turn towards the unmistakable voice of Barry Wallis, emanating from his nephew's mouth. "This isn't happening," he whispered to himself. "It's an illusion."

Edward shrieked and lunged at him. Despite his slight frame, the sudden onset of his assault caught Jonathan off guard. He rolled onto his back with the four-year-old on top. Barry's face twisted the otherwise unblemished boy's skin into a maniacal series of creases. He grinned, then opened his mouth and sank sharp pointed teeth into Jonathan's shielding forearm. The incision cut deep and proved forceful enough to draw blood.

Jonathan cried out. "What do you want?" He struggled to shake the insistent demonic midget free. There, attached to his arm, hung the little boy he loved caring for, now transfigured into some evil parody of his deceased peer. "Let go." Jonathan couldn't decide whether his statement signified a command for this creature to release his arm, release the human marionette Edward now functioned as, or both. He jerked away.

Edward's teeth tore free and his body launched across the rug. The four-year-old's head hit the Portland stone hearth with a resounding crack, and he lay still.

"Edward." Jonathan reached for the silent child. "No." He stuck his head close to Edward's mouth. Faint breath escaped his pale lips.

If he's unconscious with a head injury, there isn't a moment to lose.

Jonathan grabbed his phone and dialled 999.

"Where is he?" A distraught Penny Oldham hustled into Kent & Canterbury Hospital A & E. "Where's my boy?"

Jonathan rose from a row of plastic chairs where he sat with his parents. They'd arrived ten minutes prior, having phoned Penny at work after Jonathan contacted them from the hospital.

A male doctor idled down the hallway. "Are you Edward's mother?"

Penny pivoted on her heel. "Please tell me he's all right?"

The doctor ushered her towards the seating. "We've taken an X-ray. There's no sign of permanent injury. He suffered a nasty bang to the head and will have an ugly bruise for a time. Nurses are applying ointment and a dressing to stop him touching it. Edward cried when he awoke, but has since calmed down. He'll be out in a minute."

Penny shot Jonathan a thousand-yard stare. "How did it happen?"

Jonathan fidgeted in the chair. "He fell against the hearth and hit his head."

The doctor's brow creased. "That must have been some fall."

Jonathan's mouth dried up. How could he tell the truth? Who would believe him if he did? A lie was the only option. How much would Edward recall, and would he dispute the validity of Jonathan's assertions? "We were putting his toy cars away before bed. I'd let him stay up a little longer, and he didn't want to sleep.

So, I did the rocket ship to cheer him up. I thought if I could swoop upstairs like that, he'd settle right down."

"The rocket ship?" the doctor asked.

Penny cleared her throat and made a sweeping series of motions with her arms to illustrate. "It's a game where my brother picks Edward up and flies him around. Edward loves it."

Jonathan went on. "We were having such fun I… slipped."

Penny clenched her teeth. "You dropped him headfirst on the hearth?"

Jonathan gulped. "I'm… so sorry, Sis."

Mrs Chapman reached across her husband's lap to squeeze Jonathan's leg. "He didn't do it on purpose, Penny. It was an accident."

A door opened at the end of the corridor. Edward stepped out, holding the hand of a bubbly, big-boned African nurse. The boy spied his mother and reached his free hand towards her.

"Is that your mummy?" the nurse beamed.

She didn't have to wait for an answer. Penny shot along the corridor to pull her child into a smothering embrace.

The doctor indicated Jonathan's cut forearm. "How did you do that?"

Jonathan flushed. "I must have scraped it on the hearth when I was trying to rouse Edward."

"It's not your night, is it?" The doctor got up. "Don't leave it exposed like that. Would you like us to dress the wound?"

"No, it's okay. I'll stick antiseptic cream and a plaster

on it when I get home. It's stopped bleeding."

"All right. Take it easy." He looked from Penny back to Jonathan. "I don't envy your job of calming the waters with your sister. But you did the right thing calling an ambulance. Take comfort from that." He walked off.

Next morning, Jonathan was awoken by his phone ringing on the bedside table. He rolled over and connected the call. "Hello?"

"Jonathan? It's Penny."

Jonathan took a breath before speaking. Was she about to explode at him? "How's Edward?"

"Still asleep." She paused. "Listen, I had a long chat on the phone with Neil. We know you love Edward, but we've decided it's best if you don't babysit anymore."

Jonathan sat up against the headboard. "Sis, it was an accident."

"I know. We're lucky. Things could have been far worse. Fatal, even." Her tone brightened a notch. "Neil asked me to thank you for everything you've done, and for calling the ambulance. You've helped us out in a pinch over the last few months and we're grateful. He found out yesterday that his company have earmarked him to lead the new Ashford office, starting in a fortnight. He'll be home each evening. A nice raise in pay, too. I'll quit my job today. The three of us will manage fine."

Jonathan rubbed his brow. "That's good news." His

voice strained. "Sis?"

"Yeah?"

"Are we okay?"

An uncomfortable silence followed. "We're okay, Jonathan."

Jonathan closed his eyes. It was never a good sign when Penny used 'Jonathan' rather than 'Bro' to address him. "Are you sure?"

Penny spoke in a flat, droning voice. "Yeah. Please don't do the rocket ship with Edward again, okay?"

"Okay."

"Bye." Penny ended the call without a further word or affectionate sign-off.

Jonathan sat there in silence, an empty husk of his usually confident self.

* * *

Nick Preston slowed his Honda to a stop, wipers sweeping at full pelt amidst a blowing snowstorm. An hour after sunset, this fresh mini blizzard reduced visibility to a few yards. He'd visited a shopping outlet centre in Ashford to purchase a thicker winter coat, due to a sharp cold snap. Now, on his way back along the A28, he wished he hadn't bothered. Three cars ahead, a burly male police officer wearing a high-vis jerkin moved from vehicle to vehicle, talking to drivers. Nick pressed the power window button on auto-wind as he approached. It slipped down with a gentle whir.

"Good evening, Sir." The copper blew out red cheeks stung by icy wind and driving snow.

Nick attempted to shield his own face from the onslaught, as a flurry blew into the cabin. "Is the road jammed?"

"I'm afraid so. A van went sideways and collided with an oncoming vehicle."

"Was anyone hurt?"

"Only minor injuries to the occupants, thank goodness."

"That's a mercy," Nick shouted against a roaring wind. "Any idea how long to clear it?"

"It's going to take a couple of hours to get a tow truck here."

Nick peered through his fast-moving wipers to spy a junction on each side of the road ahead. He tapped the alternative route button on his sat nav set for '*Home*' (which he'd temporarily designated Stour Cottage as). A divergent track appeared on-screen, branching left at the junction ahead. He stuck his head back out of the window. "I'm trying to reach Chilham, safe and out of this weather. I could take a left up ahead to avoid the holdup. Is that okay?"

The policeman pulled his peaked cap lower to prevent it flying off in a stiff breeze. "You can try if you wish; I won't stop you. But, that's a single-track side road. I doubt it's been cleared or salted. If you get stuck, you'll wish you'd waited."

Nick tapped his steering wheel. "My car has part-time four-wheel drive. The rear wheels kick in when the front ones lose grip. It's got me out of tougher scrapes on the South Downs, before now."

"Fair enough. It's steep going up there before you hit

level ground towards Challock. If your ABS fails and the car slides, don't keep pushing it. Come back down; it's not worth the risk."

"Noted." Nick cranked his heater up to full as the interior temperature plummeted from the open window.

"Right you are. Go careful. Have a safe journey home." The officer stepped back.

Nick gave him a thumbs up and raised the window. He put the car in second gear, gunned the engine and eased the clutch up. The CR-V rumbled over a patch of compacted snow dusted with a fresh, loose covering. Nick overtook the vehicles ahead at a crawl, then signalled left at the junction. The officer had been correct about the lane's lack of winter weather relief. Roads like that weren't a priority. The Honda ploughed through several inches of snow. Huge white globs covered the hedgerows on either side and had long since buried the road sign. When the level, single track lane inclined upwards, Nick hunched over the wheel.

"Here we go." He patted the instrument cowl. "Don't let me down, old girl." High revs and deft drive train control saw the vehicle make steady progress past a farm and track, winding into an ever steeper climb. Interlocking branches weighed down with snow, sagged and dumped their loads onto the Honda. Each impact caused Nick to ease back until the windscreen wipers cleared enough of the pile to re-establish limited visibility. The brake pedal pumped beneath his foot with each occasional application, announcing the

ABS fighting for traction. Nick's heart fell as the car slid backward. He tugged the wheel over to correct for lateral movement and stop the Honda spinning around. The engine revved again and Nick gave it everything to compensate for the gradient. With a rumble, the tyres found purchase, and the car surged forward. Nick kept the inertia rolling. The banks were so high here, he'd bounce off each like pinball cushions if the car skidded. There seemed little chance of meeting an oncoming motorist in these conditions. He applied more force to the accelerator.

If I can keep this up, I should make the crest without a fuss.

He rounded a right-hander on the climb, still gaining speed. A tiny human shape appeared from swirling flakes at the limit of his headlights. Both beams reflected off the snow in a dazzling blaze of light. A boy with dark, thick ginger hair stood in the middle of the lane.

Nick stomped on the brake. The ABS fired again, but the car slid onward without slowing. A dull bang shuddered the Honda's bonnet as Grant's pale, smiling face smashed into the clear spot of the windshield. He locked wistful eyes with his father for an instant, before his body slid over the roof out of sight. Nick released a stricken wail and pulled the car into a snowbank where it slid to a halt. He punched on his hazard lights, then dropped out of the driver's door.

What the hell is going on? He reached back into the cabin to retrieve a torch from the glove box. *It can't be him. Did I hit someone else?* Nick slipped on treacherous black ice as he tramped around the vehicle. Memories of the article he'd copied at the library in Canterbury surfaced at the forefront of his consciousness.

Not a smiling woman, but my boy. Other than that, the incident is the same. Why Grant? He didn't die here.

He looked around to get his bearings.

I didn't recognise it in the dark and blizzard. That junction was the Wye turnoff with White Hill opposite. This must be it: the place I've read and heard so much about.

Nick checked the front of his car and found it undamaged. He climbed back inside, then zoomed the sat nav map to read its road name aloud. "White Hill."

8
Woodland Meetings

King's Wood had always been a sledging dream during snowy weather. It comprised an undulating landscape of mixed width tracks and broad grass and mud avenues flanked by thick forest. Atop the North Downs and away from the danger of traffic, kids could play without fear. Ample places existed for armies of excitable children (and several childlike adults) to rocket down the dips, sometimes two or three to a sled. For the playfully minded father, it offered a wonderful opportunity: pretend to do your wife a favour by taking the kids out to play, while in reality regressing to a nine-year-old existence. It was the recreational equivalent of buying your boy a train set for Christmas and playing with it, while being startled when he asked, *"Can I have a go now, Dad?"*

Nick Preston watched one such ebullient father climb onto the rear of a wooden sled, behind what he assumed to be his son. The lad wasn't much older than Grant. Two girls, possibly sisters, stood to one side near the trees. They huddled together in thick orange coats and fuchsia wellies. The man pushed off with his feet and the sled accelerated down a gentle, two-hundred yard dip. Nick caught the young boy's worried eyes flash past from his vantage point. He pivoted to witness the rest of their run.

Twenty yards from the bottom of the slope, the sled hit a rock or other unseen obstruction beneath the blanket of white. The homemade toboggan performed a passable imitation of a Winter Olympic bobsled crash. It careened at a forty-five degree angle, before cartwheeling into the undergrowth. The man tumbled backwards while his lad performed an ungainly, impromptu somersault into nearby bushes. Both sisters screamed.

The younger of the two yelled, "You've killed Alan, Daddy. You've killed him."

The girls slipped and stumbled downhill towards where their father stood, brushing snow from the seat of his trousers.

"He'll be fine." The man twisted to face the swaying bushes. "Alan?"

The boy struggled to his feet; wellies, nose, mouth and ears clogged with snow.

The distraught younger sister hugged her brother, then pointed at a cut on his nose. She squealed. "He's bleeding."

"I'm sure it's only a scratch, Antonia." The man approached his son. "Let's have a look." He studied Alan's nose before examining the bushes. "A thorn swiped him as he landed. It's nothing to fret about."

The other girl regained her composure with a giggle.

Alan unclogged his facial orifices and stared at his eldest sister. "What's funny, Adrienne?"

Adrienne pointed to his crotch. "You did the flying splits when you came off. Your trousers didn't survive."

Alan pulled his jacket aside to inspect the damage down below. A gaping hole widened in the fabric between his legs. An icy wind blew through the gap. Alan flushed. "Oh no."

The father groaned. "I'll catch it from your mum when we get home."

Amused by the scene, Nick trudged over as a courtesy. "Is everything all right? That was some crash."

The father stumbled to retrieve their sled. One runner had split during the incident. He held it up with a sigh. "We're fine, thank you." He wiggled the broken wood at Nick. "I guess that's the end of today's downhill action."

Nick grunted. "Just as well, if another accident was on the cards."

"I won't hear the last of this from my good lady. A minor injury and torn clothing." He slipped his arm around Alan's shoulders, before winking at Nick. "Kids, hey? Who'd have them?"

Nick offered an uneasy, flat smile and swallowed hard. "I'm sure you wouldn't be without them."

"That I wouldn't; you're right. Do you have any?"

Nick performed one solitary, stiff head shake. "No." He ascended the slope again. "Enjoy the rest of your day."

The father gathered his familial flock. "Come on, you lot. Back to the car park."

Nick walked on. He'd not driven to the woods via Challock today. Instead, he'd opted for a hike from the cottage along Mountain Street to connect with The Pilgrims' Way, as others had described. After that blizzard incident with Grant on White Hill, he didn't fancy a return trip in his car. When he'd got home that night, the emotional impact hit him like an express train. Of all the ways to encounter an apparition of his son, he'd struck him with his own vehicle in a sick parody of the boy's death. That had to be the most heartbreaking manifestation of all.

At the bottom of the next depression, a gang of twelve or thirteen-year-old boys exchanged snowballs in two loose teams. A head appeared above the open parapet of a fifteen foot wooden platform, probably used for deer culling or as a mini fire tower. Today it made the perfect fort to bombard your pals from an elevated position.

Nick sidestepped an errant, powdery missile flying wide of the mark. It struck the bark of a fir tree behind him and disintegrated with a puff. He watched the pitched but good-natured battle for a minute, then pressed on down a narrow track through a V-shaped cutting. Trees rising on either side, steep banks, and the deadening effect of snow soon closed in to mask the happy skirmish behind with a cloak of silence.

Nick stopped and shut his eyes to listen. That sledging incident had affected him deeper than he first realised. Now his heart hung heavy again with loss.

Grant would have loved it here on a day like this.

An unexpected breeze funnelled through the cutting. A boy's giggling voice echoed from the impenetrable blackness of packed evergreens on his right. Nick peered into the gloom. An identical trill of laughter rang out from the opposite tree line behind.

Nick shivered, but pulled himself together. *More kids having a lark.*

"Daddy, Baddy. Daddy, Baddy." The phrase encircled Nick like a tightening noose. It reverberated through the cutting, first from one direction and then the other.

Nick clutched his head to shut out the din. *It's not him. It can't be him. You're imagining things, Preston. Grant is dead.*

A splintering crack followed by a hissing crash, drowned out all other noise.

Nick darted back towards the gang of boys, fearful of what he'd find. Sure enough, the wooden platform had toppled - no doubt through over-enthusiastic play - and lay on its side across the tree-lined grassy avenue. By the time he reached it, the snowball combatants had vanished.

Little scamps. The Forestry Commission will be pissed once their rangers find this. Still, no injuries or they wouldn't have scarpered so fast.

He stepped over the mess of shattered wooden uprights and a ladder in pieces, continuing his walk in a southeasterly direction through the woods.

* * *

Jason Cooper shivered. A stream of cascading snow dropped from the boughs of heavy horse chestnut trees to strike his head. They overhung a bend in Mountain Street towards a blended section of The Pilgrims' Way and The North Downs Way. The snow melted on contact with his warm skin and trickled into his collar. He pulled up the hood of his parka to stave off a repeat incident. His mind flitted between the worrying e-mail he'd received from Nathan on Sunday, and a panicked babble from Adam about losing his virginity to something that looked like Samantha, but transfigured into Barry Wallis. Adam was a prankster, but no thespian. He couldn't have sounded that genuine about his supposed carnal incident gone awry, if it was a fake. He'd have given the game away or started laughing at the first indication he'd duped anyone. As it turned out, when Jason phoned Nathan later that day, Adam was calling the entire group. Nathan had just got off the phone from hearing a repeat of Adam's disturbing first attempt at coitus.

I haven't heard from Jonathan. Will he endure something awful like the other guys?

The smartphone rang from his belt pouch. Jason tore open its Velcro flap, grabbed the phone, and answered the call.

"Hello?"

"Jason? It's Jonathan."

Jason hesitated at the lifeless tone. Its absence of any vital spark was uncharacteristic of his friend. "Hey. How are you?"

Jonathan cleared his throat. "I've been better. Have you spoken with Adam?"

"Yeah, he sounds a nervous wreck."

"Wouldn't you be if that happened to you? There he was in ecstasy one moment, thinking his big day had come. Then it all turned out to be... To be... Shit, I've no idea what it was, but he's not pulling our legs. I know him too well."

"Agreed." Jason made a rocky ascent up the trail leading between the privately owned Ridge and Felborough Woods, and the public land of King's Wood. His breathing laboured from the effort. "You don't sound so good yourself. Is everything all right?"

"Penny and Neil have dispensed with me as babysitter."

Jason grabbed a branch to stop himself slipping backwards on an icy patch. "That sucks. Not quite in the same league as Nathan and Adam's woes but-"

"Wanna bet?" Jonathan cut across.

Jason reached the wooded ridge and turned left along an ancient hilltop pathway. "Okay, what aren't you telling me?"

"I was babysitting Edward, while Adam rolled out his terrifying tale over the phone. When I hung up, it was past Edward's bedtime. You know how Adam prattles on when he's full of something. Not that I blame him after that."

"Go on." Jason glanced left into The Great Stour Valley.

"I got down on the rug to help Edward pack his toys away. At first he came out with his usual cute phrases;

sweet and innocent. All well and good, until his voice turned into Barry's."

"Are you kidding?" Jason gawped.

"After everything that's happened to the others?" Jonathan took a breath. "I couldn't bring myself to look at him. Edward lunged and knocked me onto my back. I swear to God his face turned into Barry's too, Jason. I yelled at him in a frenzy. Then he bit my arm."

"Bit your arm? Why?"

Jonathan adopted a sarcastic tone. "Gee, I'm not sure. Hang on while I fetch a crystal ball and tell you."

"I doubt either of us would try a crystal ball after that Ouija board incident. So, what did you do?"

"I tried to shake him free from a manic attack. His teeth drew blood. I was in pain and shock, but also worried about hurting him. He's four years old."

Jason halted on the footpath. "This thing looks and sounds like Barry, but it can't be him."

"No shit. It gave Edward strength beyond his years too."

"What happened next?"

"I tossed him aside." Jonathan's voice became emotional. "Edward's head struck the stone hearth, and he passed out."

"F-U-C-K," Jason drew out his response in shock and deliberate solidarity. "Is he okay?"

"You mean after the ambulance rushed him to A & E for clinical attention and an X-ray?"

"You must have been bricking it." Jason started walking again. He tried to follow the gait of larger footprints in the snow from an earlier passerby.

Anything to make the going easier.

"I'm unsure what was worse: seeing Edward unresponsive but alive, or the anger and disappointment on my sister's face once she reached the hospital."

"What did you tell her?"

"That I was playing the rocket ship game with Edward and dropped him. The crappy thing is, that makes me look worse than if I'd come clean about what happened. Now I'm irresponsible and dangerous around Edward. I love that little guy."

"So Penny and Neil pulled the plug on your cushy income number?"

Jonathan sighed. "I'm not as bothered about that as I am the way they see me. I've lost their trust and respect. It's strained my relationship with Penny. We've always been close. I'm worried our bond has suffered irreparable damage."

Jason glanced over his shoulder, phone still clamped to his head. There was no-one behind him, but another of these creepy situations retold made him hyper-aware. He was isolated and scared in a place he'd always felt at home. "Are you frightened?"

"Not like I was during the incident. I suppose I should be thankful. Now, if something else happens, it won't involve Edward. God knows when Penny will let me see him next. She won't leave me alone with him."

"How's your arm?"

"It's fine. Whatever took control of Edward's body didn't turn me into the living dead or anything like that." He hesitated. "Jason?"

"Yeah?"

"I hate to say this, but…"

"But I'm the only one present at the Ouija board session yet to escape these horrors. The rest of you have suffered and I'm overdue."

"That's about the size of it. I didn't mean to worry you. Was I wrong to call?"

"Hell no." Jason looked round again. "I wish you'd done it twenty minutes earlier, though. Before I left home."

"Where are you?"

"King's Wood."

"Is that bad? You walk there all the time."

"I know." Jason considered turning back. What was the point? If this force, spirit, (call it what you will), could chase Nathan; present Adam with a living, breathing, and *fucking* facsimile of Samantha; or take control of little Edward to attack Jonathan, it would reach him wherever he ran.

Jonathan's voice evidenced mounting concern. "You're not near White Hill where Barry died, are you?"

"Not far. Technically, I'm on it. White Hill is more than the lane where Barry and his father passed away. It's an entire land mass which forms part of The Pilgrims' Way merged with a section of The North Downs Way. That's where I'm standing. A significant section of King's Wood covers White Hill."

"I wish I'd never suggested trying to contact Barry. I'm so sorry, mate."

"There's no use crying over spilt milk. Like I said before: we didn't have to go along with it. Nobody forced us." He brushed snow off a stone way marker engraved with the wording: '*THE NORTH DOWNS WAY. FARNHAM 103M 166KM. CANTERBURY 10M 16KM. DOVER 28M 45KM.*'

Jonathan grunted. "But we wouldn't all be in this fix without my bright idea. I feel such a fool. Guilty, too."

Jason set off again. "Keep in touch with Nathan and Adam, yeah? Contact me if anything else happens."

"Do you think it'll leave us alone now? Why is it impersonating Barry, or Samantha? She's not even dead."

"If I had to guess, it's because they're special to us. This entity knows stuff about our lives. It was aware of my lost car, from when Barry and I were kids. It knows about Adam and Samantha's relationship and where Adam hoped it was headed."

Jonathan gasped. "You reckon it can read minds?"

"I'm not sure. It feels more like it can sense things associated with those it touches. Deep, emotional memories or present hopes and dreams. Almost as though people leave latent energy fingerprints in time and space."

"I'm glad you're up on the subject. I wouldn't have a clue where to begin."

Jason gritted his teeth. "Neither do I; I'm hypothesising. Making logical guesses based on your accounts."

"I hope you don't wind up with an 'account' of your own. I'd better let you go."

"Cheers, Jonathan. Talk to you later." Jason hung up.

Icy wind swept up from The Great Stour Valley. Jason turned right down a track sloping away from the ridge. By the time he reached a curve near the bottom beside a small, murky woodland pond, his body no longer bore the brunt of that exposed breeze.

A sharp voice cut through from the trees to his left. "You didn't cry at my funeral."

Jason's shoulders bunched up around his ears. Barry stepped out of the undergrowth, as solid as the last time they'd met. A cheeky grin spreading across his pale countenance contradicted the serious tone of his accusation.

Barry's eyes flashed. "Have you told Louise how you feel about her yet, or are you still paralysed by fear?"

The expression *'paralysed by fear'* offered a perfect description for the lack of motive force infusing Jason's limbs in that instant. His feet were lumps of lead. Icy terror clenched his buttocks and locked his jaw.

Barry went on. "No matter. She's helping me, now."

Jason frowned. "What?"

Barry drew closer. Every footfall shuddered through Jason's tensed form. "Since you're not making use of her, I am. Or I will be soon."

Jason's nervous voice crept out of his tightened mouth in a hushed semi-squeak. "You're not him."

"What?" The apparition of Barry got right up in his face. It emanated a skin-prickling aura of cold.

The combined effects of love for his deceased friend and rage at this abomination thawed Jason's courage. He spat in his face, then shook his head and backed away. "I don't know what you are, but you're not Barry Wallis. Barry was my friend. You're not fooling anyone."

Barry's face contorted. He craned his neck upward towards a bank of trees beyond the kidney shaped pond. "What do you think, Dad?"

Jason followed his gaze.

Ian Wallis dangled from a tow rope slung over a thick branch. His puffed eyes snapped open, and he gurgled as though unable to speak.

Jason's hands trembled from a cocktail of fear and adrenaline. "That's not the tree Ian Wallis died on. It's a mile and a half away on the road downhill towards Wye."

Barry pounced and grabbed him by the scruff of the neck. His words escaped in a hiss. "You're always so particular." He forced Jason down with an iron grip. His trainers kicked Jason's legs from beneath him and a firm knee pressed into his back.

Jason witnessed his own panicked expression and Barry's gleeful, sadistic grin reflected as his face hovered over the still surface of the muddy waterhole.

The branch creaked from which Ian Wallis dangled. The noose snapped and his bloated torso plunged into the water. A curtain of showering spray soaked Jason from head to toe. Energetic ripples banished the reflections.

Barry pressed Jason's head closer to the surface. Jason struggled to resist against the insistent, supernatural strength on display. Ian Wallis' ashen head burst from below. He gripped Jason's skull with meat hook hands and tugged to support his boy's efforts. His eyes stared, devoid of life but filled with eerie clouds. A sagging, rotted tongue lolled out of his blackened mouth.

The fury which had ignited inside Jason evaporated at such overwhelming power and horror his senses couldn't escape. His head plunged into the depths. Freezing, putrid water filled every facial orifice. Strength faded from his frenzied limbs. Even desperate self-preservation lacked sufficient ability to overcome these hideous foes; ghostly monsters clad in the flesh garments of figures he'd known most of his life. Did this creature or creatures intend a similar fate for Nathan, Adam and Jonathan? Reason and logic faded from his mind as though sinking to the bed of the filthy pool. Jason's final gasp bubbled out and his torso went limp.

Nick Preston puffed along the track, ears still straining for further evidence of Grant's presence. He'd left the fallen fire tower ten minutes prior. Now the trail levelled off at the bottom of another hill leading up to the ridge. Beyond where snow-covered ruts bent ahead, a pond twenty feet across skirted the path.

Is that an animal? Nick wiped occasional flakes of snow - whipped up in a gentle vortex along the path - from his blurred eyes. He focused on an object floating face-down in the water. "Shit." The sharpening outline of a teenage boy spurred him into action. Nick stomped through ankle deep snowdrifts at the edge of the track. He slipped down to the water's edge and grabbed the boy by his ankles. Skin chilled, face lifeless and still, the teenager slid free of the pond. Nick pressed on the trunk of his body to expel as much water as he could from his lungs. He rolled him over and checked for a pulse. "Come on, Son; work with me." Nick administered CPR and blew gentle breath into the drowning victim's mouth.

"Daddy, Baddy. Daddy, Baddy." Grant's giggling voice warbled between the trunks of dense evergreens across the pond.

Nick ignored the call. *Whether in my mind or caused by something else, this isn't the time*. He continued working on the motionless figure.

A cough and spluttering froth of rank water spewed from the teenager's mouth. His eyes flicked open. Stare filled with terror, he convulsed in shock.

Nick grabbed hold of him to subdue a fit which might cause further damage. "Easy, Son. Easy." His voice calmed. "Look at me. Here; this way. Steady your breathing. That's it. Can you tell me your name?" Nick hoped his request would cause the trembling figure to relax a little and think.

"J-A..." The teenager struggled to speak at first. "Jason. Jason Cooper." His teeth chattered with cold.

"Good." Nick pulled him tighter, then rubbed his limbs to quell rapid shivers rippling through the drowned rat. Now they were both soaked through. "We should get indoors and dry off. Do you live far?"

"Mountain Street, near Chilham." Jason snapped his head around as though searching for something or someone.

Nick glanced about. "Was somebody else with you?"

Jason met his eyes. He shook his head and looked away. "No."

"Let's see if you can stand. I live that way too, at the bottom of School Hill. We've still a stretch to go." Nick helped him up.

"Thank you," Jason gasped. He put his weight forward on one leg, which wobbled and almost gave way.

"Steady." Nick supported him. "Lean on me until your strength returns. Let's start by making it up that hill."

The going was slow. By the time they reached the way marker Jason brushed snow off earlier, he'd recovered enough energy to speak. "You didn't tell me *your* name."

"Nick Preston."

Jason let go of Nick and hobbled along on his own. "I don't recall seeing you in the village before."

"I'm new. A temporary resident at Stour Cottage near the primary school. You look familiar, though. Were you at the Winter Fair?"

Jason descended into a coughing fit.

Nick patted him between the shoulder blades. "Easy. Don't feel you have to answer or speak. You've suffered quite an ordeal."

Jason flicked water from his hair. "I was at the Winter Fair. A bunch of my friends and I had a kick about with a football."

Nick snapped his fingers. "That's where I've seen you. Hey, there was a talented guy there running rings around everyone else."

Jason grimaced. "That was Barry."

"Does he live in the village, too?"

"No, he *lived* at Challock. Barry was killed after being thrown from his dad's car, on the way home from athletics practise."

Nick's cheeks paled. "I read about that. Didn't his father die soon after?"

"Yes. He hung himself at the spot Barry lost his life."

Nick's mouth dropped open. "That's awful. I'm sorry. Losing a good friend is tough at any age. You must have been through the mill." Nick paused, then spoke with a cautious lack of confidence. "Is that how you ended up in the pond?"

Jason stared at him, unsure how to respond.

Nick attempted to draw the subject out further. "I know how hopeless life seems when you lose someone you're close to. Believe it or not, I'm here because I've struggled with the death of my young son. My wife and I needed a break from each other."

Jason bit his lip. "I didn't throw myself in the pond."

"Oh." Nick wondered if he'd needed to roll out his sad story after all. For one moment it felt like casting pearls before swine. He shook the discomfort aside and changed tack. "Did you slip?"

They reached the downhill path leading back to the lane.

Jason rubbed his arms to instil warmth. "No. You'd

think I was mad or find me ungrateful if I told you the truth of what happened."

"Really?"

"I still can't believe it myself, and I'm open to a lot of weird shit. Thank you for saving my life." He sighed. "Those words don't begin to cover my gratitude."

Nick shrugged. "You're welcome. Take it from me, kid: I never believed in anything before I moved to Chilham. I've listened to bizarre tales and experienced odd stuff on more than occasion in the last few weeks. It's challenged my worldview. Why don't you try me?"

Jason puffed. *Okay. If this guy wants to hear it, he's going to get it. Who cares? I'll be home in ten minutes if he becomes annoyed and kicks off.* "Barry pushed me into the pond and held my head down, with help from his father."

Nick stopped and eyed him with that unreadable stare he was known for. He spoke in an even, emotionless voice. "Are you kidding, or do you believe that's what happened?"

This wasn't the response Jason was expecting. It caught him off guard. "You're not insulted by that statement? Even after resuscitating me and getting soaked?"

Nick drew nearer to study his face. "What the reality is, I couldn't say. But, you're telling me the truth; or you think you are. Either way, there's no mischief involved."

Jason's eyes fixed on him. "I never thought to hear that from an adult." He shivered. "Can we keep moving?"

"Sure."

They stepped onto Mountain Street, heading for the first row of cottages.

Jason stamped his feet on the tarmac road to shake water from his clothing. "Four of us friends tried a Ouija board after Barry died. I suppose we wanted to speak with him. A chance to say goodbye. Does that sound stupid?"

"Inadvisable, maybe. But less stupid than you realise." Nick looked away. "I understand. You wanted to know he was in a good place, yeah?"

Jason's eyebrows raised. "Like your son? I'm sorry to hear about him. I should have said so before."

"That's okay. Did you contact Barry?"

Jason's face darkened. "We contacted something, but it wasn't Barry. Our session went haywire. Ever since, my three other friends have all encountered things that looked and sounded like Barry. One was an apparition; another a solid, living replica of that guy's girlfriend; and a third something that took possession of his four-year-old nephew. The child's face and voice altered to mimic Barry's. The same happened with the girlfriend. I was the last of the four to endure this insanity. Barry stepped out of the undergrowth near that pond. Then I saw his father hanging from a tree. Not the tree he died on; that was at-"

"White Hill," Nick interrupted.

"Yes. Are you familiar with it?"

"By account and reputation to begin with, then first-hand experience." Nick folded his arms.

"Have you seen the road ghost?" Jason's eyes

widened.

"You know about that?" Nick blinked.

"I've an interest in the supernatural. It's one of my hobbies." Jason paused outside an attractive cottage. A sign on its front gate read: '*The Orchard*.' He rummaged around in his pockets and his face fell. "Oh no."

"What's the matter?"

"I must have lost my house keys in the water. Mum and Dad are out. I was hoping to wash and dry my clothes before they got home."

"And avoid a ticking off?" Nick smirked.

"Yeah."

"Well, you can't stay out here in the cold, soaked through to your skin. You'd better come with me the last stretch to Stour Cottage. We'll pop your clothes in the wash. You can wrap yourself in a bath towel next to the woodburner, while I warm up some soup."

"Thanks, Mr Preston."

"Call me Nick."

They continued along the lane, past rear gates to Chilham Castle. The elegant structure sat on a promontory in the distance, above its delightful formal gardens.

Jason found his voice again. "I asked if you'd seen the road ghost at White Hill, but we got distracted when I realised I'd lost my keys."

"I didn't meet the white woman. But I encountered… something there during a recent blizzard."

"How do you know about the white woman, if you're not local? I assume you didn't move from down the road?"

"You're a bright lad." Nick stretched. "I'm from Midhurst in West Sussex. No, I became interested in White Hill after my new neighbour died."

"Mr Brockman?"

"That's right. I suppose you knew Charlie?"

"And his wife. I grew up playing in King's Wood. They always walked there."

"Charlie claimed to have seen June in the woods, soon after her death. It piqued my interest, because ever since I arrived I keep seeing and hearing my dead boy, Grant." His brow furrowed. "That's a thought: Why would Barry's ghost attack all of you?"

Jason's eyes half closed. "It wasn't Barry. No way. Something spiritual, yes. Something sinister. It knew stuff about him and us, but that wasn't my best friend."

"Its appearance must make this harder to bear."

Jason sighed. "Have you ever been angry and scared at the same time?"

"Rarely, but I'm beginning to understand the concept." Nick pointed at Stour Cottage. "Here we are. Let's get dried off and light a fire."

Nick entered his lounge carrying a wooden tray with a steaming bowl of soup and two wholemeal rolls. "Is winter vegetable okay?"

"Great, thanks." Jason perched on a pouffe close to the pulsing orange glow of ignited logs in the burner.

Nick handed him the tray. "Balance it on your lap

and stick close to that fire. Are you warming up?"

"Yeah."

Nick disappeared, then returned with a tray of his own, which he set down on a coffee table. He dragged an armchair close beside Jason and passed him some folded sheets of photocopied paper. "After a charity walker died on White Hill, I conducted a little research at the library in Canterbury. That incident caught my attention, so soon after Charlie's death near the same spot."

Jason unfolded the papers, soup spoon balanced in his other hand. He read the title at the top of the page. "I have this one in my collection. It's an excellent book. Short on detail, but I suppose we'd all like more."

Nick tilted his head. "Would you still like more after what happened today?"

"More information, then."

Nick kept watching him. "The ghost I encountered on White Hill was my son. The one I keep seeing and hearing."

Jason held up the pages. "Did you strike him, like in these reports of the white woman?"

Nick nodded. His eyes watered. "A hit-and-run driver killed Grant in Chichester, more than a year and a half ago."

Jason dropped his spoon with a clatter, splashing soup. "No. Err, sorry."

Nick watched him with a knowing expression. "I see you appreciate the significance. Imagine what I felt when his darling face mashed against my windshield, before he rolled off the car and vanished."

Jason hesitated. "Did he... smile?"

Nick's face stiffened. "That made it a hundred times worse. Then during my walk today, I heard him in the trees. I didn't see him. It happened again while I was administering the kiss of life to your bedraggled body."

"I'm glad you weren't distracted." Jason picked up his spoon again.

Nick clamped his hands together in front of his face in a thoughtful pose. "First Charlie Brockman, then that dead walker, and now the stories you've told me about these visitations by an imitation friend. I can't help feeling this is all connected. Linked to the area somehow." He tapped his foot. "At first I thought my experiences of Grant were borne of grief or a by-product of alcohol. A combination of the two, perhaps. Now I'm sure they weren't. I want it to be Grant." His voice softened. "I *need* it to be Grant. But something tells me an unseen presence or power realises that too. It's using my need."

"Like with Barry and my friends?"

"That's logical."

"But why?" Jason handed him back the photocopied pages.

Nick stared into the fire. "Now that is a question."

9

Seeking Answers

Nick Preston rapped a brass door knocker at The Orchard. In the four days since his drama with Jason, rain and warmer temperatures reduced the snow to icy, melting clumps. Now it lay amidst the welcome, re-emerging greens of an underlying rural landscape.

Helen Cooper opened the door. "Yes?"

"Oh, good morning." Nick smiled and peered across her shoulder. "Is Jason home?"

"He's upstairs. Would you like me to fetch him?"

"If you wouldn't mind."

Helen hesitated, her hand pulling away from the door. "Whom shall I say is calling?"

"Nick Preston."

"Hold on a moment." Helen left the door ajar and called up the staircase. "Jason? There's a Nick Preston at the door for you."

Footsteps sounded on the stairs.

Nick caught a hushed exchange, interrogating the teenager about his adult visitor. A minute later he appeared at the door and Helen drifted into the kitchen.

"Hi, Nick. How are you?" Jason asked.

"Fine. Better now the snow is melting. Are you any the worse for wear from your pond incident?"

"No. Mum noticed nothing odd about my clothes when I got home. I caught hell for losing my keys though."

Nick snorted. "I'll bet. Listen, I wondered if you'd like a walk up to the woods? Given everything that's happened, I'd enjoy some company. I figured you might feel the same."

Jason's shoulders lifted as though casting off a heavy burden. "I haven't been for a walk since it happened. Thanks. I must seem a wimp."

Nick lowered his voice to avoid being overheard. "After drowning at the hands of two murderous evil spirits? What are you, mid-teens?"

"Sixteen."

"They should pin a medal on your chest. I'm forty and I wobbled over taking another walk there on my own. Nothing has attacked me, yet. Not like you."

"I'll grab my coat and put on some shoes. Hold on." Jason disappeared back inside. A gruff, male voice barked at him. "Don't forget your replacement house keys. Try not to lose them this time."

Nick wandered back to the cottage gate where he lingered.

Jason closed his front door and hurried down the path towards him.

"Was that your dad?" Nick asked.

"Yeah. He'll be rubbing my nose in the missing key situation for a fortnight."

"That's parents for you."

Jason zipped his jacket up beneath his chin. "I don't mind. It makes a change from him bugging me over his favourite subject."

"And what's that?" Nick followed him out into the lane.

"Girls. Or rather, their absence in my life. He enjoys telling me they're curvy people with higher pitched voices, longer hair, bumpy chests and different plumbing."

Nick half-coughed, half-laughed. "Do you know, I'm familiar with them?"

Jason managed a lacklustre smile. "Barry was popular with the girls. Dad labours that point from time to time. I could do without it now he's dead. It's tough enough coming to terms with his loss."

Nick placed a momentary hand on Jason's shoulder and squeezed it. "On top of becoming a man and all that entails? I hear ya. Try to understand that he means well and wants the best for you. I realise that's not easy."

"I know." Jason kicked a fallen pine cone down the road. "I've always enjoyed reading. I get swept away with literature sometimes and use it to hide from the world. Ordinary life seems dull by comparison with the power of the written word. Or it does to me."

"Your supernatural books?"

"Those and fantasy fiction. Barry and the rest of us grew up playing sword and sorcery role-playing games." Jason's voice sped up as though excusing an offence. "We weren't nerds, or anything. All of us enjoyed sport and other activities. Barry also built radio-controlled cars." He stopped walking for a second and flushed. "Okay, *I* might be a nerd."

Nick looked Jason up and down. "Would it matter if you were? It's a label. A pejorative term applied to those who don't fit someone's bigoted worldview of 'normal.' Give it a few years; you'll soon realise many nerds end up as business leaders. They employ the cocky little shits who once insulted them, as low paid subordinates. Sometimes justice prevails. Not always."

"Thanks, Nick. If I'm honest, I retreat into imaginary worlds. They're exciting, but… safe. Dad calls me a dreamer."

"As long as all that dreaming translates into action eventually, what of it? You're a deep thinker. From our limited interactions, I'd assess you as enjoying high emotional intelligence. That's a sought-after quality in the workplace these days. Trust me, I've worked with enough corporations to know."

They reached the track to the woods.

Jason shuffled his feet. "There is a girl I like. I've liked her for years."

"From school?"

"Yes. She's pretty and popular now. But I admired her when we were still pudgy-faced kids."

"Are you close?" Nick shifted.

"We kind of stopped speaking since the age of thirteen."

"Did she ignore you, or did you struggle with emotional and physical changes? You know: things that caused you to panic and clam up when she drew near?"

Jason gulped. "How did you know?"

An understanding light flitted behind Nick's eyes. "Because I was thirteen once too." He started up the narrow, uneven hillside climb. "Don't beat yourself up about it. Try to remember the honest admiration you felt for that pudgy-faced kid. Then talk to her from that place with no agenda other than friendship. It might surprise you how lonely *'pretty and popular'* girls often feel inside. If nothing else, chatting with a genuine guy who isn't playing insincere games to jump her bones will prove a tonic."

Jason thumped his chest with a fist. "I'm not buff or cool. Average build and appearance. It's hard to compete for her attention."

"Then don't compete."

"Huh?" Jason scratched his head.

"Be yourself, but confident in who you are and what you like. Quiet confidence and a caring nature are masculine traits too. Attractive ones. Observing before acting - while lacking aggression and huge biceps - doesn't make you a loser, Jason. I'll wager when the chips are down and someone threatens a person or thing you love, you'll draw upon more courage and fortitude than you ever imagined."

Jason stopped to catch his breath. "Nick?"

"Yeah?"

"Um, I don't want to add to your pain, but..."

"But what? Spit it out; I won't be cross."

Jason watched him. "You'd make a wonderful father. I realise I'm gushing, but I'm sorry Grant didn't get to experience even five minutes of the supportive, grown-up advice you've just given me. He'd have matured into a confident man."

Nick's eyes glistened. "Thank you. Now if I can sort myself out, my wife, Alana, may even take me back. I don't seem such a life guru when you throw our separation into the mix, do I?"

"Is she younger than you?"

"Yeah. Thirty-five."

Jason started walking again. "There's still time if you wanted another child."

Nick rubbed his chin and glanced aside. "Anyway." He looked back. "So, have you heard any more from your friends?"

"I told them what happened at the woods. I wish I hadn't mentioned it to Adam. He's the guy who suffered that girlfriend manifestation. I'm worried he's close to a nervous breakdown or something."

"Any further Barry incidents?"

"No."

"Nothing unusual at all?"

Jason shook his head. "How about you?"

"Odd flashes of movement and sounds at the cottage. I'm trying to tune them out as a deception. Grant and I were close. He wouldn't tease and abuse me like this. It's not helping my recovery, but I don't want to run either. I've done enough of that."

"My pals have come off easier, then. The others don't live in Chilham. They're not far."

"Do you think proximity to White Hill, combined with our emotional upheaval, is significant? I'm not knocking the suggestion, if you do. I've reached the same conclusion."

"No idea. These woods are known as a place ghosts roam among the trees and witch covens meet after dark."

Nick raised an eyebrow. "Romantically put. Did you make up that last bit about witch covens, or are there other stories I haven't heard?"

"Rumours. It's not unusual for occult groups to congregate in places like this. I could show you a spot I suspect it happens at King's Wood. I don't know if they're witches."

"Okay, lead on. Oh, I almost forgot: When I visited the village shop yesterday, I ran into an old boy I've seen a few times. A chap called Larry."

Jason grinned. "He's full of wild stories."

"You're right. The shopkeeper likes to lambast him over them. I quizzed him about people meeting dead loved ones, on or near White Hill. It delighted him someone took an interest."

"What did he tell you?"

"He's knows of a woman called Martha Keep, who claims to have met her dead sister in these woods as a youngster. She ran a local shop herself until retirement. Some place called Old Wives Lees. I haven't looked it up yet."

Jason turned. He walked backwards along the ridge and pointed behind them. "Old Wives Lees lies on a hill across the A252 from Chilham. It's only a couple of miles away."

"Is it big?"

"No, tiny. A pub and some houses. The shop closed

when I was a kid."

Nick joined him facing backward and moved his gaze to the right. Canterbury Cathedral shone like a beacon in rays of sunlight stabbing down through a break in the gunmetal firmament. "Do you know Andrew Stallard, the local vicar?"

"I've spoken with him. Our family aren't churchgoers, but he always chats with my folks at village events."

Nick's eyes narrowed on the cathedral. "I've pondered speaking to him about all this. When I met him after Charlie Brockman's funeral, he seemed level-headed and open."

"Won't he dismiss us for believing stuff contrary to his religion?" Jason asked.

"I can't be sure. I'll keep it in my back pocket as an option. So, Larry says this Martha lady isn't shy about telling her tale."

Jason turned down a narrow bridleway. "It sounds interesting."

"Yeah. How about I try contacting her? I'll say we're amateur paranormal investigators, researching the area. Larry didn't think she'd require much inducement to lay her whole story out. It might be a load of old guff. Chances are we won't learn anything new. But if we don't try…"

"I'm up for it." Jason pushed bracken aside. "Here we are."

Nick stepped through and whistled. "That *is* a little odd and no mistake."

A tiny clearing, a hundred yards long and forty

wide, emerged amongst thick evergreen forest. Set in a spongy woodland floor of coniferous brown needles, stones painted white were laid out in a rectangular keyhole shape. Traces of ash mingled with melting snow at the bulbous, circular end.

Jason kicked the assorted cold piles. Grey fragments blew into the air. "I found this spot when I was twelve. From time to time someone repaints the stones."

Nick squatted for a closer inspection. "It's not a weird forest sculpture? I found a few of those further over."

"No, those are commissioned and indexed. This isn't listed among them; I've checked. Besides, who'd light a fire in a sculpture? I've often found ash in the circle."

"Good point. Of course, there's no definite correlation between any rituals that may have occurred here and our supernatural disturbances. Have you ever seen anything?"

"No." Jason walked the length of the keyhole shape. "When I first discovered it, I used to dream about sneaking out after dark and catching sinister individuals summoning demonic spirits. I'm sure some of that was fuelled by the books I read, both fiction and non-fiction. But I've never acted on the fantasy."

"I'd say you're wise. It's doubtful whoever made this would react well to an intrusion or being spied upon. I'm not sure I'd want to be caught out here in the pitch black woods, at the mercy of people who believe goodness knows what."

Jason adjusted his jacket for comfort. "You asked me to show you."

"I did, and I'm grateful. I wonder what Andrew Stallard would make of this?" Nick pulled out his smartphone and snapped off several images of the scene from different angles. "I'll keep these for reference, like those library photocopies."

An ear-splitting crack made them whirl about. Nick's foot slipped down into an animal burrow and stuck. A tall, nearby conifer swayed at an alarming rate as he attempted to dislodge it. Without further warning, the trunk bent over towards Nick, casting a shadow across his form marking its intended path of collapse. Jason rushed to his side and knelt. He scooped out earth and pulled tangled roots away from his ensnared shoe. Nick pulled free and scrambled aside with Jason. Both dived headlong into a patch of moist earth. The tree gave way and toppled with an ear-splitting crash and a shower of melting snow. Its fallen trunk lay across the arcane ground symbol, but failed to dislodge the stone markers.

Nick picked himself up, then brushed down his clothing. "At least we're not soaked this time." He reached a hand to Jason and helped him stand. "Are you okay?"

"Scared shitless," Jason puffed between gasps. "But I'm in one piece."

Nick moved to examine the lower end of the tree. "There's no sign of it being cut." He crouched and tested the exposed internal wood for moisture. "No flakes of damp or decay, yet it split right near the base."

Jason joined him. "There's no wind either." He

exchanged uneasy glances with Nick.

Nick rose. "Okay, let's return to the main forest trails."

Jason made to leave.

Nick called after him. "Jason?"

Jason looked back, surprised by Nick's outstretched hand. "What?"

"I'd say this makes us even, wouldn't you?"

Jason shook it. "I suppose. I hadn't thought about it."

Nick nodded. "That's because you're the man of integrity I described on our way in; not some thuggish narcissist. Shall we head back?"

"Sure."

* * *

Lower Lees Road at Old Wives Lees followed a contour halfway up a hill opposite Chilham. Now and again, between houses and trees, a fine, sweeping vista of a bend in The Great Stour Valley opened up below.

Nick pulled his Honda up to a kerb opposite a converted oast house. On the pavement side, an attractive row of well-maintained, white terraced cottages faced the former agricultural structure. "It turns out Martha still lives in what was once the shop." He opened his door, while Jason climbed out on the other side. "This is it." Nick indicated a cottage sporting an attractive carriage lamp above the door.

"How was she when you spoke with her?"

"Keen as mustard. Larry was right: she won't take much squeezing to extract juicy details."

Gravel covered the tiny front garden. Shrubs in pots, six to a side, lined a path stretching five short paces to the door. To its right, net curtains twitched behind a living room window.

"More than a shop." Nick tapped a round ceramic house name plaque which read '*Post Office Cottage*.' He waved at a shadow behind the moving curtains.

The front door swept open. A weathered but well-proportioned hourglass figure mixed matronly warmth with well-preened poise in the form of Martha Keep. Glossy red lipstick stuck out against her pale, ghostlike complexion and ash grey hair. Intelligent eyes suggested a late sixties pensioner in the early years of retirement. The kind who wouldn't easily become a victim of scams targeted against her demographic by the unscrupulous and immoral. Her obvious lucidity reassured Nick the pair weren't about to be subjected to endless, senile ramblings. This woman appeared sharp as a pin in both grooming and intelligence.

"Mrs Keep? I'm Nick Preston. We spoke on the phone."

Martha ushered them inside. "Splendid. I've got the kettle on. Nice to see you're both punctual."

Nick nudged Jason. "This is Jason Cooper, the lad I told you about."

Martha smiled at the teenager. "You'd better remove those jackets, or you won't feel the benefit. I don't enjoy the cold. A curse of approaching old age. My central heating remains set high."

Nick and Jason unzipped their outer layers.

Martha waved at a set of hooks on the wall. "Pop

them on there, then settle yourselves in the living room. I'll bring the tea through."

When Martha strode into the living room lugging a tray laden with teapot, china and relevant sundries, she found Nick and Jason admiring a framed photographic print above the fireplace. It depicted her thirty years prior, serving behind the counter of a packed country store. "That's how this room and the ground floor once looked. I closed a decade ago. It still throws me sometimes, moving about the place."

"You were postmistress and shopkeeper?" Nick asked.

"That's correct. Trade dropped off in the end. I couldn't sell the business, so literally shut up shop. My husband passed away that year. I sold our large old house and converted this building back into a cottage again. It was easier to manage and holds so many fond memories. I chose to live here instead."

Nick joined Jason, who'd settled on a two-seater sofa.

Martha eased herself into a worn armchair beside the fireplace. "Tea is brewing in the pot. It won't take long." She sat back to examine her visitors. "So you're both keen ghost hunters?"

"Unintentional ones," Nick replied. "Jason and I have each experienced unexplainable, err… visitations - for want of a better word - over in King's Wood. An old boy in Chilham said you'd a similar tale to tell. I suppose we're hoping to find answers. That or reassurances we aren't both nuts."

Martha's pleasant face turned a shade more serious. She poured out the tea through a strainer into three cups. "I was a teenager around the same age as Jason, when I had my experience. It may have been half a century ago, but the whole encounter proved so shocking I can recall everything as though it were yesterday."

"Do you have a good memory for other things?" Nick asked.

A wry smile crept up one side of Martha's powder-white face. "Are you concerned over my accuracy?"

"Not at all." Nick pulled himself up. "Quite the opposite. You seem on the ball."

"Sugar?" Martha asked without looking up.

"No, thank you," the pair returned in unison.

Martha handed Jason a cup first. "Less startling events also stay with me. You become observant when you're the keeper of a small shop, day in, day out for an entire career. I can even recall a minibus full of schoolchildren who used to pull up on the way home sometimes, during the 1980s. A jolly boy among them called Digby, regularly bought a box of Jaffa Cakes. Silly little things like that stick. Were I an artist, I could draw you a picture of the scene with great detail." She passed a second cup and saucer to Nick.

"Thank you. That's impressive." Nick took it.

Martha lifted a cup of her own, then settled back into the armchair again. "My beloved twin sister, Saskia, died a year prior to that day in King's Wood. An undiagnosed hole in the heart. It shocked the entire family."

"It must have been awful. Were you living in Chilham at the time?" Nick asked.

"That's right; on Mountain Street."

"I live at The Orchard," Jason piped up.

Martha's eyes glittered. "We were three doors down. Saskia and I loved to play in the woods as girls. During our teenage years, we still took walks there for private chats about boys and such. It was a place we could bare our souls without provoking parental disapproval."

Nick shifted in his seat. "I'm sorry to sound indelicate, but may I ask where Saskia died?"

"At home, in bed. We still shared a room then. I awoke one morning, eager to tell Saskia about a dream I'd had. When she didn't respond, I crossed the room and shook her. She was ice cold to the touch. That's the moment I realised she'd passed away in her sleep."

"I'm sorry." Nick sipped his tea.

Martha watched him. "Did you wonder if she'd died in the woods, where my scare occurred? Or perhaps on that lane up White Hill, where many a motorist has endured a supernatural fright?"

Jason's eyebrows raised.

Martha's observant face noted his change of expression. "That's right, I'm familiar with the accounts. In those days nobody knew of the white woman. I read in the paper that she's believed to be a murder victim from the last twenty years. Strangulation, wasn't it? Anyway, White Hill was known as an uneasy and haunted place, long before that occurred. Saskia and I could both have sworn we heard screaming one night, when we were late walking back along The Pilgrims' Way. Older tales report the ghosts of murdered women or their unseen killers chasing people through those woods. Mostly, it was a pleasant place during daylight. As sisters, we never experienced undue concern. That's why I carried on walking there after Saskia died. It became a haven to grieve and reflect. To talk to her, as one talks to God up in the sky or an unseen friend conjured by the mind."

Nick put down his cup and saucer. "You said Saskia died a year before your experience?"

"I did. A year on, her bed across the room still felt empty and sad. I'd lost my drive and lust for life. One morning I arose and needed to talk with her more than ever. I must have been wandering for over an hour when I experienced an odd chill. It was a warm midsummer day, so that surprised me."

"Go on." Nick placed both palms on his knees.

"I'd reached a dark section of The Pilgrims' Way near White Hill proper. A place the track narrows and tree canopies interlock like an organic archway. 'God's Natural Cathedral,' Saskia called it when we were children. The bushes parted on one side and my sister stepped out, large as life."

"Were you scared?" Jason remembered his encounter with Barry near the pond.

"Startled," Martha replied. "Remember, I wanted more than anything to see her again. Part of me almost collapsed in shock, yet I wondered for a moment if this was a gift from God."

"And on The Pilgrims' Way to Canterbury, too. I'm not surprised." Nick nodded.

"Saskia drew nearer. I ran to hug her, but something stopped me in my tracks."

"What?" Nick and Jason were on the edge of their seats now.

"A light in her eyes. A peculiar smile on her lips. Odd minor details which added up to a terrifying realisation this wasn't my sister after all. And if not her, then who or what?"

"What did you do?" Jason finished his tea.

"I wanted to run. It felt wrong to even speak with that thing. My head spun; I became faint."

"Did you pass out?" Nick said.

"No, thank goodness. I took a breath and turned around. I was about to walk away, when a freezing iron grip latched onto my arm. Saskia stood at my shoulder. She fixed me with those odd, twinkling eyes and said, *'Where are you going, Sister Dearest?'* That term of endearment felt anything but. It dripped with mockery and cruel intent. In that moment, I believe whatever it was enjoyed my fear; like some diner presented their favourite dish. It devoured or absorbed the waves of terror shaking my body."

Nick blinked. "You should have been an author; that's quite a description. How did you get away?"

"I was rescued. Saved by a group of walkers hiking the entire route from Winchester to Canterbury. They appeared on the trail, climbing uphill behind us."

"Did they see Saskia?" Jason asked.

"No. To my relief, she vanished when they

appeared. I recovered my wits and greeted the group. They'd not long left the church at Boughton Aluph and were on their way to Chilham. I explained I was headed in that direction and asked if I could accompany them and hear the story of their trip."

"I imagine they agreed?" Nick smiled.

"Of course. Not that I wasn't interested, but it provided a perfect subterfuge to make it home without bumping into that thing again. I never went back into King's Wood and I haven't since."

"Have you experienced any more visitations from Saskia, or something that looked or sounded like her?" Nick asked.

"No. Mum and Dad sold our house the following month. Dad went to work for Canterbury City Council, and we moved to a place at Littlebourne. I didn't come back this way until I married. Even then, I couldn't bring myself to settle in Chilham itself. I know the village is lovely, and it hardly suffers Pluckley's reputation for ghosts. But, there were too many links with the past and that awful day."

Nick looked at Jason, then back to Martha. "Thank you for your time and the tea."

"Did it help? I've enjoyed our chat. It gets lonely here now with no work and my husband a memory. Most of the old customers I knew have either died, gone into care, or moved away. Still, it's a pleasant spot if you enjoy peace and quiet."

"If nothing else, it's encouraging to hear another reliable human being who's drawn similar conclusions to ours."

Martha sighed. "You know your own business. But, if you've met the thing I ran into that day, I'd be inclined to give it a wide berth."

Nick's muscles tightened. "We may not have that option."

Martha stood and reached for the tray.

Jason beat her to it. "Please let me carry that out for you."

Martha grinned. "I'm only in my late sixties, young man; not a decrepit invalid." She caught his sheepish expression. Her mock indignation softened. "But I appreciate the gesture. Please do, if you'd like to." She regarded Nick. "If you're seeking assistance or answers, a neighbour told me something interesting. A woman over in Mystole helped her brother quieten disturbances at a house he'd bought in Garlinge Green."

"Mystole?" Nick asked.

"I know where that is," Jason said.

Martha shuffled out into the hallway while Jason deposited the tray in her kitchen. "Emily said the woman was a 'Light Worker,' or some such title. Once she attended the home, her brother had no more trouble."

Nick retrieved their jackets from the pegs. "Can you remember the light worker's name?" He winked to gee her up. "I know you've such a great memory."

Martha folded her arms, an amused smirk widening across her countenance. "As it happens, I can: Erin Parsons. I've always liked the name Erin. Her surname stuck, because it amused me to find a New Age practitioner with such an ecclesiastical moniker. I'm sure she's in the phone book. If not, call me and I'll get her contact details from Emily."

Nick handed Jason his coat. "We'll look into it. Thanks again for today."

Martha opened the door. "I wish you both well."

10

Consultation

A Neolithic and Roman long barrow, the mound atop Julliberrie Down comprised a 44 metre long, 15 metre wide and 2.5 metre high covered chalk structure. Findings included a flint axe head dated around 2000 BC and a later Roman coin hoard. A ditch extended on the eastern and western sides, along with the mound's southern end. Four Romano British burials were discovered in its upper layer. A black, skeletal tree crowned the burial site's northern extremity. Commanding views of Chilham and the A28 towards Godmersham could be had from this elevated position high above a bend in the River Stour. To the residents of Chilham, it sometimes felt as though the dead kept watch. Locally referred to as 'The Giant's Grave' or 'The Grave,' due to folktales that either a giant or army and their horses were buried there, passing tourists drove by without giving the hill a second glance. Whether its etymology originated from one of Caesar's tribunes buried at the site, a conjunction of another person's name with a corruption of the old English word for hill, or more fanciful associations with a giant or witch had been lost in the mists of history.

It was a dry day in March, hinting at warmer weather ahead, when Nick and Jason nipped over a level crossing on the other side of the A28 below the hill. They traversed a narrow bridge, beneath which gently flowing water gurgled, to approach a five-storey brick and white weatherboard clad watermill. An expansive millpond stretched around the majority, while Julliberrie Down rose behind. Jason had already filled Nick in on the legends and history of the topographic feature, before their arrival.

"We could have driven to the light worker's house, but this was a good suggestion." Nick started up the hill.

Jason skidded on a patch of dewy grass. "We both enjoy our exercise. I thought this would make a pleasant change from King's Wood. It's a relief to walk in the opposite direction for once." He drew level with Nick. "Mystole lies a mile and a half further along The Pilgrims' Way from the top of Julliberrie Down."

"A six mile round trip from the village? Okay, we've a nice day for it." Nick took in the rising mound of earth that marked the barrow. "You'd think if anywhere had a right to feel creepy, it would be this place. Ever heard of weird happenings up here?"

"No." Jason paused for a look back across the valley to where Chilham Castle and the tower of St Mary's stood proud. "Whenever I come up here, a profound sense of peace overtakes me. I don't know why I didn't walk this way after Barry died, instead of King's Wood."

"Habit and the convenience of your proximity to

regular haunts, I'd say. King's Wood never gave you issues before, so why change?"

"I suppose. The trail runs behind those trees ahead." Jason set off again. "How did this new lady react to your phone call? What did you say?"

"The truth. I told her we'd heard of her work quietening troublesome spirits and wondered if she'd be willing to discuss something similar." Nick accompanied him onto another section of The Pilgrims' Way.

"Does she think we live in a haunted house?"

"No. I told her the disturbances came from deceased connections we'd encountered at King's Wood and White Hill."

"How did she react?"

Nick waved an energetic finger in the air. "With great interest. She greeted my mention of King's Wood - and especially White Hill - with considerable enthusiasm. Even offered to talk things over via a free consultation to begin with."

Jason pretended to wipe his brow. "That's a relief. I'm short of cash and haven't found a part-time job yet."

Nick smirked. "Don't worry about the money. If she seems legit and offers concrete solutions, I'll cover any expenses."

"Did you mention my friends?"

"No. Should I?"

Jason shook his head. "I'd rather keep them out of it. Nothing else has happened since those initial frights." He picked up the pace. "You could ask this woman to visit Stour Cottage. She might sense what's going on there."

Nick scratched his chin. "I doubt it. It's not the house. If anything is haunted, it's me as a person rather than some structure. The manifestations look and sound like Grant; but, he's never been here. Certainly not to Stour Cottage. His visitations aren't confined to the building, as you know."

"That's true."

Nick inhaled a deep lungful of invigorating fresh air. "We'll see what this light worker has to say about everything, then take it from there."

The pair skirted sloping fields, until they emerged between an avenue of trees and hedgerows onto a bend in a deserted, single-track tarmac lane.

Nick stared down an additional, rougher road to their right, which ended at the corner. "Which way now?"

Jason pointed ahead. "Straight on. 'Nailbourne' is on the left-hand side."

"That's an odd name. 'Bourne' refers to a river, if I'm not mistaken?"

"It does. The Nailbourne is one of three, fast-flowing intermittent streams that rise from chalk downs in East Kent. Some locals refer to them as 'Woe Waters,' on account of associations with bad events."

Nick's attention followed the ridge of Chartham Downs rising on their left. He spoke with a distant voice. "No doubt an old wives' tale."

"It's not unusual for them to remain dry for years at a stretch. Next thing you know, there's a burgeoning watercourse bisecting your land."

Nick grinned. "I can tell you're an avid reader. You should speak with Andrew Stallard, the vicar. I suspect the pair of you would find a lot in common. He's keen on local lore and history. So do these 'Woe Waters' run nearby?"

"One of them crosses the valley towards Penny Pot Wood." Jason indicated a line of trees on their right. "I imagine that's how the house got its name."

"That figures. There's a building on the left up ahead."

"That should be it."

They approached a substantial, smart detached country home with a long, sweeping tiled roof and tall chimneys. It sat back from the lane beyond a driveway flanked by thick hedgerows and a low picket fence.

Nick hesitated at the front gate to give the place a once over. "If she bought this off the back of being a light worker, I'm in the wrong business."

Jason pushed through the gate and ambled down a flagstone path towards a sheltered white wooden door with wrought iron hinges. He jangled a rustic brass bell while Nick examined a carved wooden house sign in flowing text that read: *'Nailbourne.'*

High heels clipped on wooden floorboards within, crossing to echo on stone. A sturdy latch lifted, and the door eased open.

Tall, leggy and toned with layered ebony hair down her upper back and sparkling eyes, people often assumed Erin Parsons to be an outgoing fitness or dance instructor rather than a stay-at-home New Age entrepreneur. The forty-three-year-old's appearance - dressed in a black, soft rib cropped vest and denim jeans - suggested a woman who'd failed to escape the 1980s. A fulsome perm and dangly silver earrings added further weight to such assessments. She fluttered mascara-laden eyelashes at Nick, who drew back in discomfort at an overt suggestiveness in her stare. Those bright eyes ignored Jason and remained fixed upon him.

"Ms Parsons?" Nick offered.

"Erin. You must be Nick." She extended a slender hand from which dangled a silver charm bracelet bedecked with astral symbols.

Nick gave her hand a quick squeeze with as few fingers as possible. Despite his rapid, uneasy greeting, she still caressed his digits. He cleared his throat. "This is Jason, the lad who's shared similar - though scarier - woes to mine." He inclined his head towards the carved sign. "Like the waters."

Erin's eyes narrowed for a second. "Does the return of energy in liquid form suggest woe to you? Some think the Nailbourne signifies new life. That's why I named my home after it."

"Are the waters up this year?" Jason asked. "I haven't noticed."

Erin kept her visual grasp on Nick as she answered the lad. "No, but energies are always in flux around here. Even the dullest of spiritual wits can sense this area courses with ancient power." Her face brightened. She rose on tiptoe to peek across Nick's shoulder. "Where did you park?"

"Nowhere," Nick replied. "We hiked over from Chilham."

Erin massaged Nick's body with her eyes as much as she had his fingers with her hand. "That doesn't surprise me. You look fit." She noticed his wedding ring. "Has your wife experienced the same issues? With these apparitions, I mean?"

Nick bit his lip. "My wife is back in West Sussex. We're… going through some stuff right now. Most of it surrounds our dead son, who I keep seeing and hearing. So, as I'm sure you can appreciate, I'm eager to lay everything to rest."

"I see." Erin pursed her lips to disguise what Nick fancied a predatory grin. "You'd best come inside." She stepped back.

Nick gestured for Jason to go first. Anything to provide a barrier between himself and the flirtatious temptress. His life was complicated enough, without travelling the one-way road to relationship ruin her 'come hither' manner invited.

Erin led them into a comfortable study, painted deep purple. Broad, sanded beams supported its roof. Exposed timber frames in the walls ran at odd angles typical of period properties. Erin signalled them to sit upon red cushioned rattan chairs, filling the primary space. A sturdy oak desk stood against one wall, adorned with spiritual tomes of an esoteric nature, a green-feathered quill fitted with a ballpoint nib and a cut glass paperweight featuring a pentagram motif. "This is my consultation room. I like to minimise background distractions from the house while sounding out potential clients."

Nick sat. "Business appears fruitful." His eyes wandered around the room. *This place must cost double the value of our home in Midhurst. What else does this woman do?*

Erin joined them on the chairs. "Let me guess: You're wondering how a flaky, New Age weirdo earns enough to own a house like this?"

Nick flushed. "It's none of my business. I'm sorry."

"Don't apologise. My ex-husband was a banker who made a small fortune in arbitrage. This house counted as chump change to him, after we split. I could have dug my heels in for more, but that doesn't fit my ethos."

Nick squirmed. Despite her coming onto him, he felt a chump for making obvious snap judgements based on assumption.

Erin stretched to open a drawer on the desk. She pulled out an incense stick, then positioned it in an elegant holder Nick failed to notice earlier, near the books. She struck a match, lit the top, and then blew it out. Coils of sandalwood smoke wafted across the room. "I find this helps people relax and centre themselves." She took a slow breath from her diaphragm. "Shall we begin?"

Nick's nostrils twitched, unused to the heady aroma of incense. "Where would you like us to start?"

"You've come to Kent in the last few months?"

"That's right. Like I said, my wife and I struggled after losing our boy."

Erin drew in some smoke. "Did you experience

manifestations of him at your family home?"

"No. Only since I arrived here."

"Have you tried talking with him?"

"He's never around long enough. Deep down I know it isn't Grant."

Erin raised one immaculately plucked eyebrow. "How can you be so sure?"

"The way he treats me. It's more than childish mischief. There's something else behind it: malice. I realise that sounds weird. It's not a word I thought I'd ever associate with my six-year-old. That's why I know it can't be him."

"If it's not his ghost, then what is it?"

Nick frowned. "I was hoping you'd tell me. Jesus, I didn't come here for you to ask the same questions I pose myself every day."

Erin took another elongated breath. "Please calm down, Nick. I've suggestions to offer. First, I require a feel for how you perceive the situation, before I colour that perception with one of my own."

"Oh." Nick relaxed. "Well, I think it's a spirit or force. Intelligent, nasty, vindictive. It's playing at being someone I miss: my dear boy who I'm trying to adjust to life without. Jason's experiences of his dead friend run in a similar vein."

Erin looked at Jason for the first time. "What happened?"

"My childhood best friend, Barry, was killed in a car accident on White Hill. That's-"

"I know where it is." Erin's eyes swelled, then resumed their normal size. "Long ago?"

"No. A few weeks." Jason toyed with mentioning the Ouija board incident, but stuck with his instincts. Better to keep his friends and their encounters out of play for now. "He stepped from the bushes while I was walking in King's Wood, then scolded me for not crying at his funeral."

Erin read his body language for any hint of dishonesty or a cover-up. "He appeared as solid as I am before you now?"

"Yes, but it wasn't him. Then he forced my head down and tried to drown me in a pond. I even saw his father, who'd hung himself after Barry's death. He joined in the attack." Jason elbowed Nick. "I'd be dead myself, if Nick hadn't come along and revived me."

Erin smiled at Nick again. "You're quite the hero."

Nick shook his head. "Right place, right time; nothing more. Jason returned the favour by saving me from a falling tree."

"On the same day?" Erin gasped.

"No, the following week. We were inspecting the site of some occult ritual or other. Could that be a cause for any of this?"

Erin scratched one side of her slim nose. "I shouldn't concern yourself with that. People believe what they want to believe. There are cults and covens aplenty in the vicinity. Unless you're involved with them yourselves, it's unlikely to prove a factor in your troubles."

"That's one piece of good news," Nick replied. "I was going to chat with the local vicar about it."

"Andrew Stallard?" Erin smirked. "I wouldn't

bother about him. Not unless you require a jumble sale or coffee morning organised for pensioners."

"You don't have a high opinion of Andrew?" Nick sat forward.

"I've no time for either him or his religion. A derelict minister of a derelict faith, devoid of spiritual life or reality. He's ignorant of the psychic torrent flowing all about us." Erin composed herself. "I'm sorry. I didn't mean to bring negative energy into our proceedings."

Nick eased back again. "So what do you think this is?"

Erin closed her eyes, took three more breaths, and then opened them again. "Several stories suggest White Hill (and King's Wood crowning it) draw in spiritual energy like a beacon. I put it to you that's only half the truth."

"What's the other half?" Nick clasped his hands together.

"That it draws in spiritual energy of a particular sort."

"You mean evil?"

Erin eyed him. "Define evil?"

"Let's start with imitating my dead son and running into my car on White Hill. Why don't we follow that up with an attempt to kill Jason, disguised as his best friend?" Nick's temperature rose with his voice.

Erin remained calm. "Is death evil?"

"Murder is."

"And when a soldier from one country murders a soldier from another for the political ends of their masters?"

Nick fell silent, slack jawed.

Erin sat straighter. "Forgive me, Nick. I'm trying to help you see that you're judging this entity or entities by your own shallow morality. That's an artificial construct you're applying to forces beyond your ken or realm of existence."

Nick ran a hand through his hair. "When they cross into *my* realm of existence and make life a misery or endanger others, I'll apply any damn judgement I see fit. Spirits masquerading as folk we're connected to (or people who died in the vicinity), will be held to the same standard as the living." His brow furrowed. "Stick that in your fucking incense burner and smoke it." He lurched to his feet. "I don't need to hear this."

Erin rose at a gentler rate. She reached out a hand to touch his shoulder.

Nick recoiled.

Erin's eyes turned down. "I'm sorry. I realise you're upset and didn't mean to offend. You came here for answers, but I've offered little else than doubt. Please forgive me."

Nick swallowed hard and took his seat again.

Erin lowered herself back into the rattan chair. "These recent disturbances could be a product of your grief. You're both suffering with great intensity and giving off wild energy. I can sense your auras." She ran her hands in an invisible outline, as though drawing around them in midair. "It's possible forces attracted to and encircling White Hill are enticed by that. Some wish to live again, but retain no memory of their former identity. If powerful recollections of departed loved ones rest atop your subconscious, that may be why they take such forms. It's like a blueprint they can adopt."

Nick gasped. "You're saying these things are enjoying a spiritual fancy dress party using my boy and Jason's friend for costumes?"

Erin bit her lip. "To express it in crude, earthly terms."

Jason held up a hand. "Wait a minute. You said, *'recent disturbances.'* Nick and I spoke with a woman who went through a similar ordeal with a mimic of her deceased sister. That was fifty years ago."

Erin tapped his knee. "You're thinking in the lower plane terms of a mortal lifespan. Try to appreciate that time is also an artificial construct. It doesn't work the same, beyond the veil of our existence. I've expressed disdain for the Christian faith today. But, one Bible verse puts the concept of time into an understandable perspective."

"Which one is that?" Nick asked.

"That one day is with the Lord as a thousand years, and a thousand years as one day. To some of these entities, Julius Caesar setting up an encampment at Chilham was like last week. Wrap your head around that."

Nick exchanged glances with Jason. "Okay, so how do we stop it?"

"Stop what?"

"These ghosts (or whatever) from plaguing our lives."

Erin shook her head. "I don't think they're all

departed souls. I've visited White Hill many times. In my opinion, some are spiritual beings far older, wiser and more powerful."

"Fine. How do we defeat or drive them out?"

"Have you heard nothing I've said to you?" Erin squinted.

Nick counted to ten to avoid flying off the handle again. "So we have to put up with it or move somewhere else, is that it? What if one of those things has another go at Jason? What if it kills him?"

Erin sighed. "I'm sorry, Nick. The harsh but realistic answer is: he won't go anywhere he wasn't already destined once his mortal candle extinguished. Death is nothing to fear."

"Try saying that when apparitions of your dead best friend and his father are drowning you." Nick stood up, slower this time. "This is going nowhere other than a trip to the doctor for my blood pressure." He gathered himself. "I realise you mean well, Erin. You look at this stuff from a different viewpoint. Maybe that helps some folk, but if the best you can offer is: *Tough, you'll both have to suffer*, then I'd say we're through."

Erin stood in time with Jason. "As you wish. Like I mentioned on the phone, there's no charge for a consultation."

"I appreciate that. You've given us food for thought and reinforced some of our ideas. For that I'm sure Jason and I are grateful."

Erin led them back into the hallway. "You're frustrated because I can't offer a resolution. I understand." She opened her front door. "I hope you find peace." She stopped on the doormat. "This one thought I offer: If these entities are drawn to your pain, then healing that pain is the quickest route to dropping off their radar." She slouched back against the wall, door in hand. "They may lose interest. Just a suggestion."

* * *

Fingers of morning sunlight crept over Julliberrie Down towards Chilham. Jason Cooper sat up from reclining on his bottom bunk with a fantasy novel. He held up the picture of Louise Squires. *I wonder if she's still seeing that older guy from Canterbury?* His heart ached. He inserted the photograph as a bookmark again, then placed the paperback beside his bed.

Something rattled the board forming his top bunk bookshelf. The slats it rested upon above Jason's head creaked. Noises of paper sliding on wood accelerated into a whoosh. A book on life after death and astral projection flew across the room and smacked into the window. It dropped to the floor and lay still.

"What the?" Jason gripped the mattress either side of his legs. He wobbled off the bed and crossed to the window.

Another sliding sound behind caused him to whirl. A hardback volume on ESP walloped him in the face. Jason fell back against the window, its cold glass pressing into his shoulder blades. Panic rose, ready to blare out like a steam whistle. Jason remembered

Martha Keep describing how her sister's apparition fed on her fear. Erin's words about their out-of-control energy and auras followed close behind. He balled his fists and steadied his breathing. A glossy paperback shot from the top bunk. This time Jason caught it. He held up the book entitled, '*Supernatural Kent*.' A determined grimace of victory at his interception faded into a look of twisted pain. Billowing smoke, followed by raging flames, engulfed the pages in a flash of searing heat, burning his hands. Jason tried to let go, but the title stuck fast to his fingers as though coated with industrial strength adhesive. He cried out as tongues of fire licked upward to sear his forearms.

Heavy footsteps pounded along the landing from his parents' room. Raymond Cooper burst through the door. His frustrated face at being awoken from a pleasant Saturday lay-in, evaporated before the frantic scene. Black clouds filled the room, smarting his eyes. He tugged a belt sash clear and removed his dressing gown, then ran towards Jason clutching it. Father and son collapsed to the floor, rolling in a flurry of arms and legs. Raymond beat against his dressing gown fabric to deprive the fire of oxygen. Jason stopped struggling and lay still, apart from the rapid rise and fall of adrenaline-fuelled breathing.

Raymond peeled back the smothering, ad hoc fire blanket to reveal his son's face. "Are you all right, boy?"

Helen appeared in the doorway. She coughed at the smoke and waved her arms as though karate-chopping it into squares. "What happened?"

"I was about to ask the same question." Raymond's initial concern began a steady descent towards annoyance.

Jason lifted the last charred remnants of his book. Blistered skin peeled around his wrists and stung like fresh licks from a cat-o'-nine-tails. Silent tears flowed freely from the corners of both eyes.

"Oh my goodness." Helen put a hand over her mouth and hurried into the room. "Raymond, he needs a hospital; right now."

Raymond got up. "I'm not even dressed."

Helen darted back to the landing and stumbled downstairs. "I'm calling an ambulance."

After the hospital burns unit released Jason - hands and forearms wrapped in bandages reminiscent of race horse legs - he knew tough questions would follow. The family car drew up outside The Orchard with Raymond at the wheel and Helen beside him. Jason fumbled to open a rear door with his bandaged hands.

"I'll get that for you, darling." Helen unfastened her seatbelt.

Raymond followed suit, but twisted to lock hard eyes on Jason. "What on earth were you up to that caused a fire? Were you smoking something?"

"No, Dad. And I'm not on drugs, before you ask." Jason hoped his mother would reach the door and let him out before the grim car atmosphere intensified.

"What then? Help me understand." Raymond clutched the back of his seat. "Fire doesn't start on its own without an ignition source. Were you lighting a candle?"

Jason knew his father would never accept the truth. Rather, he'd fly off into a rage, adding fuel to the regular lambasting Jason already received.

"Yes. I was thinking about Barry while reading a book on the supernatural in Kent. It felt the right thing to light a candle for him."

Raymond rubbed his eyebrows. "That makes a little more sense. I didn't notice a candle. It must have rolled under the furniture during our struggle. What was it, a night light?"

"Yes." Jason lowered his eyes.

"Thank goodness it didn't burn the house down." He studied the bandages engulfing Jason's tender hands and forearms. "I'd say you've learnt a tough lesson about taking care around fire; even night lights. We'll leave it at that. Try to be more careful."

Helen opened Jason's door. He was about to swing his legs out when Raymond spoke again.

"No more candles in your room, okay?"

"Okay, Dad."

* * *

Grant Preston ran out between parked cars on a sunny, Chichester back street. A motorist nipping down the popular cut through, way over the speed limit, gripped his steering wheel in shock. The red-haired six-year-old hammered into his front bumper, then flew across the road where he bounced, rolled and lay still. Panic set in for the driver, mixed with guilt and a sudden realisation of potential prison time if caught. Foot to the floor, he peeled away in a cloud of burning rubber.

Alana Preston screamed and dropped the mobile phone she'd held clamped to her head moments before. It shattered on the kerb before she even reached the limp, wide-eyed rag doll of her son's lifeless body.

Nick Preston awoke in a cold sweat at Stour Cottage. He'd been further away in town, awaiting his wife and son on that fateful day; the day Grant died. Yet, these vivid dreams pursued him like some tenacious bounty hunter. Imagination had a way of filling in the blanks for a scene he'd never witnessed in person. He suspected the actual incident passed quicker and with greater anguish than any pictures his unconscious mind painted.

He checked his bedside clock. *7 AM. Sod it, I'm off for a walk to clear my head and I'm going to the woods.* He was still riled about Erin Parsons' almost sympathetic attitude towards the unseen creatures adding to his torment. Yet they existed in another place. Was it a world beyond or somewhere in-between? Might Grant inhabit that realm too, despite these sickening deceptions? If he dwelt there, could the power of White Hill summon him forth?

Nick batted the idea aside. *Ever hopeful, you stupid fool. White Hill draws in the wicked. Grant wouldn't respond to it, even if he heard its call. I'm sure he wouldn't.*

He washed, dressed, and then started the day with a simple cuppa and a biscuit. At that moment Nick couldn't face food. He donned his walking kit and set off from the bottom of School Hill along Mountain Street. At The Orchard he doubled his pace, lest Jason spy him. *I'll give the kid some peace today. The way I'm feeling, no evil entity will dare mess with me on my lonesome.*

It came as little surprise to find himself mistaken. Alone in King's Wood, Grant's familiar laughter and shouts of 'Daddy, Baddy,' encircled him from trees lining every track and trail.

Nick stopped and clutched his head. He dropped to his knees, crying out in rage and anguish. "Why? Why are you doing this? Leave me and my boy alone." His outburst melted into a blanket of morning mist. Nick half expected an apparition of Grant to emerge from the undergrowth and attack him. The idea fell in line with those experiences of Martha Keep, not to mention Jason and his pals. Instead, the forest fell silent bar an intermittent hammering from a woodpecker drilling a tree trunk. *Do these things derive sick pleasure by depriving me of a face-to-face with Grant? Do they understand that's what I yearn for more than anything?* He picked himself up and pulled damp trouser cloth stuck to his knees, clear of the skin beneath.

"Shit. Oh well, it'll dry on the way back."

As he reached The Orchard again, Jason emerged from his front door.

Nick's jaw dropped upon spying his hands and arms wrapped in white bandages like an Egyptian mummy in training. "Jason. Cripes, what happened?"

Jason struggled to fasten his jacket while walking down the garden path. "I was on my way to visit you."

Nick squinted. "Was it Barry - or that Barry thing - again?"

"No, but I've little doubt about the source."

Nick opened the gate for Jason and the pair set off towards the village.

"Have you eaten today?"

Jason shook his head, then glanced over his shoulder. "Hey, were you up at King's Wood?"

"Yeah. I thought I'd leave you in peace, this morning. From the state of you, it was the right choice. Listen, I only had a biscuit earlier. It seems we've some catching up to do. Why don't we stop for breakfast at The Copper Kettle? My treat."

"Thanks. I could use a change of scene and sympathetic company."

Over a cooked breakfast, juice and coffee beside Chilham's medieval market square, Nick and Jason caught up on their latest experiences.

On the way back down School Hill, Nick folded his arms across his chest. "No voices or manifestations of people, this time? That's new."

"It was more like a Poltergeist," Jason added. "With everything that's happened, I don't think these entities stick to one type of behaviour. I tried to get a hold of myself before the book caught fire, like Erin suggested. The pages ignited regardless." Jason stopped. "Nick?"

"Yeah?"

"You *do* realise you could clear off home and never worry about this again?"

"That won't happen."

"How come? I mean, I'm glad. But, I wouldn't blame you if you did. I still can't fathom why these spirits hassled my friends. Our Ouija board session took place in Canterbury, not locally."

"Were you all together, sharing your grief around here after Barry's funeral?"

"We were. That was the day we agreed to try contacting him."

"Maybe they latched onto the four of you at the time. They're leaving your pals alone, now. That's something. If White Hill draws in these forces with its energy, perhaps they've gravitated there again?"

"I guess."

Nick presented a resolute face. "This has become personal for me. I'm unsure how you get payback on something that's not technically alive. Not as we measure life, anyhow. But, these things have abused and sullied the memory of my boy. I won't let that stand." He relaxed and sighed. "Besides, if I go home to West Sussex now, I'll always wonder about this place. It's unfinished business."

"And if we can't alter anything, as Erin hinted?"

"I don't know." They started walking again. "I just don't know." He stopped outside Stour Cottage and his face creased. "What the fuck?"

Jason followed his gaze.

The silver Honda CR-V stood in its usual parking space at the rear. All the windows and mirrors were smashed. Tiny heaps of safety glass cubes littered the upholstery.

Nick stormed along the driveway to examine his damaged vehicle.

Jason followed. "The Calendars must be out. Their car is missing."

"They'd have investigated when they heard the glass break, if they were here." Nick stuck his head into the vehicle's cabin. "There goes my insurance excess." He walked around the car. "The bodywork isn't damaged. Some vehicle glazier is about to have a fantastic day." He rubbed his fingers together in the universal gesture associated with taking money. "How did this happen?"

11

Louise

"What will it be like?" Louise Squires pulled away from kissing Wayne Hood in the backseat of his parked car. Silhouettes of swaying trees cast shadows across her uneasy face. With blemish free alabaster skin and perfect eyebrows displaying nary an errant strand, Louise stunned her male, sixteen-year-old classmates. Centre-parted fair hair framed a heart-shaped face of slender nose and pale, pouting lips. Smoky grey eyes fixed unblinking on any subject of her attention. For the shyer and less confident members of the opposite sex, it was enough to fluster and send them running from the scene. Few things frustrated Louise more. Like many girls her age, she sought reassurance and affection from brasher boys, several years her senior. In recent weeks, she'd doubted the wisdom behind that approach.

Louise's boyfriend shot her a fiendish wink. "What will it be like? Like nothing you've ever experienced." He touched her right forearm. "Hey, I also thought it was nonsense until I noticed amazing coincidences happen in my life. Positive ones. The Circle has tapped into genuine power, Lou. It's awesome."

A lanky bad boy on the make summed Wayne Hood's appearance to a tee. Gelled hair, short enough to spike at the extremities, vanished in a number three fade above folded back ears. Clean-limbed and surging with hormones, the twenty-year-old Canterbury exhaust fitter represented prime catch boyfriend material to impressionable teenage babes. Especially those who didn't yet know who they were, nor grasped their own value. Wayne didn't care, as long as those girls proved moist, tight and easy to manipulate. He collected female innocence like a western gunslinger might notches on a gun belt. Many a parent raised their daughter right, only to have such efforts shattered on the backseat of Wayne's yellow boy racer, SEAT Ibiza.

Louise fidgeted amidst the cramped space, hemmed in by fogged up windows. "I don't know; it sounds kinda weird. They're not into devil worship or anything? You know: sacrificing stuff and drinking blood?"

Wayne roared with laughter. "Our High Priestess is saner than that. No, we don't kill anything or anyone. The rituals are great fun."

"So it's run by that woman? The one you took me to regarding my sick grandmother? She was supposed to send out rivers of energy and heal her."

Wayne's eyes narrowed. "She can't do everything. Summoning and working with these forces isn't like popping pills for a headache. It was your Nan's time, that's all. I'm sorry."

Louise wrinkled her nose. "High Priestess? It's a cult,

then?"

"No. There's no brainwashing or slavish obedience. We're a loose collection of individuals looking to better our situations. To achieve that, we've connected with something unseen. An ancient presence, real and powerful." He moved in closer to nuzzle her neck. His hot breath reminded Louise of the attraction she'd felt the day the pair met.

"What would I have to do?" Louise's breathing grew heavier.

Wayne whispered in her ear. "Be open, that's all. Be open and keep your mouth shut afterwards. The Circle must remain a secret." He unfastened her blouse and bra, then massaged her breasts. His tongue flicked with practised precision against the stiffening peaks of her tender nipples.

Louise gasped. "Open to what?"

"Just open. Show me how open you can be." Wayne stepped up his arousal of her erogenous zones.

One splayed female hand pressed against the rear SEAT passenger window. It slid down the glass like the surrender of a dying soul giving up the ghost.

Minutes later the creaking, rhythmic jostling of Wayne's Ibiza joined other vehicles rocking on suspension springs at various points in King's Wood car park.

* * *

Two days later, Louise sat beside Wayne in the front passenger seat. His car pulled off the A252 between grassy banks lining Bagham Road into Chilham. Headlights illuminated the village sign. Warm illumination from The Woolpack Inn drew them closer. Wayne signalled left at the pub, following Hambrook Lane past scant houses to a sharp left-hander where School Hill fed into Mountain Street.

Louise pulled at her seatbelt in discomfort. She was desperate to cut through the silence. "There's a boy in my class at school I used to be friends with. He lives down here."

Wayne's curled bottom lip registered little interest. At length he spoke. "Former boyfriend?"

"No." Louise watched a series of cottages appear on the left. "We've spoken little since puberty."

Wayne shifted down and eased the car over to let an oncoming vehicle past. "His loss. You're amazing." He moved his hand from the gearstick to rub her upper thigh.

Louise jumped.

"What's wrong?" Wayne frowned.

"Nothing. Cold hands." Louise swallowed hard, uncertainty blazing in her eyes. She'd not intended to lose her virginity to Wayne that night in the woods. Once he started, there was an insistence to his advances which brooked no refusal. She'd been curious about sex and turned on at the start, but the experience left her feeling underwhelmed and used. Now she wished she'd never agreed to pull over for a cuddle.

Wayne made a cocky clicking sound with his tongue against the roof of his mouth. "I'd best stick them somewhere warm then." He slid his fingers up her skirt.

Louise intercepted them before they reached the crotch of her panties.

Wayne almost collided with a telephone pole. He detached his wandering hands to tug the wheel over, face reddening. "What's the matter with you this evening?"

A tingle of fear caused Louise to cringe. She'd never seen Wayne like this. He was angry and treating her differently than before.

Louise looked away, out of her side. Upstairs in a lit cottage bedroom, a teenage boy with bandaged hands drew drapes across a sash window. Louise's eyes watered. She whispered under her breath. "Jason."

"What was that?" Wayne barked.

"Nothing. My old friend I mentioned, burnt his hands. I meant to ask him about it after school. He left before I had a chance."

Wayne snorted. "Daft prat. He should try being an exhaust fitter like me. I could tell you some stories about guys suffering burns."

Talking about Jason Cooper opened a deeper chasm of worry and dissatisfaction in Louise's tummy. She changed the subject. "This isn't the way to King's Wood car park."

"No. Those of us who drive to the meetings don't leave our cars in such a public spot. Not on ritual nights. There's a rough gravel parking area on a bend ahead. This is a no through road; quiet and with good access to the woods via an uphill track."

"I'm not sure I want to do this, Wayne." Louise's voice trembled.

Wayne pulled into the gravel area he'd described beside three other empty cars. He yanked up the handbrake and tugged a hip flask from his jacket pocket. "Listen, babe," his voice sweetened to a playful, almost helpless tone. "I was the same, my first time out. It's fear of the unknown; nothing more. You'll have fun." He opened the flask cap. "Here, take a few sips of this. It'll calm your nerves."

"What is it?"

"Something to take the edge off your anxiety." He handed Louise the flask, then unfastened his seatbelt.

She took a few short, hesitant gulps. The liquid tasted sweet, with an alcoholic after burn that made her cough.

"Easy." Wayne patted her between the shoulder blades. "Gentle sips, you crazy wild boozer."

Louise wiped her mouth. His soothing words and fresh attempts to inject humour into a fractious situation eased her tensed muscles. Whatever was in that flask already loosened her up.

Wayne opened his driver's door. "You enjoy a nip more, while I fetch our bag."

"What's in the bag?" It surprised Louise that her eyelids grew heavy without warning.

"Robes. I've one each. Nothing to worry about; we always dress up at the ritual site. It's a mark of respect."

Louise swallowed more of the calming liquid. She capped the flask and got out of the car.

Wayne closed the boot, a sports bag in one hand. He grinned. "There she is, ready to transform her life for the better. You're going to love this, Lou." He slipped an arm around her waist, its hand shining a pocket torch ahead of them.

The pair wandered onto a rough footpath, disappearing into a long stretch flanked by trees and hedgerows. Rodents scurried in the undergrowth and an owl hooted overhead.

* * *

The following morning Louise awoke in her bed with a thumping headache.

Her mother knocked at the door. "Louise? Louise, are you awake? It's after ten."

Her father's voice grunted as he crossed the landing outside. "It's a good job she doesn't have school today. I'm not sure about that boy she's hanging out with."

"Many girls her age have their heads turned by older boys," Mrs Squires replied.

"Did you notice the state of her when she came home last night? Our daughter acted like a zombie." His voice trailed away as both parents descended the stairs, still in discussion over her relationship with Wayne Hood.

Louise rubbed her eyes. *What was in that drink Wayne gave me yesterday?*

Someone slammed the lid on their wheelie bin in a

garden next door. The sound echoed through Louise's sensitive cranium like a pneumatic drill. She eased herself up, plumping pillows for extra support. The moment she finished on the second pillow, her face froze. Snatches of memories, woolly and indistinct, floated through her mind. A dull ache throbbed from the region surrounding her pubic bone.

What happened last night? What happened at the woods? I can't remember much after we set off along that track in the dark. I know I rested my head against Wayne's shoulder and felt relaxed. Her mouth dropped open. *Oh my God, we stripped naked before donning those robes! There was a bonfire in the woods with dancing. Men and women whirling about and...* She screwed her eyes tight and shook her head in a violent realisation. Images of leering men pawing at her, forced themselves into Louise's consciousness. They invaded her mind the same way those lecherous fellows had invaded her pliant, intoxicated body. *What about their leader? The High Priestess, Wayne called her. That occult practitioner from the foot of Chartham Downs. She wasn't pleasant like the day Wayne took me to see her about Nana.* Louise tugged the ends of her hair, lips quivering. *How she laughed as they used me; her hands lifted high before those dancing flames.* A delayed replay of Wayne's supposedly fun ritual rolled on before her dazed face. Louise broke down and sobbed into her pillow.

Chilham Railway Station was an isolated stop on the Canterbury West line from Ashford. It sat devoid of buildings or an office, with only a handful of covered benches to ward off the elements on either platform. Easy to miss, the halt proved one step up from a solitary request stop. Louise Squires stepped down onto Platform 1 beneath a steel grey afternoon sky. A stiff breeze rustled bare tree branches behind a metal railing fence. Thanks to the seasonal absence of foliage, she discovered a striking view across Chilham Lakes beyond.

Rapid warning tones sounded from the train as its electrical doors slid shut. A whine of engines from the bogeys beneath accompanied the yellow and white conveyance slipping away towards its next stop at Wye.

Louise crossed a footbridge to the other platform and a simple open gate to a tiny car park and busy A-road. Cars whizzed by as she crossed at the junction of the A28 and A252. St Mary's Church crowned the hill ahead, clustered about by trees and a higgledy piggledy assortment of roofs indicating the village centre. After composing herself from the upset of earlier recollections, Louise had fixed a sandwich for lunch. She told her folks she was heading one stop down the line from Chartham to visit a school friend. Now on foot, she retraced part of the route Wayne had driven them the night before.

At the junction of School Hill into Mountain Street, she spied two men engaged in a deep discussion beside a silver Honda CR-V. One, a sturdy ginger-haired fellow of early middle age, tapped the car windshield as he spoke to the other; a guy well into retirement. Louise kept walking. She didn't know why she'd taken so much care grooming herself before leaving. Recent experiences of what happened when her immaculate presentation caught the attention of the opposite sex, haunted her insides like a mansion of ghosts. She glanced through impressive rear garden gates into the grounds of Chilham Castle. Her soul resonated with the emptiness of its elegant halls. A change in wind direction wafted the fragrance of Louise's favourite perfume into her nostrils. She'd washed and brushed her hair, then made herself up with restrained care to avoid coming across as a tart.

A row of cottages appeared on the left-hand side of the lane. Opposite, a high, grassy bank led uphill into overlooking trees.

Louise's manicured nails clicked against a front path gate at The Orchard. She gazed up at the window where she'd seen Jason Cooper shut his curtains during her fateful journey to the King's Wood ritual. A sigh followed, then she strode down the path and rapped on a brass door knocker.

The distinct rhythm and report of a female gait approached. The front door opened to reveal Helen Cooper's pleasant but puzzled face. "Yes?"

"Oh, hello. Is Jason home?"

"He is. Did you want me to fetch him?"

"Yes please." Louise shuffled her feet on the doorstep.

"What's your name, young lady?"

"Louise. Louise Squires."

Helen half turned, then pivoted back with happy

eyes and a widening mouth. "I didn't recognise you." She clasped her hands together, then held one down at waist level like someone estimating the height of a child. "Not little Louise Squires? We haven't seen you in years." Helen gave her an admiring once over. "You look so much like your mother."

Louise relaxed into a welcome slouch. "Thank you."

Helen ushered her into the hallway. "Come out of the chilly air. I'll call Jason." She closed the front door, then shouted up the stairwell. "Jason? Jason?"

A door opened above, accompanied by a teenage boy's voice. "What's up, Mum?"

Helen rubbed her mouth to conceal a smile of satisfaction. She relished the next statement and wanted to make it last. "Louise Squires is here to see you."

Silence reigned for a moment, then thudding steps sounded on the staircase. Jason didn't wait until he reached the bottom, leaning over the banister to gaze down into the hallway. "Hey," his voice squeaked, resulting in a follow-on, overdone manly cough that warmed Louise's troubled heart.

Raymond Cooper wandered out of the living room clutching a cup and saucer. His eyebrows raised in interest at the pretty teenage girl cluttering up their hallway. His surprise level doubled at the flustered expression stretching his son's face.

Helen sidled up to him. "Do you remember Louise, Raymond? She's come to see Jason."

Jason flushed. He wanted to shrink and disappear like a mouse through a crack in the skirting board.

"Has she, now?" Raymond stirred his drink with a teaspoon in long, deliberate swirls. "Will wonders never cease? My prayers are answered. Next thing, I'll be going to church."

Helen laughed. "In a pine box. Go back into the lounge. Let's give these two some space."

Jason bit his lip, unsure of the response he'd receive to his next question. "Can she come up, Mum?"

Helen fidgeted on the spot.

Raymond reappeared in the lounge doorway. "Of course she can, Son. You two enjoy yourselves."

Helen was about to puff out a protest when Raymond dragged her away into the room. "Don't look a gift horse in the mouth. Come on, now; what's he going to do with hands wrapped up like that?"

Louise giggled inside at their exchange. She followed Jason up to his bedroom, aware of his body language skating a thin line between euphoria and panic. She closed the door behind them and looked around.

Jason flapped his bandaged hands in discomfort. "I'm sorry it's not cooler. I like to read."

"Yes, I remember." Louise studied the contents of his bookshelves. "Though last time we talked about books, they were the children's variety."

Jason grimaced. "It's been awhile."

Louise stopped reading and shifted to face him. Her beautiful but penetrating stare turned Jason's legs to jelly. "Why *is* that? Once upon a time we chatted almost every day."

Jason ran a trembling, bandaged arm across his sandy hair. "We grew up. Both of us formed groups of new friends. All that stuff, I guess."

Louise curled her tongue thoughtfully, suggesting someone unconvinced by his explanation. "Huh. Is that so?"

Jason motioned to his bed. "Did you want to sit down? I'll settle myself on the beanbag here."

Louise eased herself into a sitting position, facing out from the mattress. She pushed herself forward to study some of Jason's fantasy miniatures. "Did you paint these yourself?"

Jason squirmed. "Yes. I… I like sword and sorcery stuff."

Louise paused from her inspection to examine him for a moment. "Don't be embarrassed, Jason. There's nothing wrong with it." She nodded at his largest bookcase. "And you also like to read about the paranormal and occult, as well as fantasy?"

"It's an interest." Jason crossed his legs on the beanbag.

"Have you spoken much with Adam?"

"We talk on the phone and via e-mail all the time. He doesn't live far from you these days, does he?"

"A five minute walk." Her face adopted a casual indifference. "So you guys tried a Ouija board to speak with Barry?"

Jason's head grew hot. "He told you that?" He clenched a fist beneath his bandages. *I'll kill him. We agreed to keep our foray into the occult out of class.*

"No, Samantha did." Louise noticed his tensing lower arms. "Don't be angry at him. When Adam wigged out around her, Sam demanded answers. He told her what happened in his garden shed."

Jason blinked. "You've heard the story?"

"Yeah. And Nathan at the cathedral and Jonathan with his young nephew. Samantha wouldn't have believed it, but she's never seen Adam so scared. You know what a big mouthed joker he is."

Jason moistened his lips. "Do you believe it?"

"I've no reason not to. If it's good enough for Sam, it's good enough for me. She's no liar. It's freaky as hell, though."

Jason let out a sigh of relief. "I'm glad those two are okay. I didn't realise he'd told her."

"She's rebuilding his confidence. Sam loves that doofus."

"He's lucky to have her."

Louise continued watching his face. "I never see you hanging out with a girlfriend. Do you have some local hottie tucked away? A girl from another school, perhaps?"

Whether this was genuine curiosity or some kind of test, Jason wasn't sure. Either way, his heart sank. He'd no idea how to broach his unwavering infatuation for the dream girl sitting three feet away on his bed. "No." Jason stared at the carpet.

"Oh. Have *you* had any scary encounters with things that look or sound like Barry?"

Jason gave a silent nod. He sat a moment longer before speaking again. "He tried drowning me, up in the woods. Barry's dead father helped. Except it wasn't them."

"For real?" Louise gripped her knees.

"Uh-huh."

"How did you get away?"

"I didn't. I drowned." Jason read the confusion written across her alabaster brow. "A guy staying in the village pulled my body from the pond and resuscitated me."

Louise placed one hand across her shapely chest. "Thank God."

Jason's mood soared at the genuine gratitude in her delivery. "I'd have met Barry again for real if that man hadn't saved me."

"How did you explain what happened to him?"

"I told him the truth."

"Are you serious? Wow. How did he take it?"

"Better than I expected. He's experienced weird stuff around here too. Nick is separated from his wife. They lost their six-year-old son to a hit-and-run driver a while back. It's put a strain on their relationship."

"I'm sure it has." Louise gestured to his bandages. "Does your injury have something to do with these scary dramas?"

"Unfortunately. I'm hoping to have the bandages removed soon."

"What happened?"

"I was sitting where you are now. Books on the top bunk shelf above your head shot across the room, as though someone was throwing them."

"Did you see anything?"

"No, but when I caught one, it ignited in my grasp and I couldn't let go."

Louise moved her hand from chest to mouth. "Jason,

this is awful."

"You're telling me." Jason shuffled off the cushion to open a drawer on his bedside cabinet. He retrieved the charred remains of the book in question to show her.

"All because of a Ouija board?" Louise examined the blackened pages, then handed the book back.

"No, I don't think so. The Ouija board played a part, but something else is going on. That man I told you about, Nick, hasn't messed with Ouija boards or the occult. He keeps hearing and running into something that imitates his dead son. Nick's sure it's not him, the way I'm sure whatever attacked me wasn't Barry."

Louise crossed her arms and rubbed gooseflesh prickling her shoulders. "And there I was hoping to unload my problems, to see if you could help."

Jason dropped the book back into the drawer. "I almost forgot: I haven't even asked what you're doing here. Claire Cummings told Nathan you were seeing an older guy from Canterbury. You're the last person I expected to find on my doorstep."

Louise flinched. "He's part of the reason I'm here. The guy from Canterbury, I mean. After I heard that entire story from Sam, I figured my childhood friend, Jason, might offer me helpful advice."

"About older guys from Canterbury?" Jason muttered with a doubtful smirk. He shut the drawer a little too hard. His paperback fantasy novel toppled onto the floor, spilling the photograph he used as a bookmark. Jason turned five shades of crimson, then froze with his shoulders taut.

Louise reached down to pick up the photograph

between quivering fingers. She took a breath and moistened her lips. "I was a cute thirteen-year-old, wasn't I?"

Jason sat crestfallen, unable to look up into those gorgeous but penetrating eyes.

Louise swallowed. Her voice came out in a whisper. "You never speak to me anymore. Jason… Help me understand?"

Jason put his head in his wrapped up hands. "We grew up. Things changed. I wanted to be with you, but I… I couldn't tell you. Then every time I tried, it seemed an impossible mountain to climb." He clenched his teeth. "Am I weak? Am I a coward?"

Louise bent lower to connect with his shifting eyes. "Because you're quiet and observant? Because you don't charge into situations like a bull in a china shop? Because you experience powerful feelings you find difficult to express?" She placed a slender finger beneath his chin and lifted his head to face her. "They overwhelm you, don't they? I remember how you reacted to simple situations when we were kids. Stuff that didn't bother anyone else."

"Yes. Things affect me deeper than others."

Louise's eyes glistened. "I wish I'd known how you felt. I thought you'd gone off me. You know: *she's some stupid girl from the crowd, not interested in my stuff these days*."

Jason gave a violent head shake. "No. Never."

Louise wiped a brimming tear away from her left eye. "I've made the worst mistakes of my life over the last few days, Jason." She passed the photograph to him. "If I'd known you wanted to be my boyfriend, the answer would've been yes. I've always liked you."

Taking Louise Squires off the pedestal he'd placed her on in his mind and waking up to reality, broke Jason's heart. It was a painful lesson, worsened by a realisation of what he'd missed out on. He'd only himself to blame.

Louise sniffed. "You said your experiences happened up in the woods. Is that King's Wood?"

"That's right. The area stretching from The Pilgrims' Way across to the lane on White Hill where Barry died."

"I've had some experiences at King's Wood. The worst happened last night. Not ghosts or spirits, but occult related."

Jason forgot his anguish and discomfort, alarmed at the mirror of such emotions surfacing on Louise's visage. "You went to King's Wood after dark?"

"Yes. I drove past your house with my boyfriend, Wayne. Seeing you draw your bedroom curtains made me want to visit. That and my earlier conversation with Sam."

"Did you park at the bend in the road?"

"That's it. Wayne told me we were going to party at some secret ritual with a group he's mixed up in. He claimed it would be a blast."

Jason gulped. "How did you meet a bloke like that?"

"I bumped into him in Canterbury one Saturday. He's a confident, good-looking guy and knows it. Wayne swept me off my feet. Anyway, my Nan was at the hospice for end-of-life care." A single tear escaped now to trickle down her cheek. "Wayne said he knew a spiritual woman who worked with directed energy. He claimed she could help Nana remotely. It sounded weird, but I wasn't going to pass up any chance she'd recover. So we went to her house at Mystole for a consultation. She promised to undertake a solo directed energy session, aimed at reaching Nana."

"Whoa, whoa, whoa, Mystole? Is this woman called Erin Parsons?"

Louise's mouth dropped open. "Yes. Have you met her?"

"Nick and I visited. We've been seeking advice and answers for our own predicaments. I've teamed up with him. Partners in adversity, I suppose. Odd: a teenage boy and a middle-aged man. He's a nice guy once you pierce his blank exterior. I like him. Anyway, Erin couldn't do anything, although she offered a suggestion. Nick blew up at her. She rubbed him the wrong way and he got really mad."

Louise bit her lip. "Then he's an excellent judge of character. Stay away from her, Jason. That woman is trouble."

"How do you mean?"

"She's what they call the 'High Priestess' of that group: 'The Circle.' Wayne claimed they're empowered by ancient entities or spirits. I don't understand it. He probably doesn't either. It's all about him getting what he wants." Her eyes stared into space. "He has a proper talent for that."

"Did you attend the ritual?"

Louise's lip wobbled. "I wasn't minded to after Nana

died, but things progressed with Wayne. Relationships are easy to fall into, but tough to escape. That's what Sam's big sister told me. She's right. Wayne was charming and slick. I got carried along for the ride. Then the other night we... Well, I'm sure you can guess."

Jason felt like his heart plummeted through his stomach upon catching her drift. "Oh."

"Yeah. He won me over about attending the ritual. Now who's weak and a coward? I'd promised to go with him, so I did. What a total Muppet. All the way there, I was having second thoughts. Wayne picked up on it and grew angry."

Jason's face darkened. "Did he hurt you?"

Louise half-smiled at the defensive tone in his voice and protective gaze now fixed upon her. "Not then. He gave me something to drink. Said it would help me relax."

"Booze?"

"I believe so. I'm convinced there was a date rape drug in there. I became tired and my head felt fuzzy. The next thing I knew it was this morning, when I woke up in bed at home."

"You remember nothing about the ritual?"

"That's just it. After I awoke, memories of what happened swept over me. Jason, I..." She broke down into heartrending sobs.

Jason scooted to sit beside her on the mattress. His social clumsiness evaporated, displaced by the genuine affection he'd carried for Louise since the day they'd met as children. He wrapped an arm around her. She melted into his embrace, crying against his T-shirt. Jason squeezed. "Shh. It's okay." He rocked like the gentle tempo of a slow beating metronome. "Do you want to talk about it? It's all right if not. I'm here for you." He said a silent prayer for luck. "I love you, Louise. I've always loved you."

Louise lifted her head to stare at him. Her voice cracked. "I know you do. I mean, you care about me. You really care, don't you? I see it, now."

"Of course." He hesitated. "Is that wrong?"

"No, Jason. I feel safe around you. I think that also drew me here." She caught a momentary flicker of disappointment chasing across his expression. "That's not girl code for 'boring.' Not with me."

Jason choked on his words. "I'm worried about you."

Louise flung her arms about his neck and held on tight. Her voice trembled in his ear. "There was a fire at a small clearing in the woods. Erin Parsons stood there laughing while people danced around. She howled with delight as a group of men abused me. They *all* abused me, Jason. I hurt so badly in my stomach this morning."

Now Jason couldn't hold back his anguish as he clutched onto her. "You should tell the police."

Louise pulled back, shook her head and wiped her nose. "I can't. If Mum and Dad found out what I'd been involved with, it would destroy them. I'm such a fool."

Jason sighed. "Are you going to see Wayne again?"

"Not if I can help it. I'm worried about him, but

that's not your problem." She slid a hand up to touch the side of his face. "Jason?"

"Yes?"

"Would you kiss me?"

Two hours later, a gentle knock at the bedroom door was followed by Helen Cooper's voice. "Are you two okay in there?"

Jason lay on his bed, fully clothed, with Louise cuddled up in a loving embrace. He would never forget the moment his lips met hers for the first time. They'd kissed for ten minutes, then settled down to talk and snuggle like long-time soulmates. Sex wasn't on the cards, and Jason didn't care. This connection and her willingness to confide in him were all the affirmations of love he needed. Life would be different from now on.

"We're fine, Mum," Jason replied.

"Is Louise staying for dinner? Your father and I would be glad to have her join us."

Jason inhaled the apple blossom fragrance of Louise's shampoo. He kissed her crown. "How about it?"

Louise nuzzled the nape of his neck. "I'd love to, thank you. I'd better call my folks."

"Great. Afterwards, I'll walk you to the station. Unless you want Dad to drive you home? I'm sure he won't mind. Chartham isn't far."

"The station will be fine." A smile teased her lips. "Then we can have a proper kiss goodnight."

Jason rubbed her back and called out. "Four for dinner, Mum. Thanks."

12

The Vessel

A train decelerated into a nighttime Chartham station. In the short period since she'd kissed Jason goodbye at Chilham, Louise crafted a mobile phone picture message. It contained a bright, soft focus, high-resolution image of her taken during summer. She keyed in accompanying text:

'Here's a more recent photo. It's pervy ogling a thirteen-year-old, even at your age. ;o)
Thanks for today.
Luv U,
Lou.
X.'

She smiled to herself and clicked the on-screen button to send it.

Helen and Raymond Cooper had been darlings over dinner. They'd treated her like Jason had invited royalty. On the walk to Chilham Station, Jason said his father's attitude towards him had transformed in under an hour. He couldn't believe the alteration and almost choked on his food when Raymond gave him a friendly slap on the back. Helen tiptoed around gentle enquiries as to their status. In the end, Louise broke the standoff by reaching for Jason's hand and saying to his parents: *'Thank you for having me to dinner. I hope I'll see a lot more of you now Jason and I are a couple.'* That was the second time Jason gagged, but his eyes shone afterwards.

Louise stood and pressed the electric door button to open the carriage. The ache from her abdomen flared up again. She gripped her tummy. Intense pain sharpened and rose like lacerating claws inside her chest. Louise stumbled onto the platform, then hobbled towards the level crossing gates. A guard opened them after the train pulled out, then ascended a set of smart, white wooden steps to a pea green Victorian weatherboarded signal box. He paused at the top to watch Louise cross, calling after her.

"Are you all right, love?"

Louise groaned. "Girl cramps. I'm okay; I'll be home in a few minutes."

"Take care." The guard disappeared inside his signal box.

Louise continued along the flat tarmac of Station Road towards Chartham's church tower and village green. A pair of bright LED car headlights flared to life from the roadside facing her. As a rattling diesel van passed in the other direction, Louise's heart sank. Its beams illuminated the bodywork of the parked vehicle; a yellow SEAT Ibiza.

"Oh no," Louise muttered under her breath. She closed her eyes for a moment. "You can do this, Lou. Tell him to take a hike." Stomach pains stabbed again. "For goodness' sake, the bastard had you gang raped." She set her face like flint and doubled her pace with determined steps, storming past the car.

Wayne Hood threw the SEAT into reverse and backed up, electric window sliding down as he came. "Hey? Lou, it's me."

"Leave me alone, Wayne." Louise hurried on.

"What's the matter?"

Louise stopped dead and spun on a heel that crunched amidst roadside gravel. Her mouth fell open. "What's the matter?" She started walking again.

Wayne continued reversing the car to speak with her. "Are you upset about last night? Babe, you were wild. Once you let go, the whole clearing went nuts. We knew we'd chosen the right person."

Louise's nostrils flared. She halted once more. "Chosen the right person? As what, a boy toy to abuse?"

Wayne frowned. "Abuse? What are you talking about? You gave yourself willingly."

"Thanks to your hip flask. I noticed you drank nothing from it." She fought back a rising urge to blub again. No way would she show this manipulative user tearful eyes. "I didn't even know where I was, let alone what I was doing."

"You performed like a star."

"A star? What, a porn star?" Louise clenched her fists, voice rising in pitch from increased stress.

"No. You're The Vessel. Our High Priestess has nominated you. Her choice is acceptable to The Old Ones. How cool is that?"

"Old Ones? You mean those middle-aged perverts who screwed me while I was drugged or intoxicated?"

Wayne shook his head. "No." He waved a hand towards the sky. "The Old Ones."

Louise held up a stiff, flat hand. "Stay away from me, Wayne. I want nothing to do with you or your sick friends. It's over. God, I wish I'd never gone out with you."

A sadistic grin flashed across Wayne's face. His voice dripped with a domineering, self-assured certainty. "You can't stop it now the marriage process has begun. You're The Vessel, Lou. Nothing can reverse that now."

Louise clamped hands over her ears, then darted through the churchyard. Wayne gunned his engine and roared away into the night.

"How was your dinner at Jason's? Is Helen Cooper well?" Mrs Squires poked her head into the hallway as Louise wiped her feet on the doormat.

Louise slipped her shoes off. "We had a pleasant time. Mrs Cooper was fine. She said I look like you."

Mrs Squires grinned, then her amusement faded. "You look flushed, Louise. Are you okay?"

Louise fidgeted. "I might be coming on early." It was a reasonable deception. *Thank God I'm not coming on early, after what happened at the woods.*

"Oh dear. Well, a good night's rest won't hurt. You were out late yesterday with that lad from Canterbury." She bit her lip. "Your father and I are worried about him."

Louise hung up her jacket, back turned. "Don't be; it's over. Wayne was a dreadful mistake."

"How dreadful?" Cautious and concerned vocal tones accompanied her question.

Louise didn't answer.

Mrs Squires couldn't disguise relief in her voice at this development. "We all make them. Are you and Jason an item now?"

"Yes."

"That's marvellous. Oh, your father will be pleased." Her overdone delight felt a tad patronising, but Louise appreciated the words.

"Night, Mum." Louise kissed her mother on the cheek, then hurried upstairs. A message pinged on her phone from Jason. She flopped down on her bed to read it:

'Thanks for the pic. I'll have to print a new bookmark. Lying here, thinking of you and the time I wasted. So sorry. Can't wait to see you again.

Luv U 2,
Jason.
X.'

Beneath it he'd inserted a selfie of him resting on the bottom bunk where the pair had cuddled. Louise saved the image to a directory and associated it with his number so it would flash up whenever he called. For a moment she considered phoning him to describe her encounter with Wayne. *What was that 'Vessel' and 'Marriage' talk about?* After thinking it over, Louise decided against bothering Jason further. She'd unloaded on him enough for one day. *Mum is right: a good night's rest won't hurt. I'll think clearer in the morning. Wayne is full of crap. I hope that's the last I'll hear of him.*

At the foot of Chartham Downs a short distance away, a yellow SEAT Ibiza drew up outside a fine, rustic property labelled *'Nailbourne,'* in the hamlet of Mystole. Wayne Hood decamped and sauntered towards the picturesque country home's front door. It opened before he'd reached it, the owner alerted by noise from his engine.

Erin Parsons folded her arms and pressed against the frame, signature black soft rib cropped vest and denim jeans adorning her leggy torso. She flashed a whitened smile at her fit subordinate, twenty-three years junior. "Hello, stranger."

Wayne halted on the doorstep. "Stranger? You saw me last night."

Erin slid long-nailed fingers into the top of his shirt to stroke a patch of chest hair. "Our unions on White Hill are different. Holy. Spiritual."

Wayne huffed. "Are you going to invite me in?"

Erin pursed her lips. "Why should I? You didn't come round for a session this week. What was I supposed to do with my excess energy?"

Wayne shrugged. "I don't know; sort yourself out?"

Erin flicked her tongue behind one cheek in playful circuits, then poked it out and curled the tip before him. "I suppose you were busy breaking-in The Vessel? How was she? The acolytes enjoyed her."

"Tight and stressed the first time, if you must know. She's just split up with me."

Erin drew him inside by the arm and closed her front door. "Is that surprising? It won't do her any good, now the process has begun."

"I told her that." Wayne wandered into Erin's lounge and plonked himself on a dark blue, Alcantara sofa.

Erin poured them both a shot of Jamaican rum in two crystal tumblers. She draped herself over the sofa next to Wayne and handed him his drink. "How did she react?"

"Louise didn't grasp what I was talking about."

Erin knocked back her glass of spirits in one gulp, before putting it down. "Of course she didn't, the foolish child. No matter; she'll understand soon enough." She slipped off her shoes and played footsie with Wayne while he sipped his drink. Her voice grew husky. "Now, how about you finish your rum and fill *this* vessel?" Erin unfastened her jeans with sensual fingers.

Wayne put down his glass on a side table and reached for her.

* * *

Jason Cooper rolled over in bed, a second pillow clutched tight to his chest. Sunlight teased his face through a gap in the curtains. He squinted, then rubbed his eyes. Something solid pressed against his right temple. He lifted his head to discover the smartphone that always lived on his bedside cabinet overnight. Yesterday, however, he'd fallen asleep mooning over the picture Louise sent him until the phone fell from his unconscious grasp. He illuminated the screen whose wallpaper now compromised that stunning, soft focus shot of his new girlfriend.

"Morning, Lou." He grinned to himself, then put the phone down in its normal spot. *Get a grip, Jason. You're gonna scare her off if you become all clingy. She likes you the way you are.* He sat bolt upright at that joyous realisation. "Holy shit, she does," he blurted aloud. *Should I call her? What's the time? Is she cranky in the morning? Ugh. Stop over-thinking this.* He swiped open the directory and initiated a call.

"Morning, Jason." Louise's voice came soft, followed by a yawn.

"Did I wake you?"

"I was stirring. How did you sleep?"

"The best. How about you?"

Louise groaned. "Uneasy." She registered an uncomfortable silence at the other end. "Not on account of you, silly. I ran into Wayne outside Chartham Station last night. He was waiting for me."

"What did you do?"

"At first I tried ignoring him. He kept backing his car up level with me and shouting through the window. Wayne seemed surprised I was upset. He even claimed I joined in that debauched orgy in King's Wood like a prize harlot."

"How did you respond?"

"How do you think? He said their High Priestess - that New Age bitch, Erin - had nominated me as 'The Vessel.' And that 'The Old Ones' found her choice acceptable. I thought he was referring to those crusty coots who sexually assaulted me." She lowered her voice, worried her mother might pass the bedroom door and overhear snatches of their conversation. "Now it looks like a reference to whatever they worship or bow down to."

"That's disconcerting." Jason sounded thoughtful.

"Disconcerting?" Louise giggled. "Trust you to come out with such a fine example of understatement." A moment of laughter brought temporary, blessed relief to her ongoing anxiety and horrific memories.

"Sorry." Jason backpedalled. "I'm not making light of what happened."

"Just teasing. I told Wayne I never wanted to see him again and wished we'd never gone out. He informed me nothing could stop it, now the marriage process has begun."

"Marriage?" Jason coughed.

"I know. Weird, right? Like I'd marry him, even were I ready to wed anybody."

Jason relaxed with his head sunk into the pillow.

"That's odd. From the way you described Wayne, he doesn't sound like the commitment type. More of a shagger." He caught himself. "Oh, Lou. I'm sorry, I didn't think that comment through."

"It's okay. You're right, he is. I wish I hadn't been so naïve."

"Could the term refer to you being this nominated 'Vessel' of theirs? I don't want to bring up painful memories, but they…"

"Treated me like a vessel? That's true." She clutched her chest. Fresh fire spread from her abdomen upward, like tearing talons seeking purchase. Louise tried to ignore it.

"How's your tummy this morning?" Jason batted away thoughts of what Louise must have suffered that night in the woods, less than a thirty-minute walk from his home.

"It's still giving me grief." Louise lay back. Her grey eyes glinted and a playful lilt filtered into her lowered voice. "Where are you, Jason?"

"I'm in bed."

"Uh-huh. Did you think about me last night?"

"Yeah. I've a confession to make."

"What's that?" A warm smile spread across her face.

"I fell asleep looking at that photo you sent me."

"Anything else?" Louise's cheeks bunched up with a cheeky wrinkle of her nose.

"No. But that's why I slept so well."

"Oh. Well, I suppose we both resolved stuff yesterday." She rested one hand on her tummy, desperate to reach out and engage romantically on her own terms, rather than through the abusive, grooming initiatives of Wayne Hood. She released a deliberate sigh. *I so want him to relax around me.* "Jason?"

"Yeah?"

"I'm thinking about you."

Jason frowned. "Of course you are, we're on the phone."

Louise sucked her teeth. "You don't have an ounce of guile, do you?"

"Huh?"

"Never mind. What I was about to say is: I'm thinking about you and my hand is resting on my tummy."

"Oh." Jason wasn't sure where this was headed.

"If you're in charge and want to make your girlfriend happy, where should I move my fingers next?"

Jason gulped, his gaze drawn to the half-lob morning wood that became a full-bore salute at Louise's last sentence. *Easy, fella. Remember how you feel about her and demonstrate affection.* He lowered his voice. "Slide your fingers downward."

"Okay. How far?"

"Are you wearing panties?"

"Pervert."

"Hey. No, I…"

Louise giggled again. "Only kidding. I love this. Yes, I'm wearing panties. Skimpy white ones."

Jason's tone became emboldened. He couldn't believe she was communicating with him on these terms. But then, after everything she'd been through that week, perhaps it made sense? A way to dismiss or counteract her violent sexual abuse through normal, loving sensuality. *Jesus, she's got more courage than I have.* He stopped his ruminating again and cleared his throat. "I want you to slide your fingers under the waistband and keep moving them down."

"Yes, Master." Louise's cheeky tones drifted into laboured breathing. "Mmm." Her purr of pleasure ached with arousal. "Jason, that feels good. This is your hand I'm touching myself with."

Jason's imagination worked overtime to fill in the visual gaps. Resolve destroyed, he moved his own free hand in a series of frantic, intimate tugs. *Oh God, I love this girl.*

Louise moaned under her breath. "You're touching me." She panted. "I'm so wet."

Jason dropped the phone, then fumbled to retrieve it. "Lou?"

Louise's voice gurgled at the other end.

Jason puffed to keep control. *Wow, she makes some amazing noises. I didn't know girls really did that.*

The gurgling deepened to a guttural croak. Louise's sweet voice swam like a discordant multitude of tortured creatures. It hissed a frustrated demand in his ear. "Leave White Hill alone."

Jason's arousal vanished. Blood drained from his cheeks to match his genitals. *Oh God, not this.*

The myriad voices spoke again. This time they slurred like a slowed-down tape recorder. "Leave White Hill alone, or you'll lie-down with your dead friend."

A roar thundered from the speaker, causing Jason to drop the phone once more. When he picked it up, Louise had disconnected the call.

"Do you think the transformation in her voice was similar to what happened with your pal and his nephew?" Nick plonked two mugs of stiff black coffee on the dining table at Stour Cottage.

Jason stared at the wall, picked up the mug and burnt his lips on the drink.

"That's not long off the boil." Nick sat down, face strained. "You're not with it, are you? I can't say I'm surprised."

Jason stiffened. "There were so many voices. None of them sounded like Barry. If they'd impersonated him, they wouldn't have warned me about laying down with my dead friend."

Nick rocked back against his wooden chair, causing it to creak. "The fact they referred to him in the third person represents a noticeable alteration from previous experiences. And you say Louise won't go to the police over what happened at King's Wood?"

"No. She's ashamed and worried it would break her parents' hearts."

Nick drummed the fingers of one hand on the table. "Unwise, but I understand. She sounds like a strong young woman with a good heart."

Jason nodded. "No argument from me."

"That makes what Wayne did to her more reprehensible, somehow. So Erin Parsons was leading the entire show?" Nick stopped drumming and slammed his fist down. Coffee slopped over the lip of his disturbed mug. "I knew something about that woman wasn't right. I never liked her."

Jason blew across the surface of his drink. "When Louise came round to explain what happened and seek my advice, neither of us connected my spiritual encounters with her ritual nightmare. Not beyond them taking place at King's Wood, within the vicinity of White Hill."

"Why would you? They were horses of a different colour."

"Until that call this morning." Jason jolted. "Crap, I almost forgot: Barry's apparition at the pond said he was using Louise, or about to. It slipped my mind. That must be what he - or it - was referring to."

Nick squinted. "Have you phoned Louise again?"

"No. I'm worried whatever manipulated her, might do more harm if I try. I couldn't bear responsibility for that."

"How about messaging her later? Nothing too involved. '*We got cut off earlier. Are you okay?*' Then wait and see what comes back."

"That's not a bad idea. I'll send one after I get home. I wanted to let you know. Other than her, you're the only person I trust with all this. I'm still keeping as much from my other friends as possible."

Nick grunted. "Hmm. What with your burning books and my broken car windows, we're drawing unwanted attention from somewhere. It's as well to keep anyone not stuck in the middle, out of it. Erin was right about one thing: the best way to avoid these creatures is to stay off their radar. That's assuming she's not responsible for some of it herself."

"Directly?" Jason asked.

"Her or 'The Circle' you mentioned." Nick rubbed slow fingers across his brow. "We're getting out of our depth with all this."

Jason gulped down his coffee. "We're like unarmed, naked warriors facing a horde of demons." He pulled at an earlobe with thumb and forefinger. "That's me and my penchant for fantasy."

Nick collected his mug. "It's a fine analogy. Worrying, but fine. I wonder how far removed from the literal truth it is?"

"A long way, I hope. Thanks for the coffee and hearing me out, Nick. I'm happier having shared all this with you."

"I'm glad you did." Nick got up. "Should either you or Louise need a safe spot away from your homes to seek refuge, my door is open, Jason. If you want a ride somewhere or a friend to watch your back, don't stand on ceremony. None of us should face this alone. We're stronger together."

"I'll leave you in peace." Jason walked towards the front door.

"Hey?" Nick called behind him.

Jason glanced back as he unfastened the latch.

Nick cracked a weak smile. "I'm happy about you and Louise. That's good news. Such a shame it took those horrors to make it happen."

Jason zipped his jacket. "I'm waking up to new

worlds on both sides of mortality." He blinked. "Right now, I wish it were only this side."

Nick approached him. "I'm no prognosticator, but sometimes things happen for a reason to the right people. At the right time, too."

"Are we the right people?"

Nick grimaced. "I've a feeling we'll soon know. Go easy, buddy."

"Cheers." Jason stepped down into the lane and made for home.

Nick leaned around the door frame to watch him go. Once Jason cleared the bend, his eyes wandered across to the summit of Julliberrie Down.

"It's a magnificent place. Have you been up there?" Andrew Stallard's voice made Nick jump.

"Good morning, Andrew. I must have zoned out for a moment."

Andrew adjusted his dog collar for comfort underneath a padded coat. "I hope I didn't startle you."

"I've had worse." Nick smiled. *Oh boy have I had worse. And all since I arrived here.* "Yes - to answer your question - I have been up there."

"That hilltop resonates with history." Andrew rocked on his heels like an athlete preparing for a race. "Are you well?"

Nick watched a car drive up School Hill. "My health is fine. But you weren't enquiring after my physical wellbeing so much, were you?"

Andrew cleared his throat. "You're an astute fellow. I won't pry, but since we're chatting I'd like to reiterate my offer of a non-judgemental, listening ear."

Nick crossed his arms. "When we spoke after Charlie Brockman's funeral, you mentioned us being in a spiritual war."

"It's the essence of the Christian faith. Not only the Christian faith, either. Many belief systems feature conflict between non-corporeal higher beings, with humanity stuck in the middle or occupying an uncomfortable periphery."

"Non-corporeal higher beings? I like that description."

"In relation to what?" Andrew straightened his octagonal glasses.

Nick's attention darted back to the bend Jason had disappeared around. *If I'm going to lay this out, I'd need to tell Andrew everything. I won't do that without Jason's permission.* "I did some reading up on the area. Ghost stories and such. Charlie piqued my interest with those assertions about meeting his late wife in the woods."

Andrew intertwined his fingers. "Interesting. But the non-corporeal higher beings to which I referred, are more than mere departed spirits of ordinary humans."

"Might they pretend to be people we know, if they appeared to us?"

Both Andrew's eyebrows lifted high. "Like June Brockman?"

"Or anyone?"

Andrew wanted to counter with *'your son?'* but a big heart and temperate nature kept both the question and general probing curiosity in check. Had this tragic widower experienced similar grief-induced apparitions to dear old Charlie? "To what end?"

"A nefarious one." Nick chewed an imaginary cud. "Like a way to afflict or torment the living who might otherwise exist beyond their reach?"

Andrew stepped aside to greet a passing dog walker, before turning back to face Nick. "You've put some thought into this. Well, in my religious tradition we consider the Devil '*The Father of Lies*.' Malicious deceptions are well within his purview, so why not others among the cohorts who fell from Heaven with him?"

Nick derived scant comfort from this minister, buttressing his assessment of recent events. Events he'd yet to reveal with any clarity. His earlier comment to Jason about being out of their depth resurfaced in his uneasy brain. "I may call on you for a deeper chat about this sometime, if you'd be willing to discuss it further?"

"I'd be delighted, Nick. Local history - even the ghostly kind - spiritual interpretations and experiences are my bread and butter, as you know. Evenings are best, but call anytime you like."

"Have a good day, Andrew."

"You too. Goodbye." Andrew continued down the lane as Nick closed his front door.

* * *

The vicarage at Chilham stood a square-cut Georgian structure, spread across two sash-windowed floors plus twin attic dormers and a well-concealed basement. This spacious, red brick residence nestled out of sight behind a white, five-bar gate amidst tall trees at the rear of St Mary's churchyard. It amazed Andrew Stallard the Diocese hadn't liquidated the property to fund church upkeep costs during years of dwindling attendance. He would have been content with a modest flat or two-up, two-down cottage rather than the semi-manorial pile he rattled around in. Even a minister with a wife and nine children wouldn't lack for space. Andrew had no such affective attachments.

His conversation about non-corporeal higher entities earlier in the day, caused his mind to work overtime.

Nick is a pleasant fellow. Guarded over his emotions, but who can blame him for that? How much fragility is concealed behind that blank exterior? How much pain does he bear alone, because he is unable or unwilling to share it?

Andrew twisted newspaper sheets and stuffed them into a grate around a fresh, seasoned log in the parlour. A collection of aged leather books sat on a hexagonal, polished table before one of the elegant Georgian residence's enormous windows. Each sash comprised four rows of three glass panes between white painted wooden bars. A rose pink hue of dusk in the air outside, accompanied by cawing crows, blended with a snap and crackle of kindling catching in the fireplace. Andrew tossed a match singeing his fingers into the growing blaze. He stood there for a moment to warm his hands. A considerate man, Andrew kept the vicarage's central heating on low; favouring instead multiple layers of jumpers for warmth. Every room in this expansive property featured high ceilings. The entire structure would require an executive income to heat at a reasonable level. Andrew counted his discomfort as nothing compared to the sufferings of Christ. Church funds were tight. Profligacy over running costs wasn't an option. His favourite mentor at seminary always told him: *'Don't crank the heating on your minister's residence too high. Otherwise St Peter may believe you prefer it and send you elsewhere once you arrive at the pearly gates.'*

Andrew chuckled to himself and crossed to sit at the table. He picked up one of the leather-bound volumes and studied its gold leaf spine lettering: *'Historia Ecclesiastica gentis Anglorum - Vol 1.'* He stroked the spine, then placed it down again with its four companion volumes.

"Ah, The Venerable Bede. What times you lived in; what things you saw."

A shuddering bang sounded from the rear of the property. Andrew sat up sharp. *Something must have fallen in the kitchen.* He pushed away from the table, then wandered out into the hall. A broad oak staircase with low risers and brass grippers secured a plush crimson carpet to its mid-section. A hinged kitchen door beside, which swung in both directions, spoke of days when the local minister's house enjoyed catering staff. Were it not for a grand castle across the square, St Mary's ecclesiastical accommodation would never have blossomed into such opulence.

Inside the kitchen, a gust of strong wind rattled a range of dangling copper pans against one another. Each hung from a cast iron hook in a rack above a broad worktop. The source of the disturbance took Andrew aback. The kitchen's sash window had been pulled open. This required a feat of considerable strength, as he knew well. Yet other than himself, the vicarage remained empty, and he'd not opened that window since autumn. He sidled around a long, rough central table and tugged at the sash to shut it again. The clattering copper pans stopped swinging; their uncoordinated music replaced by an unbroken scratching like a gouge through wood. Andrew fell back against an enamel sink. His eyes focused on splintering marks on the rear of the bi-directional door he'd entered through. Written by an unseen hand, the paint sliced apart into two spidery words of text: 'Salvet animan.'

Andrew stood there, jugular throbbing as the last letter appeared and the scratching ceased. He kicked his startled brain into Latin translation mode. *Salvet animan - Stay home*. His brow furrowed. "Stay home from what, or where?" His words boomed in the large culinary space.

One by one the copper pans dropped from their hooks, bounced from the worktop and clattered onto the tiled floor. The cacophony reached such a deafening volume, Andrew darted from the kitchen back into the hallway. He spun at the report of heavy stomping feet on the staircase. The thick-piled carpet depressed on every step, as though some unseen giant were storming down to reach him. A rise and fall of furious breathing filled the expansive hallway. Hot blasts of air buffeted Andrew's face. He struggled to stand firm, voice quivering as a prayer of protection poured from his mouth.

"Visit, Lord, we pray, this place and drive far from it all the snares of the enemy. Let your holy angels dwell here to keep us in peace, and may your blessing be upon it evermore; through Jesus Christ our Lord. Amen."

Doors opened and slammed throughout the structure. A howling wind whipped down the stairwell, causing Andrew to lean into it lest he topple to the floor. He shouted against the hurricane; every word a battle of faith and belief in the aid of a higher power.

"Whoever dwells in the shelter of the Most High, and abides under the shadow of the Almighty, shall say to the Lord, '*My refuge and my stronghold, my God, in whom I put my trust.*' For He shall deliver you from the snare of the fowler and from the deadly pestilence."

The wind increased its power. Andrew hooked his arm around the handle of a closed door for support and continued his spiritual invocation.

"He shall cover you with His wings and you shall be safe under His feathers; His faithfulness shall be your shield and buckler."

The carpet indentations quickened pace until they stopped before him. Fiery wind scalded his face as though blown from the nostrils of something ten feet high.

Andrew roared on.

"You shall not be afraid of any terror by night, nor of the arrow that flies by day; of the pestilence that stalks in darkness, nor of the sickness that destroys at noonday. Because you have made the Lord your refuge and the Most High your stronghold, there shall no evil happen to you, neither shall any plague come near your tent. For He shall give his angels charge over you, to keep you in all your ways." Andrew pulled a silver cross on a chain from beneath his layers of jumpers. He kissed the talisman once, then held it towards the blasting heat. "In nomine Patris et Filii et Spiritus Sancti." He took a deep breath from his diaphragm and shouted in righteous indignation one final Latin phrase. "Apage Satanas!"

The main vicarage door blew open behind him. Andrew turned to look. A rushing force struck him in the back, knocking him face down to the floor. He lifted his head as one final wave of heat surged from the building and the portal slammed shut. The residence remained in silence and Andrew lost consciousness where he lay.

13
Her Cup Runneth Over

Time off school was never to Jason Cooper's delight. On that bright day amidst the transition from winter to early spring, little choice existed. First, he had a hospital appointment for the removal of his bandages. Second, the night before his mother received word her sister had been rushed into hospital, up in Cambridge. As soon as the family returned from his appointment, Jason's mother and father were off to visit.

"I've left some cold casserole in the fridge to warm up for your dinner. We should be home by tomorrow night. Uncle Bernie will put us up." Helen Cooper placed a folded change of clothes into a black holdall resting atop her mattress.

Jason watched from his parents' bedroom doorway. "I'm sure Uncle Bernie will be glad of the company. Give Auntie Alison a kiss for me. Tell her I hope she makes a swift recovery."

"I will, darling. How are your hands and lower arms now?"

Jason examined the tender new flesh. "Like a baby's bottom; soft and delicate."

"Be careful if you go out walking. Don't forget to rub

that cream in tonight that the doctor gave you."

"I won't, Mum." He noticed unusual crow's feet crinkling the corners of her eyes. "Auntie Alison is in the best place."

"Uncle Bernie said she'd felt rough for a week. He came home to find her with an enormous, swollen belly, as though pregnant. When the ambulance reached Addenbrooke's, nurses drained three catheter bags of waste water from her body. Another half an hour and they reckon her bladder would have burst with fatal consequences."

"Now they'll find out what's wrong. She'll be right as rain, Mum. You'll see."

Helen zipped the bag. "Have you spoken with Louise today?"

"Not since yesterday morning." He paused. "I don't think she was quite herself." The mobile phone almost burned in his pocket, still lacking any response to the text he'd sent Louise twenty-four hours earlier.

"It might be that time of the month. Don't think ill of her, she's a nice girl."

"Yes, she is. Thanks, Mum."

Jason waved his parents off during the early afternoon. His phone remained silent, though he checked it many times. Each examination saw him linger over the digital wallpaper image of Louise.

As darkness descended, he retrieved his bowl of casserole from the fridge and warmed it on the hob. A soft rap on the front door disturbed his busy stirring.

He set a wooden spoon down on a trivet and sauntered into the hallway to answer it.

"Hey." Louise stared at him through worried, soulful eyes; voice almost a whisper on the doorstep.

Jason gasped. "Are you okay? I was so worried." He reached out his hands to clasp her icy fingers, then moved in for a kiss.

Louise responded with marked discomfort that wasn't lost on her new boyfriend. Her fingers chilled Jason's hands.

"Gosh, you're frozen. Come inside."

Louise shuffled into the hall, lacking her signature bold spark. "Are your parents home? I didn't see their car out front."

"No. Mum's sister was taken ill. They're spending the night with my Uncle Bernie in Cambridge." A rich, steamy aroma of meat and vegetables wafted from the kitchen. "I was warming up casserole for dinner. There's enough for two. I could swear Mum thinks I'm wasting away."

Louise shrugged. "Okay. Thanks, that sounds good." She kept her hands clasped before her abdomen as they went. "You've had your bandages removed. How is it?"

"Tender, but I'm glad to get shot of those wrappings." Jason pulled two china bowls from a cupboard, then ladled out helpings of casserole. "Do you want tea, juice, cola, what?"

"Cola would be nice." Louise tugged at her heavy pullover, then sat down at the kitchen table.

Jason bustled around, setting an extra place and

pouring her drink. "Almost done."

"Jason?" Louise watched his face as he delivered their dinners without making eye contact.

"Yeah?"

"I got your text message."

Jason sat next to her. "You didn't respond. Can you remember what happened during our call?"

Breath caught in Louise's throat. "That pain in my stomach kept spreading upward. It still is. But it's more than physical discomfort. It feels like something... many somethings are inside me, or pushing their way in from I don't know where."

Jason picked up a spoon. "We were..." He cleared his throat. "Um, chatting. Then your voice changed into a sound of *many somethings*."

Louise touched his arm before he could spoon up some casserole. Her eyes shone for a moment. "I remember our conversation before. I was so happy."

Jason flushed. "That makes two of us."

Louise let go. "The next thing I knew, I woke up in bed an hour later with a dry mouth and more internal pain." She gulped. "What did I say when my voice changed?"

"*Leave White Hill alone. Leave White Hill alone, or you'll lie-down with your dead friend.* Your exact words in the freakiest, most horrific voices I've ever heard. The line disconnected right after."

Louise reached a hand to her mouth. "Oh, my God. What did you do?"

"I ran up the road to tell Nick about it. What else could I do? I was scared if I called back, those things would hurt you. Nick suggested I send you the message."

Louise tried some casserole. "I wanted to call, but I didn't know what was going on. When I joined Mum in the kitchen before lunch, I pulled a knife out of the drawer and crept up behind her."

Thick, steaming liquid dribbled off Jason's tilted spoon, held halfway between bowl and mouth. "Were you aware of what was happening?"

Louise nodded. "Yes, but like an observer. Something else was controlling my body. I couldn't even scream a warning at Mum. The kids next door kicked a ball that walloped the kitchen window. Mum ran out the back door to tear them off a strip. Thankfully, I got control again and put the knife away."

Jason sat with his mouth open. The gormless expression of concern directed at her caused Louise to spoon some of her own casserole into his slack orifice. Jason swallowed. "You must have been terrified."

Louise kissed his cheek. "I spent the whole of yesterday afternoon trying to resist whatever this is. By sundown I was exhausted. This morning I pulled a sickie from school and stayed in my room. It seemed the safest bet until I could see you in private. Explaining everything on the phone was a non-starter."

Jason slipped his arm around her waist. "You appear calm, all things considered. You've so much courage."

Louise's face darkened. "No, I'm bricking it. But I've noticed those things find it easier to take hold when

I'm upset or emotional. So I'm trying to run on an even keel." Her eyes watered. "I'm worried I'll hurt you, like I almost did Mum. But I don't know where else to turn. Am I possessed?"

Jason held her close. "We should visit Nick. I'm not sure what he can do, but he recommended we stick together in all this."

"Okay."

Jason let go and pointed to Louise's bowl. "Get some food down you; it'll keep your strength up. Then we'll walk up the road." He carried his empty bowl and glass to the kitchen sink and ran some water. The zesty fragrance of lemon washing-up liquid faded to a rank odour somewhere between rotting meat and fresh manure. Jason sniffed at the overflow. *Is the drain backing up? Yuck, that's foul.* He looked round to find Louise standing four feet away, staring at him with intense pupils from a lowered head. A toothy grin spread across her face. Her bosom heaved in time with a rattling growl.

"No." Jason pushed himself back as Louise lunged, both hands locking onto his throat. Fingernails dug into the flesh surrounding his windpipe. Louise pinned him against the worktop; wild, cue ball eyes almost popping out of her skull. Her breath stank with a medley of every corrupt odour Jason's expansive imagination might conjure. He struggled for air, fingers tugging Louise's arms wide at the elbows. In the narrowing tunnel of his oxygen starved sight, Jason fancied he spied Louise as a lost soul, pursued by taloned spectres inside the pretty but altered orbs of her smoky eyes. *How can I fight the girl I love? What if I hurt her?* Self-preservation and overpowering affection for the young woman who owned his heart, blended into one last, hopeful course of action.

"Louise." His voice croaked from near strangulation. "I love you, Louise. Fight back. Don't let them hurt me."

Louise released her grasp, body spasming into a doubled-over fit. She whirled from side to side, a pitched battle raging somewhere deep within. Jason reached for his throat and gulped down air. He ran water from the tap into his empty glass and took a sip between heaving rasps. Louise crashed into the kitchen table and fell to the floor in a heap.

"Easy. Sit up slow and drink this." Jason helped Louise raise her head from the kitchen floor at The Orchard. She'd been out cold for ten minutes before her limbs started twitching again. He lifted a tumbler of cola to her lips. "Small sips. The sugar will help."

Louise took in some sweet liquid. Her eyes moistened, lips quivering. "Jason?" She reached a hand to stroke his face. "Are you okay? I was so scared I was going to kill you."

"I'll live, this time. You snapped out of it when I addressed you by name." He administered more cola, then wiped her mouth. "I remembered reading in one of my occult books that a person lost in possession requires an anchor. Something for their identity to cling onto during a moment of chaos. Any aspect that's definite and emotive from their individual life will do. I took a gamble on your love for me running deep and went with it. Thank God I was right; it paid off."

Louise sniffed. "I heard your voice through the brain fog. It helped me wrestle for control." She sat straighter and touched her stomach. "Whatever this is, hasn't gone away. It's a temporary reprieve. Even now I can feel them scratching at my insides."

"Then the sooner we reach Nick, the better. If nothing else, he can help me restrain you safely."

Louise pressed their foreheads together. "Jason." Her breath came in short pants. "I don't want to die. But if it comes to it, do what you have to for your own sake. Even if that means hurting me."

Jason scrunched his face and shook his head. "I can't, Lou. I can't hurt you. How could I live with myself? Jesus, how would I even explain it, let alone cope afterwards?"

Louise tried to stand. Jason rose to steady her.

"I'll clean up later. Let's grab our coats and go."

"Jason? Hey, how are you? Wow, this must be Louise." Nick opened the front door at Stour Cottage, shedding a beam of welcoming light onto School Hill.

Jason stepped closer, clutching his girlfriend. "Whatever took hold of Lou on the phone yesterday, almost made her stab her mother. She just tried throttling me in the kitchen."

Nick gawped. "Are your folks there?"

"No, they had to go away for the night."

Nick pushed back his short ginger hair with a tense hand, mind grappling for a suitable response.

Jason broke the standoff. "I brought her here for safety. With two of us present, we can monitor her and deal with the situation if she loses control again."

Nick studied the sheepish girl's downcast face. "You poor lamb." He inserted his feet into a pair of slip-on shoes.

"Where are you going?" Jason asked.

"*We* are going to speak with Andrew Stallard, the vicar. I don't know about you, but I've no idea how to help someone who's possessed. Shit, I didn't even believe in all this stuff until a few weeks ago."

Jason released Louise and folded his arms. "Andrew Stallard? The jumble sale/coffee morning guy?"

Nick pulled on a jacket. "I wouldn't set any store by Erin Parsons' assessment of him. If anyone can offer help or advice right now, it's got to be Andrew. I don't know anyone else, do you?"

"No, you're right. Okay, what have we got to lose?"

"My sentiments exactly." Nick checked his pocket for house keys, then ushered them back into the lane.

The trio hurried on foot up School Hill into the square; Nick in the lead with Louise and Jason holding onto each other behind. Folk music rippled amidst a lively throng inside The White Horse as they passed by on the path leading to St Mary's Church. Strains of '*Brigg Fair*' escaped into the night air. Jenny the barmaid bobbed her head in time and pulled a pint. The passing group didn't stop to listen. They skirted the church tower until they reached the tree-lined boundary and white, five-bar gate leading to the vicarage. Lamplight blazed from the front parlour window. Nick unfastened the gate, let his companions through, and then secured it behind them. They crunched up a short gravel drive to ascend a short run of concrete steps outside the front door.

Louise emitted a low whine which twisted into a guttural snarl.

"Oh God, she's going again." Jason clamped both arms to her sides and held on for all he was worth.

Nick rang the front doorbell with great insistence.

Dull footsteps approached. Andrew Stallard opened the tall, white portal in time for Louise's eyes to roll upward, exposing their whites. She hissed at him like an angry cobra, rearing to strike.

Nick was taken aback by a distinct lack of surprise on the reverend's face.

Andrew glanced from Nick to Jason to Louise and back again. He stepped aside and opened the door to its full extent. "You'd better bring her inside."

"Do you want to fuck this sweet, girlish body, repressed Nazarene?" Louise leered at Andrew Stallard. She fidgeted against robe cords securing her wrists to a sturdy wooden chair in the expansive vicarage cellar.

"Good God." Nick Preston covered his nose to block out a rancid odour like rotting excrement.

"Louise…" Jason stood, arms limp at his sides, watching her pretty face contorted into an expression of domineering, superior mockery.

Andrew Stallard uncorked a vial of oil, face calm. "Don't respond to it."

Louise threw back her head, mouth stretched wide. A howling tumult of tortured voices screamed. The deafening outburst rumbled against dusty shelves and whitewashed cellar walls.

"Don't respond to *them*," Andrew corrected himself.

"When you opened the door, I expected us to shock you. Have you dealt with this stuff before?" Nick asked.

"No. I endured a warning from some of these things, yesterday evening."

"A warning?" Jason said.

"Yes. I've long been aware of a rising tide of spiritual darkness along The Great Stour Valley." He looked at Nick. "You and I danced around suspicions neither of us felt able to share, when I passed your cottage."

"Over June Brockman's appearance to Charlie?"

"That's right. You've seen your dead boy too, haven't you?"

Nick hung his head. "It's not him, but yes."

Louise rolled wild eyes towards Nick and puckered her lips into a meek expression. Unblinking, she spoke with the timbre of a small boy. "Daddy Baddy, Daddy Baddy."

Nick struggled to shut out that beautiful child's voice he loved so much.

Andrew read the anguish straining his face. "I understand, Nick. Whatever has targeted you, disliked me offering help. For now we must stand firm and free this young lady, if it's not too late."

"Too late?" Jason's eyebrows lifted.

Andrew placed a reassuring hand on the teenager's shoulder. "I'll explain, later. I suspect it's way past time we all had an honest discussion. Now, Son, tell me: has she manifested like this before? You must have experienced something unsettling to darken my doorway."

"Yes, she tried throttling me earlier. Louise was lured into a ritual at King's Wood. Something about her being chosen as 'The Vessel,' though she didn't know that at the time. I suppose this is it."

Andrew's eyes widened at the term. "Then there isn't a moment to lose. How did you stop her?"

"I appealed to her love for me. I'm not a religious believer, but I've read about this stuff."

"Smart lad." Andrew tipped some oil onto his right thumb. "We're in a battle of spiritual wills. You did the correct thing. Did you say her name was Louise?"

"Yes."

"Louise is lost inside her own body, like a carjacked driver thrown into the rear of their vehicle. That you were able to call her back for a time, suggests the transformation isn't permanent or complete, yet."

"What can we do?" Jason asked.

"All three of us must draw upon unwavering emotions within. I don't know this girl, but my faith is the rock upon which I stand with resolute certainty. From what you've told me, a love for Louise is yours." He looked at Nick. "For you, it's the knowledge this tormenting beast is not your son, and the fire that burns within you when it mimics him." He sighed. "Rest assured, it will test all those strengths before this is over. Gather around her."

Nick positioned himself at Louise's right arm, with Jason opposite. Andrew stood before her. Oil glistened on his thumb as he lowered it towards her forehead.

Louise panted in time with heaving shoulders. She stared up at the approaching thumb, cheeks blowing out and nostril's flaring. The voice croaked a sinister command, blending a deep, slurred tone with several high-pitched squeals uttering the same phrase in unison. "Keep your dirty, fucking church hands off this body, underling."

Andrew spoke with even, subdued authority, unshaken by the infernal vocal assault. "Cleanse and sanctify our sister, Louise, oh Lord. You who knit her together in her mother's womb, drive out all that is wicked and unholy from this sacred vessel."

Louise hocked back a gob of saliva and spat in Andrew's face.

Andrew pressed his thumb into her forehead and smeared the sign of the cross. "When the enemy comes in like a flood, the Spirit of the Lord shall lift up a standard against him. I anoint this child with oil, a symbol of your Holy Spirit. In the name of the Father, and of the Son, and of the Holy Ghost. Amen."

Louise cackled. "*She* let us in. We're staying. This bitch is ours now."

Andrew placed his phial of oil on a side table, then picked up a plastic bottle of water.

Louise licked her lips, hate-filled eyes focused on the

minister. "I know what you want, preacher of propaganda." She spread her legs as far apart as the chair would allow. "You want to anoint her tight little cunt with your seed."

Andrew unscrewed the cap from his bottle, half covered the opening with his thumb, and then flicked a stream of water first vertically, then horizontally across Louise's restrained form. "Release her, banished and accursed ones. I expel you to the outer darkness. You have no authority here. Leave this vessel at peace, in Jesus' name. And they overcame him by the blood of the Lamb, and by the word of their testimony, and they loved not their lives unto the death."

Louise shook the chair, wrists struggling against the cords. Overhead lamp bulbs flickered and swung. Dust rained down from floor joists above.

Andrew nodded at Jason. "Call to her."

Jason reached a tentative hand out to touch Louise's left shoulder.

Louise snapped her head round to glare at him. "Limp dick coward. How long do you think this fertile creature would stay by your side? You couldn't satisfy your own hand."

Jason witnessed a multitude of lights sparkling in her chaotic eyes. Were they the beasts within, or a mere reflection from the swinging bulbs? He fought back against the heartbreaking slur and squeezed his hand tighter. "I know you can hear me, Lou. It's Jason. I love you. I've always loved you. Deep down I know you've always loved me too."

Louise rocked her head from side to side, mimicking

his voice. "I love you. I've always loved you." She snarled. "Love is weak. Love is nothing. Power is all."

Nick's anger flared. He clamped Louise's right shoulder. "Love is everything. If you feel anything at all, feel my love burning within for my son, Pretender. That same love drives you back into the pit whence you came." Nick amazed himself at his own semi-religious use of language.

Louise sneered with a wide-mouthed grin. She gnashed her teeth. "Love is everything? Hypocrite. You who hate your own wife and blame her for Grant's death."

Nick recoiled, snatching his hand away.

Andrew frowned at him and shook his head.

Louise laughed. "Grant burns in hell."

"No! It's not true. None of it is true." Nick grabbed her shoulder again. "Leave this girl alone." His shouting voice echoed around the cellar.

Doors banged in the vicarage above them, as they had the previous evening during Andrew's encounter with an invisible presence. He made the sign of the cross with holy water again, then placed his hand atop Louise's struggling head. "This is the pivotal moment." His voice rose in volume to make himself heard above the growing din. "Whatever happens, whatever it says or does, don't take your focus off love for this girl and the vision of her liberation. Channel your emotions into it."

A row of shelves dropped from steel brackets on the far cellar wall. Sundry tools, boxes and dusty junk bounced and rolled around the floor.

Andrew closed his eyes and spoke a quotation from the book of Psalms. "You are my hiding place; you will protect me from trouble and surround me with songs of deliverance."

The temperature plummeted.

Jason wanted to let go and rub his arms. Instead, he pressed down on Louise's shoulder to still her frantic body. He willed every ounce of love his battered heart could summon into focusing on her spiritual emancipation.

Andrew continued with more passages of scripture. "The thief comes only to steal and kill and destroy; I have come that they may have life, and have it to the full."

Louise wailed. "You can't have her back."

Andrew spoke on. "The righteous cry out, and the Lord hears them; He delivers them from all their troubles."

Saliva poured from the corners of Louise's mouth. A gurgled rebuke arose. "She's not righteous; she's a fornicating whore."

A freestanding cupboard toppled with a bang, missing Andrew by a whisker. He shouted from bursting lungs. "And I heard a loud voice saying in heaven, Now is come salvation, and strength, and the kingdom of our God, and the power of his Christ: for the accuser of our brethren is cast down, which accused them before our God day and night."

Louise whined like a wounded dog.

Andrew, Jason and Nick held her fast, pouring out every light-filled desire for the troubled girl's deliverance their collective souls could summon. The electrical power failed, plunging them into blackness and silence.

Underneath Jason's hand, corded muscles straining Louise's shoulders slackened. Quiet sobs teased his ears from the darkness. Two seconds later the lights flickered and came back on.

Andrew lifted his hand from Louise's head, but stopped Jason embracing her. "Not yet. We must be sure it isn't a trick."

Louise vomited down the front of her outfit in a single stream, then raised tearful, confused eyes to the curious, dog-collar wearing man before her.

"Were you baptised, child?" Andrew asked.

Louise nodded.

"Will you take communion?"

Louise looked from Andrew to Nick to Jason and nodded again.

Andrew reached back to a box on the table. He said a prayer and administered the host, before supplicating God to fill Louise with His grace and bar further access to the evil one.

"So that's the entire story to date." Nick settled into a leather armchair upstairs in the vicarage's impressive library.

Louise hugged Jason on a matching sofa, four feet away.

Andrew thumbed through a battered leather volume resting on a green ink blotter atop the library's sturdy mahogany desk. He sat up against a semi-circular backed chair and wiped his thin-framed octagonal glasses. "Apparitions, Ouija boards, occult rituals, poltergeists, demonic deceptions and possessions - it's incredible." He put his glasses back on. "We've been fortunate."

"Fortunate?" Nick almost choked on the word.

"Fortunate we released Louise in time." Andrew shifted his chair round to face them.

Jason rubbed Louise's back. "You said you'd explain that, later."

Andrew reached over to lift the battered tome. "I've recently acquired a copy of rare writings attributed to Nothhelm, a former Archbishop of Canterbury who died in AD 739, long before Thomas Becket or the pilgrims. He was a contemporary of Bede and Boniface, who gathered works while researching the history of Canterbury and its environs to help Bede in his own writings." He sighed. "I adore Bede. I've been re-reading him over the last few months. But Nothhelm... Well, he's something else."

"How is that relevant to our situation?" Nick asked. "Forgive me. I realise you're a keen student of history, but…"

Andrew flicked through several pages with an idle finger. "Nothhelm's obscure text describes twin spiritual beacons along the North Downs to Canterbury. He attests that the burial site of Julliberrie Down pulsates with holy energy, while across the Stour Valley, White Hill forms an inverted beacon. One summoning all that is opposed to God's light in this world and the next."

"Erin Parsons was very interested in White Hill when we mentioned it to her," Jason said. "She suggested something similar."

Andrew grunted. "She's the one who leads that cult Louise was sucked into?"

"Yes. That term they used for Louise, 'The Vessel,' is something you've heard before, isn't it?"

Andrew smiled. "Like I said earlier, you're a smart lad. Nothhelm - or whoever the author was - speculated that entities drawn to White Hill were seeking a bride to dominate in a diabolical parody of Christ and His church. It's an old game: take something pure and holy, then flip it."

Nick fidgeted in the armchair. "Is it possible Louise was selected by The Circle to fulfil that same desire?"

Andrew nodded. "No doubt in exchange for the cultists receiving promised earthly power. Nothhelm believed that if a vessel containing White Hill's accumulated entities attended the sacred site at Julliberrie Down, those dark beings could be forever banished."

"Would that stop all the nonsense? The apparitions and road ghosts?" Nick asked.

Andrew tweaked an eyebrow. "Who can say? We're talking about the musings of a man from around 1300 years ago; if Nothhelm even wrote them. Like I said, he gathered works: local histories, myths and legends for editing and collation. How the originator came by such a belief is impossible to fathom. Was it spiritual revelation or pure speculation?"

Louise reached for Jason's hand. "Do you mean if you'd dragged me up that hill on the other side of the river, you could have sent this evil packing?"

Andrew put the book down, then carried his chair over to sit facing her. "The text suggests a vessel, once filled to completion, would become a plague upon the living. They'd exist in a state of permanent manipulation, losing everything of the person who went before. Nothhelm's solution may be little more than a fancy, though I worry about his accuracy regarding a vessel. Dragging you up the hill as you suggest, wasn't a realistic option. Besides, though well underway, the transformation wasn't complete. You were still yourself, some of the time." He addressed the others. "In that we've also been fortunate. Our adversaries and their schemes are thwarted, if Louise is no longer the designated instrument. They'll have to find another, though it will rankle them."

"Why is all this happening now?" Nick asked. "Why has it taken so many centuries?"

"Do you remember what Erin Parsons said about time, Nick?" Jason replied.

"Oh yeah, that Bible verse. What was it? One day is with the Lord as a thousand years, and a thousand years as one day."

"2 Peter 3:8," Andrew interjected. "She's a curious High Priestess, your cultist. A dangerous and wicked dabbler, I'd suggest. In this case, it's a helpful use of scripture. The passage of time differs a great deal beyond our limited existence and perception. That much is certain." He faced Louise again. "How is your tummy now?"

"Better, thank you. Whatever was inside me has vanished. I feel myself again. Weak, but myself."

"That's good news." Andrew studied her companions. "We must watch over Louise and each other. Down in the cellar we experienced a taste - a mere glimpse - of the ancient evil these principalities and powers might unleash. I doubt we've heard the last of them."

"Could we report the cult?" Nick asked. "If they're drugging and abusing people…"

Andrew shook his head. "And achieve what? A short delaying action at best, for beings with eternity to burn. I put it to you we'd face tough questions and receive little help from the authorities."

Nick caught Jason's concerned expression. He remembered Louise's refusal to report her sexual assault. "Okay." He checked his watch. "We should run along." He stood and extended a hand towards Andrew. "There aren't words to express our gratitude for what you did this evening."

Andrew shook it. "I'm glad you trusted me enough - or were desperate enough - to visit. After yesterday, I no longer find myself alone. Believe me, the last twenty-four hours have tested my faith and resolve to the core. There are few in the church I can go to with something like this. Isn't that ridiculous?"

Jason and Louise rose.

Louise pulled a handkerchief from her pocket and blew her nose. "I'm sorry for the things I said downstairs, Reverend Stallard. I was aware of them, though unable to stop myself."

"Bless your heart. Call me Andrew. *You* said nothing, Louise. Those creatures respond and give utterance to the baser parts of our weak flesh. Witnessing it for the first time with my own senses was a shock, but their fallen nature is well documented." He waved a hand across the shelves of theological and historical volumes about them. "Now you must rest. Take heart and strength from the genuine love of your fine young man here. I didn't deliver you on my own. Religion be damned; Nick and Jason played their part." He walked over to a drawer and retrieved three small plastic bottles of clear liquid, similar to the one he'd used downstairs. "I'd like you each to keep one of these close by."

"Is that holy water?" Nick pursed his lips.

"Humour me." Andrew placed a bottle in his hand, then passed the others to Louise and Jason. "Unlikely as it sounds, this water represents an intersection of the spiritual and physical, infused with powers of light. Maybe it will aid in protecting each of you from the intersection of chaotic spiritual and physical powers raised against us. You witnessed the reaction when it came in contact with Louise's manipulated physicality."

Nick popped the bottle into his pocket and tapped it. "All the sensible old rules I used to believe governed my existence, have vanished. I suppose it's time to take a few things on faith, even if it's not my own."

Nick hesitated outside Stour Cottage. "Do you guys need a ride anywhere? Should we drive Louise home?"

Louise clutched onto Jason. "Can I stay with you tonight? I don't want to be alone; not with people I can't talk to about this. How can I tell my folks?"

Jason gulped. "I'll fix up the spare room."

Nick pulled out his house keys. "You two stay safe. Any problems, Jason, call me right away, yeah?"

"Ditto, Nick. If those things become enraged, I don't like to think of what might happen."

"Goodnight." Nick frowned and disappeared inside.

Louise and Jason strolled arm in arm through the dark. A stale aroma of crusty, dried vomit caused Louise to wrinkle her nose.

"Can I put my clothes in the wash before bed?"

"Sure." Jason looked up into a clear sky dotted with bright stars. "Are you scared, Lou?"

"About these demons or whatever they are? Who wouldn't be? I think Andrew's old writings are correct. There was a tug of war happening inside while you tried to free me in the cellar. Every new entity that showed up became a pressing weight, squashing me down into nothing. Your voices drifted further away, like I'd fallen down a well."

Jason unlocked the front door at The Orchard. "I'll finish cleaning the kitchen in a bit. Don't worry, I can vacate the room while you chuck your stinky clothes in the wash."

Louise nuzzled his neck. "If seeing your girlfriend

naked scares you, I'll stick my jacket on."

Jason scratched his neck. "I was being a gentleman. Why don't you go through to the washing machine? I'll make up the bed in the spare room."

Ten minutes later Jason descended the stairs. A churning from the washer's drum greeted his ears. "You're all set." He entered the kitchen to find Louise standing in her jacket with bare legs and feet. The sight of her toned thighs and shapely calves diverted his eyes to resist a sudden, growing arousal.

"Jason?"

"Yeah?" Flustered, he collected the remaining dinner things to wash up.

"Please look at me."

Jason placed the items in a bowl at the sink, then turned to face her.

Louise gave a gentle smile. "Those creatures made me say I wouldn't stay with you. That's not true."

"I know." Jason tried not to cultivate the seeds of doubt, planted in his mind earlier.

Louise's voice grew bolder. "The only truth in our exchange was when you said we'd always loved each other." Her eyes shone. "Tonight you stood by me, as I'll always stand by you. If I didn't know that before, I realise it now." She reached up to lift the zipper of her jacket between lithe fingers. The fastener came down in a long, whirring sweep and her last item of clothing dropped to the floor.

14
Unexpected Visitors

Jason locked his front door and swung a school bag over his shoulder. Louise waited at the gate, clad in her laundered clothing from the night before.

"I'll have to run home and change when we get off at Chartham. I can't turn up at school dressed like this."

"Will your folks mind that you stayed here? Are you going to tell them the truth?"

Louise stepped into the lane with Jason at her side. "Not the whole truth. I may catch a few disapproving looks, but Mum and Dad are pleased I'm no longer seeing Wayne."

Jason inhaled a lungful of crisp morning air. He bobbed along like an inquisitive bird until Louise reached for his hand.

"You're full of life this morning." She stifled a wry smile.

Jason stopped to look in her eyes. "Lou, I can't believe what happened last night."

Louise adopted a coy pose. "You mean me being delivered from demonic possession?"

"Well, that too; but I meant…" He stopped and snorted. "Oh, I see. You're teasing me."

Louise slid her arms around his neck "I'm thankful for what happened. It meant so much."

Jason couldn't tear his eyes away from her stare. A welcome change of habit and boost in confidence. "I could conquer the world."

Louise whispered. "I'm glad our lovemaking agreed with you." She pressed her lips against his.

If Louise's foot lifted a touch from the pleasure of their connection, it sank again in time with familiar, boisterous tones from a burbling, bean can exhaust pipe. She looked around as Wayne Hood's yellow SEAT Ibiza screeched to a halt near the bend into Hambrook Lane. The driver's door flew open, and an angry-faced Canterbury exhaust fitter stormed towards them, shouting.

"So that's what it's all about, is it?" He grabbed Louise's arm.

Jason reached to remove it, but Wayne shoved him away with a sharp hand to the chest. "Keep your nose out of this, school boy."

"Hey, leave her alone." Jason balled his fists.

Wayne let go of Louise and connected an uppercut to Jason's jaw in one fluid movement. Jason dropped onto the wet verge, seeing more stars than the night before on that same spot.

Louise kicked Wayne in the shins and yelled. "Never touch either of us again."

Wayne hobbled about, then slapped her cheek with a resounding backhander. "Bitch. What have you been up to? Erin went mad last night. She said you've undone the ritual."

Louise touched her reddened, stinging cheek as she backed up. "Stay away from me, Wayne. If you've any sense, you'll stay away from Erin, too."

Wayne paced forward. Jason recovered his wits and barrelled into the older man's torso. They rolled onto the tarmac road, a flailing mass of limbs and hollered profanity. Wayne got the upper hand, piling his fists into Jason's face.

"Oi!" a sharp voice barked from a cottage across the bend.

Wayne pummelled away for a further ten seconds, before two muscular arms pulled him clear and shoved his fuming frame six feet up the road.

Louise crouched by Jason's side. Nick Preston wiped his hands from the intervention, standing over the pair in a defensive posture.

"Who the fuck are you?" Wayne regained his feet.

"Your worst nightmare if you lay a hand on these two again." Nick's voice cut cool and clear, filled with an assurance he'd make good on his promise. That unreadable stare chilled Wayne's ire with uncertainty. Nick pointed at the SEAT. "Now get in your shit-box boy racer mobile and clear off."

Wayne Hood's ego was larger than his brain. He straightened, sauntered past casually, then pivoted and swung a punch at Nick's head.

Nick dodged the blow, allowing the inertia of Wayne's attack to carry him into a raised fist of his own. A sharp crack and a shower of blood erupted from Wayne's nose. He staggered back against his car, then slid to the ground near its offside front wheel arch.

Louise mopped blood from a cut beneath Jason's eye with a pack of pocket paper tissues.

"Is he all right?" Nick bent over them.

Jason touched a welt on his left cheek, then pulled his fingers away at the stinging sensation. A salty taste of blood coated his tongue. "Thanks, Nick."

Wayne tried to pick himself up.

Nick jabbed a finger at him. "Is that the guy who took you to the woods, Louise?"

Louise nodded.

Wayne half opened his car door before Nick kicked it shut. He grabbed the bleeding assailant by the scruff of his neck and shoved him face down across the bonnet. "I don't think so, buddy boy." He addressed Louise. "I realise you have views on reporting certain issues, but would you support an assault charge? If this idiot knows he'll do time, he might think twice before bothering you again."

Louise helped Jason to his feet. "Okay."

Wayne attempted to lift his head. Nick took great pleasure in slamming it back down. All Nick's rage at the creatures who'd impersonated Grant, infused his limbs with a liberal interpretation of 'necessary force.' He pulled a mobile phone from his pocket. "Louise, my front door is still open. Take Jason inside. You'll find a first aid kit with plasters and ointment in the second kitchen cupboard on your left. I'll join you once the Old Bill show up."

Louise and Jason staggered across the bend towards Stour Cottage. Nick dialled the police. He relished delivering another head slam as Wayne resisted his restraint.

"Where did you get to this morning?" Adam Little sat down in the Chartham school cafeteria, clutching his packed lunch. It was as he opened the Tupperware lid he noticed Jason's facial bruising. "Shit. What happened to you? Not more weird stuff?"

"Louise's ex-boyfriend is what happened. Or rather, his fists. He pulled up in his car and set upon us near my house this morning."

Jonathan Chapman sat down with a frown. "What was Louise doing near your house?"

Adam grinned. "Haven't you heard? She dumped her twenty-year-old geezer for Jason. Samantha just told me all about it."

"No way? Dude, I'm impressed." Jonathan stretched a hand across the dining table. "You kept that quiet."

Jason shrugged and shook it. "It's a recent development."

Adam licked his lips. "He's too modest. Louise told Samantha our guy here reached her in ways that older bloke never could." He slapped his knee with a jovial hand. "What kind of monster do you keep tucked in those trousers, Jason? Is it strapped to your leg?"

"Trust you to take it literally," Nathan Bishop joined them. "I imagine Louise meant at an emotional level." He waved a reassuring hand towards Jason. "Though I'm sure our pal measured up magnificently in other respects."

Jonathan winked at Nathan. "An emotional level? Says the guy who shagged Miss 'So, *do you want to do it?*' That's rich."

Adam peeled a banana, mouth spreading wide in a dopey grin. "One skin, two skin, three skin, fo-"

"Oh, grow up." Nathan cuffed the back of his head, then regarded Adam with a thoughtful stare. "I suppose we shouldn't complain. You turned into a basket case for a while back there."

Adam's face grew serious. "Wouldn't you if something like that happened? I don't know how I'd have kept myself together, if it weren't for Samantha. Man, for a week or more I couldn't even touch her, you know? I was shit scared."

"Lou said she helped you through," Jason piped up.

Adam sighed. "It's funny. Before, I couldn't wait to get in her knickers. Since she looked after me while I was acting like a spas, I've experienced…"

"I believe the word you're looking for is 'love,' mate," Nathan added. He placed a hand across Jonathan's mouth. "Don't say it. I know I had sex with a girl I'd only said hello to a couple of times, okay? I won't make a habit of it." He clapped an arm across Adam's shoulders. "It's good news, Adam. You too, Jason."

Adam bit his banana, then spluttered at Jason with a full mouth. "How did you get away from Louise's ex?"

"My new neighbour up the road is a reliable friend. He emerged from his cottage, restrained the guy, and then phoned the police. After they took our statements and processed Wayne, Nick drove us to school via

Lou's place so she could change."

"He sounds a decent sort," Jonathan punctured a carton of orange juice with a thin plastic straw.

"Yeah, he is. So, has anyone experienced more weird happenings?"

A general round of head shakes followed, setting Jason at ease.

Nathan poked his face across the table. "How did you and Louise get together in the end?"

Jason thought for a moment. "I'll tell you another time." He'd heard all he needed. His friends appeared safe for the time being, and he intended to keep it that way.

"I know we only made it in late morning, but it still felt like a bloomin' long day." Louise strolled out through the school gates that afternoon beside Jason. "Did Adam tease you about us? I told Sam. Hope you don't mind?"

"Of course not. He was - how can I put this? - he was 'Adam' about it."

Louise laughed.

Jason hesitated to let some younger kids run past. "Once upon a time, that would have been annoying. Today it was a relief, after his scare. None of the guys have a clue what's happened in *our* lives. Did you tell any of that to Sam?"

"No. For her safety, if nothing else."

"That's my angle on the situation too." Jason adjusted his school bag shoulder strap.

Louise looked both ways as they crossed the road. "Jason?"

"Uh-huh?"

"Wayne said Erin went mad last night and claimed I'd undone the ritual."

"That's reassuring, isn't it?"

"Yes, but how did she know?"

"If she's open to those entities, they must visit or communicate with her. I assume that's how she formed her group and established rituals in the first place. She doesn't strike me as a scholar. Not someone who'd read historical Latin, Greek, or Old English texts like Andrew Stallard."

"I owe him so much. Nick, too."

"We're gonna beat this, Lou. We have to. What happened at the vicarage last night was our first victory. We'd been tormented and pursued the whole way, until then. If Wayne's restraining order goes through, that'll be another blow for the good guys."

Louise squeezed his waist. "You're the original 'good guy.' Shall I walk you to the station?"

"Sure, if you're not worried Wayne will appear or follow you home."

"I won't organise my life around fear of that bastard. He's an opportunist and a coward. That much was obvious when the police showed up. They gave him a proper scare."

"And a caution," Jason smiled to himself.

"Yeah, that too. He'll be crapping himself that I'll drop his little group of sinister perverts in it, now. I'm still not going there, but enjoy him squirming over the notion." She changed tack, mood brightening. "Will your folks be home?"

"They should be. I hope Auntie Alison is okay."

Louise kissed him on the cheek and winked. "Have you got your holy water in case of emergencies?"

Jason slipped Andrew Stallard's plastic bottle out of his pocket to show her.

Louise mirrored his action with her own. "I shouldn't joke. I'd be a puppet plague upon humanity if it weren't for your local vicar; assuming those writings are true. My possession experience was authentic enough. I might have killed you or my parents by now."

"Did you feel anything when Andrew sloshed holy water over you?"

"Now you mention it: yes. Not pain, although those creatures hated the sensation. It felt like somebody cutting shreds in a thick, black curtain to let light through. Both times he did it, my personality drew strength to fight back. The same with that oil he rubbed into my forehead. Was it faith, willpower, or the stuff itself? I couldn't tell you."

"Maybe there's something to this religious paraphernalia after all?" Jason tucked his bottle away.

At Chartham Station, Louise waited for Jason's Chilham bound train to pull out. She waved, then turned for home. One hand stroked the bottle bulge in her pocket, with the respect accorded a loaded pistol.

* * *

"Thanks, Jenny." Nick Preston lifted two pints saluting the barmaid, then squeezed between patrons at The White Horse. Andrew Stallard watched him sit down opposite at a compact, square dark wooden table. "There you go, Andrew."

"Thank you, Nick." Andrew received the drink. "You're settling in around here now."

"What makes you say that?" Nick glanced from side to side. Headlights flashed against the windows as a car pulled around the square to disappear down Church Hill, skirting the quaint old inn.

"You called Jenny by name."

Nick twisted in his seat to regard the barmaid. "I suppose I did. Do you know, with everything that's happened, I hadn't noticed?"

"Have you heard from Jason and Louise?"

"Not since the morning after our adventure at the vicarage. Louise's cultist, onetime boyfriend, showed up on the lane near my cottage. Jason and Louise were walking towards the station for school. That guy, Wayne, pulled over and laid into them."

"Cheers." Andrew lifted his pint and clinked their glasses together.

"Your good health." Nick took a sip. "It was lucky I'd stepped outside for a minute and could intervene. We phoned the police. He's not allowed anywhere near those two, now."

"Were they injured?" Andrew's eyes narrowed.

"Louise took a slap across the face. Jason came off

worse. That brave fella tried fighting the guy. He received his fair share of cuts and bruises for the trouble."

"He's a dedicated young man; though, I suspect he doesn't recognise qualities in himself that are obvious to the rest of us."

"Yeah. I'd say he hovers somewhere between genuine modesty and low self-esteem. I imagine Louise will wipe away the latter."

"How's she bearing up?"

"Like a trooper, despite that skirmish with Wayne. When I drove the pair to school, she told me Wayne said Erin Parsons threw a hissy fit over her undoing the ritual."

Andrew pressed both palms together in a thoughtful, prayer-like gesture before his nose and mouth. "She knows, then?"

"Who, Erin? Sounds like it. Through supernatural means, no doubt."

"Hmm. Those creatures are using her like they do everyone else."

"Yup. But, she's too high on their supply to wake up and smell the coffee," Nick replied. "Why didn't they inhabit and dominate *her* as their vessel? It would've saved them a world of trouble."

Andrew savoured his beer for a moment. "I suspect any rituals thus far were used to strengthen emerging powers at White Hill. Weird manifestations are increasing, and now the perpetrators are ready to take their 'bride.' That's why it couldn't be Ms Parsons; she'd already assumed another role in proceedings.

One that's still necessary."

"Like a bishop can't become a choir boy and still lead service?"

Andrew grinned. "Succinctly put. They deemed Louise acceptable in their sight. We may have closed the door for now, but I imagine they'll still want her."

"Will it stop them using another girl?"

Andrew mopped his brow with a handkerchief. "I don't know. I doubt it. But, I'm worried they'll target Louise again, even if they find a fresh host during the interim."

"I'd keep that little nugget to yourself until it becomes an issue. There's no sense scaring her and Jason further."

"Agreed."

Nick looked around the pub. "We've covered my news, but I haven't asked how you've been? Any further disturbances at your residence?"

"No. You?"

Nick shook his head. "All quiet on the western front. I'd be a fool to think it's over, though. They're regrouping, I have no doubt."

"Someone slashed my car tyres."

Nick stared. "You're kidding?"

"No. It looks like a knife blade did the job. All four needed replacing."

"Someone broke the windows on my Honda. That was right after Jason and I visited Erin Parsons. I suppose there could be a brain-dead vandal targeting Chilham vehicles. It's rather a coincidence you getting hit too."

"An expense I could do without. But, if it's The Circle and the worst they can manage is vandalising cars, that's an easier foe to vanquish."

Nick finished his pint. "Can I get you another?"

Andrew drained his glass, then stood. "No, thank you. I'm glad we had a check-in, Nick. Please keep me apprised of any developments."

"I'll do that. You too. Have a good evening, Andrew."

Nick whistled to himself, hands in pockets while strolling from the square back down School Hill. He smiled at a red and white sign screwed to the side of St Mary's Primary School beside a multi-paned Gothic window: *'We learn to love and we love to learn.'*

Near the foot of the hill, his pace ground to an abrupt halt. A tall, slender feminine outline stood silhouetted beneath the lantern outside Stour Cottage. Side-parted, shoulder-length blonde hair outlined an unmistakable teardrop head.

"Alana?" Nick's mind wrestled to reconcile his wife's presence with the environs of Chilham and his rented bolt hole. "What the…?"

Alana collapsed into the wall of the cottage, gasping for air.

Nick rushed to her side. "Are you hurt? How did you get here?"

Alana's aquamarine eyes swam with pain and confusion. "Nick?" She drew in a sharp breath and clawed at him. "I've found you. What's happening?"

"Let's get you inside." Nick looked round. "Where's your car?"

Alana shook her head and touched a bruised temple. "I... I don't know."

It was at this moment Nick noticed her torn clothing and dirt-flecked arms. He gritted his teeth. *If those bastards have harmed my wife, there'll be hell to pay.* He fished out his keys and opened the door.

Alana sat at the dining room table, gripping a strong cup of coffee between shaking hands. Her face stared into nothingness, eyes mere slits.

Nick eased himself down beside her. "I can't believe you're here."

"Where is here?" Alana's voice drifted towards an imagined horizon, like her expression.

"You don't know where you are? I'd better drive you to the hospital. There's an A & E in Canterbury."

"No." Alana grabbed his arm in a panic. "Not tonight. I'm so tired, Nick. Please, can I sleep? If I'm not okay in the morning, we'll find a doctor."

Nick sighed. "I assume you packed a bag?"

"It's in the car."

"Which you've left somewhere?"

Alana fixed him with a pained expression. Her chin wobbled, then she flopped her head forward, sobbing into folded arms on the table.

"Hey." Nick transitioned from mild frustration into tender concern. He rubbed her back. "Okay, okay. You can stay in my room. I'll crash on the sofa tonight until we sort everything out. We haven't seen each other in two-and-a-half months."

Alana lifted her head, shut her eyes and gave a gentle nod. "Thank you."

"Drink your coffee while I sort out some linens." He stood, kissed her crown, and then disappeared upstairs.

Alana slept through until mid-afternoon the following day. Nick let her rest, unwilling to rouse her from what appeared a peaceful slumber. A sharp rap on the cottage door drew his attention from ruminating over his wife's sudden appearance. He released the latch and opened it to find a male and female police officer on the doorstep.

"Mr Preston?" The man spoke first.

"Yes?"

"May I ask if you've misplaced your wife?"

"I beg your pardon?"

The female officer chipped in. "We found a red Ford Fiesta abandoned on the Challock road last night. Our vehicle check traced it back to an address in West Sussex. Your home, I believe?"

"That's right. I'm renting this place for a while."

"I see," the man went on. "When Midhurst officers attended your address this morning, neighbours informed them the registered keeper, Mrs Alana Preston, left yesterday afternoon to join you here. We're concerned for her welfare."

Nick stepped aside. "Won't you come in? My wife

arrived on foot in a daze last night. She was scuffed and bruised, with no recollection of how she got here or where her car was. I put her to bed." He motioned to the female officer. "She's been asleep upstairs ever since. Would you like to check on her for yourself?"

The woman removed her cap. "Thank you, Sir." She found her way to the staircase and disappeared up to the bedroom.

Nick shut the front door. "Can I fix you people a brew? I fear it might be a tough job prising answers out of my wife. I want some myself. Alana and I were going through a trial separation. I didn't know she was coming."

"That clears up several unanswered questions." The male officer walked with Nick into the dining room. "Tea would be grand. Thank you."

Half an hour later, Alana descended the stairs, having washed and re-dressed in torn clothing she'd done her best to brush clean.

"Can I have a word, Dean?" The female officer drew her colleague aside into the hall for a subdued chat.

Nick sat Alana down with a hot drink. She clutched onto his hands in silence, as though for dear life.

The male officer cleared his throat, and they re-joined the couple. "It seems your wife suffered a bad scare on the road after dark, Mr Preston. Somehow she stumbled into the woods and ended up on your doorstep. It's neither a short nor direct walk. Has she been here before?"

"No." Nick frowned.

"That's curious. A striking example of blind luck."

Nick hesitated to ask his next question, but it would look suspicious if he didn't. He passed them each a cup of tea. "What kind of scare are you referring to?"

Dean exchanged a hurried glance with his colleague. "We sometimes receive reports from motorists who claim to have struck a person near that spot. They're understandably upset and concerned for the individual's life. Most times we find no damage to their vehicle, nor sign of a crash or injury. No body either."

"Do you think they're making it up or taking something they shouldn't?"

"I can't speak for every case, but no."

"So what do you suppose it is?" Nick asked. He'd have almost enjoyed this interrogation, were it not for too many unanswered questions surrounding Alana's appearance.

"I wish I knew. It's a dark, lonely, tree-shrouded and winding hill. Deer leap out, occasionally." He scratched the back of his neck.

"If they hit a deer, surely you'd find damage and signs of injury?"

"Mmm." Dean looked uneasy.

"Did my wife hit a deer?"

"No, Sir."

The female officer spoke up. "Most reports we receive are sightings of a specific person. A smiling woman in white. It's all rather odd."

"You mean a ghost?" Nick attempted to sound

surprised.

"We couldn't comment on that, Sir," the woman replied. "Though in your wife's case, she claims it was…" Her jaw froze. "Someone else. She watched them appear from the trees again afterwards and gave chase into the woods. How she found her way here is anyone's guess."

Alana mouthed a silent 'thank you' to her.

Dean picked up the thread. "My colleague says your wife appears shaken from her experience, but happy to be here. That satisfies our welfare concerns. We've transported her car to an impound yard. There's a release fee. I'll give you the collection details. I'm sure she'll be glad to recover her vehicle, along with a change of clothes."

"Thank you."

"Might I suggest a medical check-up, once the lady feels strong enough?"

"We'll do that. I appreciate your visit." Nick took the offered impound yard information, collected their empty mugs and showed them out.

When he re-entered the dining room, Alana was shaking again. Now he understood, or thought he did. "Alana?"

Alana's eyes turned down at the corners, strained with fear and uncertainty.

"It's okay, love." Nick sat beside her. "I know what happened. That *'someone else'* you hit on the road wasn't a woman in white, was it?"

"No."

Nick held her close. "There's no easy way to say this.

I don't want you to think it an attack or accusation." He took a breath. "You hit Grant, didn't you?"

Tears streamed down Alana's cheeks. "Oh, Nick. It was him; I'm sure of it. His face struck my windshield, and I gazed into his eyes." She blubbed. "It was like reliving that day in Chichester all over again, except with myself as the hit-and-run driver."

Air blasted from Nick's nostrils. "I know. The same thing happened to me on that precise spot. It's a place called White Hill." His brow furrowed. "That reminds me: why were you driving up that way? Did you get lost?"

Alana touched her temple like she had the night before. "No. There were works on the main road and a diversion." She coughed. "What do you mean the same thing happened to you? You hit Grant there too? Is he haunting us?"

"I thought he was haunting *me* for a time. Here at the cottage, too. It looked like him; it sounded like him. But it wasn't him, Alana. There are things I need to tell you. Troubling things you may find hard to believe. But before we get into that, can you remember what happened after you stopped the car?"

Alana placed her elbows on the table. "I hopped out to search for him. At first there was no sign, then I caught a rustle and his laughter from the undergrowth. He appeared at the side of the road, grinned and ran back into the woods." She wiped her nose. "It couldn't be him; not alive. But, ghost or hallucination, I wanted so much to see my boy again; to tell him how much I love him and how sorry I am that I let go of his hand."

Nick's heart ached. "What happened next?"

"I pursued. We ran on, like a child's game. The next thing I knew I was alone and lost in dense forest with only my phone screen for illumination. Then the battery gave out." Her breathing quickened, fingernails gripping the table edge. "Women's voices screamed. There was a crashing amidst the trees and something chased me."

"Did you see it?"

"No. I was so frightened, I couldn't stop running despite the dark. Shapes emerged from the bushes." Her brow creased. "Everything is a blur after that. The next thing I knew, I was standing outside your door."

Nick tapped the table. "At a house you've never seen in a village you've never visited."

The edges of Alana's mouth crinkled into a fragile but hopeful smile. "Could Grant have led me here? To you; to safety?"

Nick hung his head. "I wish that were true." He bit his lip. "Alana, before I tell you the strangest, most worrisome tale you'll ever hear, there's something I must get off my chest."

"What's that?"

"Recently, I received a kernel of personal truth. It came amidst a torrent of lies from a horrific source beyond comprehension. That truth struck me to the core. I finally understood how I'd behaved around you and saw the folly of it all. Darling, I'm so sorry I blamed you for what happened to our son." He shook his head, pupils dilating. "I never meant to take it out on you; believe me, I didn't. It wasn't your fault."

Alana sniffed, voice paper-thin. "But if I hadn't been on the phone… If I'd kept hold of him…"

Nick clamped his hands either side of her face. "You didn't make that idiot speed down a rat run. He was driving too fast through double-banked, parked cars in a built-up area. That's not your fault. It was a horrible, horrible accident, and it destroys me that I've let it tear us apart. That day in Chichester, I lost one of the two things I love most in this world. Like a fool, ever since then I've done my damndest to push away the other. I love you, Alana. I love you more than anything and I'm sorry. Please forgive me."

Alana pulled him into a soft embrace. The pair rocked, kissed and wept as the afternoon drew on.

By late evening they'd returned with Alana's red Fiesta, plus a clean bill of health for its driver from a startled but unconvinced doctor. Alana climbed out of the car she'd shoehorned in beside Nick's Honda at the rear of the cottage.

"Should I be concerned the GP gave me a card with phone numbers for psychological counselling?"

Nick collected her bag from the boot. "If you'd told him half the story I regaled you with before we left, he'd have sectioned us both, not handed out business cards."

Alana admired the cottage. "You've not seen or heard anything weird here since the night that teenage girl was cured, delivered, or whatever they call it?"

"Louise? No." He walked towards the kitchen door,

then stopped. "Alana?"

"Yes?"

"I want more than anything for us to go home to Midhurst and start over. I'd load the car up and leave right now, only…"

"Don't worry, I understand. If your landlords are okay with it, I'll stay here until you're ready."

"Brian and Doreen? They'll be delighted to meet you. I'll take you next door in the morning. Right now, it's time to fix my wonderful wife a decent meal."

Alana pinched his bum. "Don't go overboard, I've a funny tummy. It must be the shock and upheaval."

Nick kissed her. "Is a funny tummy as terminal to romantic intimacy as a headache?"

Alana licked her lips and winked. "You won't be sleeping on the sofa tonight; I promise you that, Mr Preston."

15
On the Offensive

Nick Preston lay in bed at Stour Cottage with only pyjama bottoms for clothing. One naked, muscular arm cupped around Alana's nightdress-clad torso in the nocturnal stillness. His face evidenced an aura of peace and relaxation it hadn't displayed since the day Grant died.

Their lovemaking had been sincere and beautiful. True intimate connections were restored after eighteen months of robotic, dutiful, heartless grinding.

Waves of breath from Alana's nostrils rippled Nick's fine, silken chest hair, highlighted by moonlight intruding through the curtains. Uneasy dreams caused her head to move in half a dozen rapid jerks. Images of leaping fire in a wooded glade flickered through her slumber. Men and women of various ages engaged in all manner of robe-shrouded sexual activity, thrusting and writhing with carnal delight. A leggy woman with layered ebony hair threw up her hands before the flames in worshipful abandon. Her face twisted into a portrait of glee-filled revenge. Then they were on her; hooded men from twenty to fifty years, pinning her to the forest floor amidst a deliberate arrangement of stones. They showered her with intimate seed and skewered every orifice she possessed upon their turgid flesh wands. To Alana's shock, she wasn't fighting but participating; moaning and crying out with hedonistic abandon. The tall woman laughed, causing Alana to sit up in bed, panting and sweating.

What was that all about? She noticed the peace surrounding Nick's unconscious countenance. *My mind must be replaying those scenes Nick described from Louise's ordeal.* She gripped her stomach. *Ouch, that's a bad cramp. What's up with my tummy?* An insistent pulling force tore at her soul. The bedroom door swung open with a drawn-out creak.

"Oh, my God." Alana recoiled from the blank-faced apparition of Grant, stock still and watching her.

"Are you coming home now, Mummy?" He stepped closer to the bed.

Alana let slip a subdued squeal. After Nick's account of events since his arrival in Chilham, she maintained no illusions regarding their intruder's actual identity.

"Nick?" Alana rocked her husband's stirring form. "Nick, wake up." She swivelled back, now eye to eye with Grant's maniacal, tilting face. His voice slurred and deepened into a chorus of speaking entities, all falling over one another.

"You aren't as young. But, you'll bear our essence until we restore the first bride." The boy reached a tiny hand up towards her. "Let us finish what we began, yester eve."

Alana shook her head. "No. No, it can't be true."

Grant's voice returned to the child's normal, sweet

timbre. "Take my hand, Mummy. Keep hold of it this time. Not like before." A half-smile crept up one cheek.

Alana cried and screamed at the ceiling. When she looked back, Grant had vanished.

Nick sat up and rubbed his eyes. "What happened?"

Alana grabbed him. "He… I mean *IT* was here in the room." She let go and clutched her chest.

Nick shook his head, then pulled her closer. "Did it take Grant's form?"

Alana nodded. "It spoke to me. Oh Nick, it sounded like Grant to begin with. Then that voice…"

"What did it say?"

"That he and I should finish what we began, yester eve."

"Your game in the woods?"

"I don't know. Perhaps. I had an awful dream, like that ritual Louise described to you. This time I was the one taking part."

"How do you feel?"

"I've still got a tummy ache, but also a weird heartburn." Her tone wobbled. "That thing mocked me with Grant's voice about taking his hand and not letting go."

Nick pressed his head back against the headboard. "Bastards."

Alana lay against his shoulder. "Nick, I'm scared. What if that ritual wasn't a dream? Grant said, '*You aren't as young. But, you'll bear our essence until the first bride is restored.*' It was referring to me as a substitute vessel for Louise, wasn't it?"

Nick glanced at his bedroom clock. "It's not quite

one in the morning. I'm loathed to wake Andrew at this hour, but I will if we have to."

Alana wiggled her fingers against his muscular body. "Hold me tight."

Nick stroked her shoulders and kissed her head. "Try to rest. If you feel worse or like you're losing control, rouse me right away. Otherwise, we'll visit the vicarage after breakfast."

Alana pecked at his jawline, then slid her tongue down to tease his pectorals.

Nick relaxed with a stimulated whisper. "You've found more energy. I'm up for another romantic diversion, if it takes your mind off what happened."

Alana growled and snickered, speech sibilant and diabolically lustful. "Your wife is our whore." She sunk her teeth into his left nipple and bit hard.

Nick grunted in pain as Alana's teeth drew blood. He shoved his hands against her torso, but it pressed him into the mattress with escalating weight. "Get off."

Alana gripped him around the throat with one tense hand. Her fingernails dug into his neck while she smothered a pillow across his face with the other.

Nick's muffled rebukes accompanied flailing, panicked limbs. Whatever inhabited his wife's body, imbued it with physical force and density far beyond the norm. He choked and gagged. His frantic right hand clipped the bedside clock and knocked over a small, plastic bottle beside it. Tremulous, questing fingers felt for the container in a realisation this was his last chance. His thumb flicked open a flap atop its white screw cap, designed for sprinkling. With an airless gurgle, Nick flicked a stream of holy water across Alana's face. She rolled off the bed, raising the rafters with a furious scream. Nick threw the pillow clear, gasping for air. Alana flipped over with the energy of a recoiling spring. She crouched on the carpet like a puma waiting to pounce. Her features contorted in rage to match a drawn out hiss seeping between her brilliant white teeth.

Nick raised the bottle for a second flick and shouted. "Leave my wife alone. You can't have her." He brought the container forward in a sharp swipe.

Water splashed the wall as Alana dodged sideways. She tensed, then launched clear over the bed. A sharp crack of breaking glass accompanied her catlike form crashing through the upstairs window.

"Alana," Nick uttered a protective cry. He stumbled off the mattress to collapse against the window frame. Unsteady hands caught himself in time to halt an impending overbalance and tumble into the lane below. Alana had landed unharmed. She ran towards the bend, white nightdress billowing behind. A moment later she'd sprinted from sight down Mountain Street. An infernal cackle hung on the chill night air to mark her passing.

Nick dressed in a flash and shut the bedroom door behind him. Explaining this latest property damage to the Calendars would take some doing, but right now he'd bigger concerns. Pocket torch in hand, he emerged from the cottage to kick shards of fallen glass from the broken window clear of the step. He was about to sprint up School Hill towards the square, when he noticed a yellow SEAT Ibiza and several other cars round the bend from Hambrook Lane. They were headed in the same direction Alana had run. One vehicle he recognised as a Lexus belonging to Erin Parsons. *This is it. They're going to finalise those entities' diabolical access into our world. My wife is the conduit.* He zipped his jacket, then sprinted up the hill.

A minute after Nick rang the bell at the vicarage, light flared from an upstairs window. Andrew Stallard threw up the sash and leaned out. His voice condensed into puffs of vapour. "Who is it?"

"Andrew, it's Nick Preston. I need your help."

"Good heavens. Have they attacked Louise again?"

"No, though she may be their eventual target. It's my wife. Please hurry; we must reach the ritual site at King's Wood. I can't lose Alana *and* my boy. Quick, before it's too late."

Andrew coughed from the effects of damp air. "Hold on, Nick. I'll be right down."

"The Circle must have drugged and subjected your wife to their vessel ritual after they discovered her running through the woods. I wonder if those entities realised it was her, even as she drove up White Hill? They're vengeful, cruel, and we're all targets for their ire now." Andrew moved at a brisk pace beside Nick, past the rear garden gates of Chilham Castle. During their interim journey on foot down from the village, Nick had brought him up to speed on recent events. A lot had transpired since they'd said goodbye at The White Horse the previous evening.

"Alana became stronger than Louise was, that night we restrained her in your cellar. Far more than any difference in age and muscle development would account for. She weighed a tonne. I couldn't resist her powerful arms. Were it not for that holy water you gave me…"

Andrew tapped a pocket in his coat to ensure he'd brought some of his own. "One positive indicator. It appears to repel them, even when applied without specific faith. Unfortunately, it may be of little use in the ultimate struggle. So, you're telling me Alana was stronger and her transformation took a fraction of the time? It's as I feared: their power is growing by the day. There isn't a moment to lose."

A row of cottages appeared from the gloom on their left.

Nick pointed to The Orchard. "What about Jason? We need all the help we can get. Our allies are limited in number and three is better than two. Who knows what we'll encounter?"

"What of his parents?" Andrew asked.

"They're out of the loop and may be away. Their car isn't here. His mum and dad have been up and down to Cambridge, visiting his sick aunt. Perhaps they've gone again."

"We can but try." Andrew followed him through the

front gate and down the path.

Helen and Raymond Cooper's second trip to Cambridge, after Alison's release from hospital, afforded Jason and Louise a perfect, romantic opportunity. Somewhere up at Uncle Bernie's house, Jason's folks were fussing around in efforts to ease Alison's recovery. Meanwhile, at The Orchard in Kent, Jason lay back in awe, hands full of Louise's naked buttocks as she shuddered atop him in breathless ecstasy. Given the proximity of the top bunk slats and panel above, he got a front-row seat to those striking grey eyes. Louise's face hovered over him. Her passionate breath pulsed against his forehead in the final moments before his own joyous release pumped through a tensing groin.

Three hours and another vigorous loving session later, Jason lay listening to Louise asleep in his arms. A sudden intrusion of the cottage's brass door knocker, shaking the portal in its frame, stole wind from the sails of his reverie. He disentangled himself, then pulled on a top before opening the window.

Nick looked up from the doorstep. "Jason? It's Nick and Andrew. We need you."

"I'll let you in." Jason closed the window again.

Louise yawned and rose onto one elbow. "Who is it?"

"Nick and Andrew."

Louise stiffened. "Good God. Has something happened?"

"I'll find out." Jason darted onto the landing and descended the stairs in a thumping rush.

Nick and Andrew crossed the threshold before he'd even opened the front door to its full extent.

"Are your parents away?" Nick's strained face and brusque questioning raised hairs on Jason's neck.

"Yeah. It's just Louise and I."

"Louise?" Nick grimaced. "That complicates matters."

"How come?" Louise called over the banister, clad in a T-shirt and panties.

Nick craned his neck upward. "Are you decent? If you are, you'd better come down."

"I'll pull some jeans on." Louise dashed into Jason's room. She reappeared a minute later, sweeping her luxuriant mane of fair hair back over tender shoulders with an agitated hand. "Hi, Nick. Hi, Andrew." She flushed. "I might not be decent in the vicar's eyes after this."

Andrew presented a flat smile. "I'm not here to preach Christian morality at you, Louise. We've a problem."

"What's going on?" Jason asked.

Nick rubbed scratchy stubble sprouting from his chin. "Last night my dazed wife showed up on my doorstep from West Sussex. No car, nor change of clothes. It transpires she encountered that road ghost impersonation of our dead son, Grant, on White Hill. The same one I hit in the snow. She chased him into

King's Wood, but can't remember how she wound up at Stour Cottage."

"Flip me," Jason gasped.

"It gets worse. We collected her car from an impound yard after the police visited. They found it abandoned on the uphill road where Alana left it. A short while ago, she awoke to find another apparition of Grant in our bedroom. To cut a long story short, it seems The Circle nabbed her last night and performed the same ritual they used on Louise."

Louise covered her mouth with a wavering hand. "No."

"I'm afraid so. From what it said to her, she's a stand-in to carry them until they can infest their chosen vessel again."

"You mean me?" Louise's eyes bulged.

Jason reached for her, still facing Nick. "Where's your wife now?"

"After she manifested furious, possessive spirits and almost strangled me, she jumped out of the window and ran towards the woods."

"You fought her off? She must have passed by outside." Jason inclined his head in the lane's direction.

"No doubt. She was strong, Jason; stronger than Louise under their influence. The good reverend's water bottle saved the day. I guess it scared them I'd overpower and release Alana, like we did Louise. Were it not so, I suspect I wouldn't still be breathing."

Louise held tight to Jason. "Thank goodness she didn't break in here."

Andrew nodded at the front door. "I'd suggest she's

off to meet The Circle. Nick noticed cars arriving, on his way to fetch me. Specifically, Wayne and Erin's. If my suspicions are correct, they're about to perform a diabolical confirmation ceremony. One to complete the transformation process. It's something they'd have tried with Louise, had we not freed her first."

Nick shot him a stony stare. "All your suspicions have been right on the money so far, Andrew. Those obscure writings, too. The question is: how do we stop it? At least we'll have Jason to help." He regarded the teenage boy. "That's assuming you'll join us?"

"You know I'm there, Nick." He banged a fist against the wall behind him.

"Don't forget me," Louise frowned.

Nick flinched. "That may not be such a smart idea. If they're still after you, escorting their prey into the lion's den would be a fool's errand. We need you as far away from them as possible."

Louise let go of Jason and folded her arms across her chest. "If your wife becomes their vaunted 'plague on humanity,' what chance do you think I'll have? We're all in the shit."

"I don't know. It-"

"Hey," Louise interrupted Nick with a shout. She pushed away from the stairway wall with her bare foot, attention shifting from Nick to Andrew. "Didn't that Notty guy in your book-"

"Nothhelm," Andrew interjected.

"That's the one. Didn't he say a vessel filled with those beings could be purged, if brought to that other hill across the valley?"

"Julliberrie Down," Jason muttered.

Louise glanced at him, then back to the others. "Yeah, that place."

Nick huffed. "But if you're taken by them, we may not be able to subdue and bring you there. Not to mention we'll have angry cultists to tackle."

Louise shook her head and rolled her eyes. "Men. What is it with you, force, and doing things the hard way?"

"Huh?" Nick asked.

"Those creatures don't have to dwell inside *me* to be banished, as long as someone is carrying them, yeah?"

Andrew shifted his feet. "That's what the text implies, yes."

"So if those spirits want me as bad as you say and they're possessing Nick's wife, all I need do is show up, flash my rear and keep far enough ahead of her and the cult until we reach the right spot."

Andrew's brow raised in admiration. "You're willing to use yourself as bait?"

Louise's shoulders slumped. "I'm dead scared, but what choice do we have? The only problem is: I don't know the way well enough. It would take me time to find a solid route up there without hitting a hedge or fence, even in broad daylight. I know where the down sits in relation to Chilham and King's Wood, but that's about it. Plus, there's limited visibility out."

Nick's heart swelled at Louise's courage on display. "I imagine your boyfriend knows the best route."

Jason pressed his back against the staircase wall. He gave a slow, resolute nod. "Yeah, I know it."

Nick grasped Louise's hands. "Are you sure about this?"

Louise swallowed. "I'm sure. I understand what your wife is going through. She's in hell right now. We'll bust her out, if we can. Bust her out or bloody well die trying. I've had enough of this."

Nick's eyes misted. "Thank you." He nodded at the vicar. "Andrew and I will run interference behind the pair of you, slowing your pursuers if we can."

Louise shrugged. "What happens once I get up there? Julliberrie Down, I mean. I'm no holy person. What should I do?"

"Andrew?" Nick asked.

"Nothhelm didn't say. Would that were not so. I hope the presence of The Vessel on that ancient holy site will elicit some kind of spiritual reaction. Beyond that, all I can suggest is to draw upon whatever faith and willpower you're able to summon." He unhitched the silver cross and chain from beneath his jacket, then placed it over Louise's shoulders. "Wear this. It was left me by an amateur archaeologist some years ago, after his passing. He unearthed it close to the same spot."

Louise's eyes shuttered. "What if I don't believe?"

Andrew gripped her upper arms. "You don't always have to believe in something for it to be real and efficacious. I pray it will protect you."

"Thank you." Louise clasped the cross for a moment.

Jason pulled on his walking shoes. "From Louise's description of the ritual, The Circle must use that site where the falling tree almost flattened us, Nick."

Nick hastened towards the front door. "Then we'd better get a move on."

16
Julliberrie Down

Four figures - three male, one female - hurried around a bend beneath broad, budding horse chestnut trees. They overhung the lane at a point it left human habitations behind. Boughs that shadowed a horse paddock flanking the road, sighed in a soft nocturnal breeze.

Andrew Stallard muttered quiet prayers under his breath. Louise Squires gripped Jason Cooper's hand for courage and support. Nick Preston set his face in the moonlight towards a wooded ridge rising in the distance.

A fox darted from a patch of undergrowth. It paused in the middle of the road to study the curious, advancing companions, then bounced over a hedge and vanished in a heartbeat.

Jason's subdued voice cut loud enough to dominate Andrew's prayers. "We need to stay quiet and alert, the closer we get."

Nick regarded him. "That's logical. Are you floating this for a reason?"

"I read a book of personal accounts from occult abuse survivors once."

"Ear-tickling stuff," Andrew observed in a sudden break from petitioning The Almighty.

Jason shrugged. "Several victims mentioned perimeter lookouts stationed during rituals in woods and other remote locations."

"So they could melt into the landscape or accost an unwary passer-by?" Nick said. "I wonder if that's how Alana was nabbed?"

"She may have stumbled into their midst while running from whatever pursued her," Andrew commented.

"Or was herded there," Nick replied. "Good call, Jason. We'll stay sharp once we've climbed the hill. If memory serves, that clearing was near a bridleway, a fifteen minute walk from the track summit."

Jason nodded. "Yeah. If it was me running the ritual, I'd place a guard along The Pilgrims' Way above the bridleway, then another on that low, wide grass path down below on the woodland side. The one that runs beside the pond you pulled me from. Unless a body ploughed through dense undergrowth, they'd be spotted before reaching the keyhole stones. Time enough to raise an alarm."

Nick clicked his tongue. "And a body ploughing through the undergrowth would make enough noise to draw attention. That limits our chances of sneaking in close, before we're discovered."

Andrew emitted a thoughtful hum. "In our case, we've two advantages. First, we're intending to announce our presence, sooner or later. Later would be better, unless the ritual is already complete."

"And second?" Louise squinted.

"We're not clueless nighttime ramblers, thrashing around in the dark unawares. We know where the cultists are and plan on storming their site directly. Of course, we're also in the presence of unseen, adversarial powers who could alert them long before we arrive. That's a chance we'll have to take."

Louise attempted to calm her nerves through drawn out, deep breathing. "I can't believe we're doing this."

Nick nudged Jason. "Once Louise gets their attention, what's our best route out of there?"

"Over the ridge. There's a wire fence and high gate separating the woods and farmland sloping down into the valley. It's private land. But, we can climb the gate and run downhill past Deer Lodge, north of Godmersham Park."

Louise attempted to lighten the heavy mood with simple humour. "I guess we're not worried about being prosecuted for trespassing, then?"

Nick sniffed. "You can't prosecute someone for trespassing in England. It's a popular myth perpetuated by landowners."

"Are you serious?" Louise blinked.

"Yep. Those '*Trespassers will be prosecuted*' signs are known as '*The Wooden Lie*' in legal circles. My uncle was a country solicitor, trust me." He looked at Jason again. "What's at the bottom of the hill?"

"We'll skirt the Stour near woods south of Hurst Farm. We can ford the river there and cross the A28 near the pumping station, or keep to the banks and cross outside East Stour Farm. The less we're bunched up and hemmed in by tight tracks and footpaths, the better."

"That's sensible," Nick said.

Jason went on. "From East Stour Farm, it's a straight run north to the long barrow on Julliberrie Down."

"How far?" Louise massaged his fingers, trying hard not to pinch in her agitated state.

"From the farm? A mile. Uphill all the way. The entire route from the ritual site must be three miles, but there's no other option. You can't get there by car."

"Three miles." Nick stared at the moon. "And with God knows who or what on our tails."

Andrew nodded. "The problem is, we can't afford to lose them. If Alana - or whoever the vessel turns out to be - gives up or turns away, this is all for nought. We have to keep them pursuing us."

"For something which may not even work," Nick added. "Pray harder, Reverend. We're gonna need all the help we can get."

Louise froze, bringing her companions to a lurching halt.

"What's up, Lou?" Jason gripped her.

Louise stared and pointed straight ahead to a sharp turn where the lane became a farm track, while a footpath section of The Pilgrims' Way emerged from a gap in the hedge line. A collection of cars stood parked in a rough lay-by opposite. She swallowed to ease taut vocal cords. "Sorry. Memories of that night."

Jason winced. "I would say *'you don't have to do this.'*

But..."

"But I do." Louise lowered her arm. "I'll be okay. There's something else I must do, first." She brushed past him and sidled up to Wayne Hood's SEAT.

Nick grinned as she bent over in the bushes, then lifted a weighty lump of rock to shoulder height.

Jason's cheeks puffed out. "Oh, my life. Thank goodness The Circle are out of earshot." He called to Louise in a harsh whisper. "What if he has an alarm, Lou?"

Louise shook her head. "He hasn't." She threw the rock against the vehicle's windshield. Its glass shattered into countless fragments upon impact, raining down upon the dashboard and upholstery like a cascade of diamonds.

Nick winked at Jason. "Your girl's got spirit, buddy. Try never to piss her off, okay?"

Jason pursed his lips. "Yeah, I'm realising that." Deep inside it still thrilled him to hear Louise referred to as *'your girl.'*

Nick sauntered over to the lay-by, then grabbed an egg-sized stone from the verge. "I don't know if Erin has an alarm, but I'll not pass up an opportunity to fuck with the woman who accosted my wife." He dragged the stone along the vehicle's side panels, scoring the paintwork, then crouched and inserted it as a tight obstruction into Erin's already cooled exhaust pipe. "Sorry I'm not turning the other cheek, Andrew."

Andrew arrived at the spot with Jason. "We may be called upon to take more aggressive actions than these, before this night is through." He motioned towards the hedge line footpath. "Is everyone ready? We'd best move in single file and keep conversation to a minimum from here on out."

Climbing the steep, uneven track to King's Wood caused many people to wheeze on a good day in relaxed spirits. Those four shadowy silhouettes scrambling up the tree-enshrouded narrow footpath, puffed like an overnight steam train. Exertions both physical and emotional took their toll, quickening pulses and shortening breath.

At the top they recovered, reducing the noise of their rapid inhalations to an even rate.

Jason took the lead, followed by Louise. Nick went next, with Andrew bringing up the rear. Five minutes along the ridge-top path where King's Wood opened onto The Great Stour Valley, Andrew cast a glance over his shoulder. Seven and a half miles away as the crow flew, floodlights outlined the towers of Canterbury Cathedral. Its beacon of hope and the trail along which his feet hastened, infused him with romantic imaginings; pictures of the countless souls who'd passed that way over the centuries, drawing strength upon spying their goal nestling amidst the valley's distant river meadows.

Further on, Jason's arm shot up with a flat warning hand. He halted into a crouch, followed instinctively by the other members of their party. Ahead, further along a sweeping curve in the path, a tiny orange glow pulsed for a second followed by a cloud of exhaled smoke. A bulky figure in a heavy jacket wandered back and forth across the footpath, drawing on a cigarette.

"Do you think that's a lookout?" Louise whispered.

"It's an odd time and place to stop for a fag." Nick bunched up closer. "Okay, what's the game plan? Is he near the bridleway, Jason?"

"Yeah. The trail runs downhill in a straight line behind him. That clearing we visited lies to the left-hand side of it."

"We'll never get close without being spotted," Andrew mused.

Jason indicated the high gate in a wire fence he'd referred to earlier, then pointed at a nearby trail opposite, plunging downhill into the woods. "That leads to the pond. Part way down there's a place the surrounding trees aren't as dense. There'll be a lot of old twigs and debris, but Lou and I could sneak past that way."

"What about the rest of us?" Nick asked.

"Can the two of you subdue the lookout if we're discovered?" Jason studied the smoking figure still oblivious to their presence.

Nick wagged a stiff finger. "You shouldn't enter that clearing alone."

"That's not what I'm thinking. Give us five minutes, then grab the guy. We need that point clear to escape via the gate on our way out. Once The Circle's members are in pursuit, darting back under the trees would take too long. They'd flank and nab us using the footpaths."

"You want Andrew and I to lay that guy out, then

track downhill along the bridleway and hook up with you?"

"That's the idea."

Nick shrugged. "I don't have any better suggestions. Andrew?"

Andrew shook his head.

Nick patted Jason's shoulder. "Good luck."

Jason took Louise's hand. He led her away down the sloping woodland trail.

Nick inclined his head to mutter in Andrew's ear. "Let's stay low and slow. We'll move as close as we can to that bloke, while Jason and Louise have their five minute head start. The nearer we get, the easier it will be to jump him before he can raise an alarm."

Jason pulled Louise behind him over a bank into a thinner patch of trees. Moonlight glimmered now and again amidst the swaying boughs to aid their straining eyes. Jason put a finger to his lips. He drew a diagonal line in the air ahead, outlining the bridleway running perpendicular to their place of concealment. Amber hues warmed the pale night sky. Vigorous motions from many figures cast long, fire-lit shadows in random fingers through the undergrowth. They flitted and strobed across the narrow, solitary equestrian thoroughfare. Horseshoes had churned up the mud here. Slippery patches, claggy and filled with rain water were branded with imprints of the farriers trade to mark their passing.

A sudden stomping of feet caused Louise to draw a

louder breath than intended. A woman screamed behind them, deep inside the woods. Her cry of terror was echoed by another, not far downhill.

Jason gulped. "They're not alive, Lou. People sometimes hear them in the woods after dark. It's all part of the spiritual magnetism."

Louise fought not to release a sudden pressure on her bladder. "That isn't reassuring, Jason." She shut her eyes and tried to screen out the terrifying echoes of pursuits from long ago. "What do we do now?"

"We should wait for Nick and Andrew. If they're not here in two minutes, it's all down to us."

"Oh great," Louise fidgeted.

Nick made it within twenty yards of the lookout before his foot broke a twig. Its sharp report caused the figure to whirl, cigarette long since extinguished. Nick stormed from the bushes and ploughed into him. Both men rolled over, moss and old ferns mussing their hair and clothing. They staggered aloft, still locked in a thrashing bout of uncoordinated wrestling. The lookout broke free and shouted. Nick cut his outburst short by lunging forward to clamp a hand across his mouth. With the other he secured one of his opponent's arms in a Half Nelson. The lookout bit his fingers, causing Nick to let go with a grunt. A staggering blow struck the cultist's jaw. His head snapped back, knocking into Nick's like two balls of a Newton's Cradle. The pair tumbled to the ground.

Nick shook his startled skull. The lookout lay

unconscious, three feet away. Andrew stood over both, fists clenched in a raised guard.

Nick pushed himself up against a tree trunk for support. "Nice hit."

Andrew lowered his fists. "I was a boxer in my youth. I'm surprised it all came back."

Nick grinned, then shook his head in disbelief. "The need of the moment. Come on, we'd better hurry in case somebody heard him shout. Jason and Louise could be in trouble."

A formerly gentle breeze - barely a breath of wind - whipped into a sudden, chilling gust. Voices snarled and rasped on the air about them, circling downhill towards the clearing.

Jason and Louise pressed against a mossy mound beside the bridleway. The female screaming continued unabated. Jason hoped it remained out of earshot, away from Nick and Andrew on the footpath. That silent wish still lingered at the forefront of his mind when a deafening male shout rang over the ridge above and to their left. The cry was cut short, but carried enough to disrupt the rhythm of prancing silhouettes around a fire beyond.

"It's now or never." Jason staggered across the bridleway, slipping on the churned up mud. He spun to grab Louise around the waist, eyes sad. "I love you. No matter what happens, I'll always love you."

Louise blubbed then caught herself. Jason kissed her on the mouth. A howling wind shook the trees around them as she reciprocated. Harsh voices - identical to those that once filled her soul - stabbed at her ears with fury and malice. Louise ended the kiss, her resolute face darkening at the demonic wind lifting strands of her pretty fair hair. "They know we're here, Jason."

"Then so do The Circle. Let's end this."

The pair ploughed through the undergrowth, lacking clear knowledge of what lay beyond. Righteous anger burned deep within them, giving strength to otherwise tense and draining limbs.

A bonfire blazed in the top keyhole section of the ritual stones. Erin Parsons stood before it, eyes wild; smile broad enough to tear her face open from ear to ear. All about the clearing, ten robed male and female figures froze in the midst of depraved sexual activity. An attractive, mid-thirties blonde woman lay sprawled on her back, knees raised beneath a hitched up nightdress. Wayne Hood pulled out from between her thighs, rising to grin at the startled teenagers who'd interrupted his pleasure. A crack of splintering wood and swishing branches disturbed the upper clearing. Nick and Andrew stumbled through, knocking two men servicing a female cultist into a heap of arms and legs. Nick caught sight of Louise's abusive ex-boyfriend lowered over his wife. He dived for him with a roar.

Ecstasy flared in Erin's eyes as the howling wind of screeching, tormented voices whipped the bonfire's glow into a raging blaze of light. Sparks circled upwards. Erin pointed a delicate finger at Louise. "Lo, the first bride has come."

Nick's enraged form, spitting curses and pinning Wayne Hood to the clearing floor, interrupted her glee; but only for a moment.

Alana's head lifted off the ground, eyes shut. She sat up straight, neck twisting like a robot to face Nick. Both eyelids flew open. Dark, powerful orbs stained black as ebony fixed upon him, before averting their gaze to where Louise stood at Jason's side.

Jason grabbed her hand. "Run."

Louise didn't need telling twice. She pivoted, bringing her legs into an uphill sprint with a single motion. A male cultist recovered from his shock and attempted to cut off their escape like a goalie. Andrew's swinging fist connected with his jaw in a crack that sent him reeling.

"We're right behind you." Andrew's free hand pushed Louise onward between the shoulder blades.

The young couple crashed through the bushes, Jason correcting their panicked and erratic course toward the clearer - if slippery - ascent of the bridleway.

Alana threw back her head to howl with the visceral intensity of a rabid wolf.

Nick shuddered. He raised a fist, laid out Wayne with a single punch, then reached for his wife.

Alana growled and shoved both hands into his chest. Nick flew back, his spine slamming into the remains of the fallen, now sawn tree trunk that had almost squashed him and Jason.

Harsh wind whistled again, encircling Alana's open mouth. Her body stiffened, then convulsed in time with a new entry into her jerking, manipulated vessel.

Shouts raging in the wind before, now joined the throng escaping Alana's voice box.

"We must have the first bride." She powered forwards.

Andrew raised his fists, mouth at a loss for words of prayer or scripture to assist. The manifested reality of White Hill's combined demonic assembly swept him aside like a dried leaf.

Jason pushed Louise's foot up from beneath. She struggled to scramble over the high gate barring their flight from the ridge towards The Great Stour Valley. Clumps of mud flew off her shoes each time she lost footing. Her upper body folded over the top and she dropped down the other side. Jason clambered up behind. A deafening rush of blood pumped in his ears. It drowned out the inhuman screams and roars of whatever pursued them. His hands tore at the wire covered metal barrier, shaking from the effects of an adrenal gland working overtime. Further back along the ridge, a raging, shrieking something neared the top of the bridleway. Jason dropped into the grassy field beyond the gate.

Louise dragged him to his feet. "Come on. Which way?"

Jason cast his arm across the field. The pair ran downhill, fleet as angels with a devil close at heel.

Back in the clearing, Andrew helped Nick to his feet.

Erin and The Circle had given chase to Alana and her quarry, leaving Wayne Hood unconscious near the fire. Branches swayed at the lower end of the clearing. Another man in a heavy jacket burst through. Andrew felled him like a sack of potatoes with a single strike.

Nick rubbed his bruised back. "That must be the other lookout Jason speculated over."

Andrew nodded. "Thirteen, if you count both guards and Erin Parsons."

"Is that significant?" Nick scanned the clearing for any other signs of life.

"A typical number."

"Fourteen with my wife. Andrew, how can we stop her? She launched me off my feet like a feather in a hurricane."

"Me too. Now she's pursuing Louise and Jason with the ten remaining members of The Circle."

Nick moved off, still half-winded. "I hope you're up for a run."

Jason and Louise tore past the smart, isolated country home of Deer Lodge on a broad stony track skirting fields between Godmersham and Chilham. Louise lost her footing on the loose aggregate, skidding onto her side in a shower of chalk chips. Jason tugged her clear of the ground. He cast a glance back to the downs they'd descended. A bulging, corded, animalistic shape half-scampered down from the gate they'd crossed. Its lumbering movement sat somewhere between a gorilla and wild dog in appearance.

"My God, that's Alana," Jason gasped.

A cluster of shadowy figures dropped over the barrier behind her, their forms materialising and vanishing through the night in occasional, silvery aura's from above.

Jason and Louise ran on. They bore left to leave the track and sprint for a scattered line of trees. Beyond them, a thinner line snaked beside shimmering waters of The Great Stour.

"There's the river," Louise panted.

A fresh, inhuman wail echoed across the valley.

"Keep following it, Lou." Jason plunged through the tree line. "We've got to cross the river and main road before we hit the trail to Julliberrie Down."

Andrew and Nick reached the stony path at Deer Lodge as Alana and the cultists crossed to the scattered trees.

Andrew grunted. "We're gaining on them."

Nick drove himself onward. "Dear God, let those two make it across the river." He was too exhausted and preoccupied to weigh up their situation. A crushing emptiness at what he'd witnessed his wife become and his inability to intervene, compacted the contents of his stomach into a solid bung. In that moment, Nick's previous exclamation addressed to The Almighty morphed into a silent prayer. To whom it was addressed considering his lack of religion, he couldn't say. All Nick knew was that something outside himself must intervene, if they were to save the people they loved. *Please help them. Aid Louise and Jason. Deliver my wife from the onslaught of evil.*

The pair broke through the scattered trees and crossed to the river bank. Two slower members of The Circle lagged behind their comrades, now surging along the edges of the winding watercourse. Nick's fury broke loose. He tackled the nearest robed adversary, tugging the hood clear as they slowed. An angry woman's face greeted him with malevolent eyes. Nick spat in disgust, then hurled her clear of the bank. She hit the water with a splash, followed by a cartwheeling male compatriot Andrew sent in behind.

Ahead, Erin Parsons hesitated on a narrow footbridge to peer back along the bank. She pointed and hissed an order at another two of her followers. They remained behind while Erin and the others ran on.

Unperturbed, Andrew and Nick charged the bridge. No human would stand in their way.

Louise and Jason hurried across the A28 between a gap in speeding headlights. Both were losing the energy and drive to go on. An uphill dash to their destination yet remained, while sounds of pursuit drew ever nearer. Whatever infested Alana Preston, it infused her with limitless strength and endurance. Fear and desperation were all that enabled the teenagers to put one foot in front of another. Each step came slower and required more effort than the last. Ahead, up the track, a wooded crown of hills beckoned. So near yet so far.

Something shook the hedges behind them. Alana's twisted, hissing form bounded up the track; Erin Parsons hot on her heels. Bereft of the same spirit yet obeying their leader, five staggering robed figures brought up the rear.

Louise clasped the cross swinging about her neck in wild arcs. Tears of frustration and heartbreak stung her eyes. *It's all over if Alana catches me. What will happen to her once those things invade my soul again? Will the process kill her? Will it kill me?* She stumbled on, tripping in a swaying course like some punch-drunk prize-fighter.

Back down the hill where they'd crossed the road, two other forms grabbed hold of another duo of their pursuers. Louise's breath caught in her throat. *Andrew and Nick.*

Jason fell against an outstretched branch at the wayside for support. He whirled in time to see Alana and Erin surge forwards, closing the gap on their climb. He gasped for oxygen, winded and with little strength remaining. "We won't make the top like this, Lou. I've got to slow them down, somehow."

"No," Louise stopped in a heartbeat.

"Keep going." Jason waved her on. "I love you. Get to the long barrow. Don't look back."

Louise ran on, sniffing against unrestrained tears flowing down her cheeks.

Jason weighed up his options. *I can't stop Alana, but I*

can counter the author of our woes. He clambered up onto a wooded rise, then rummaged for a solid, fallen branch. As Alana stormed past at an inhuman velocity, he readied the makeshift weapon. It struck Erin Parsons square in the face, the power of his swing sending her into a semi-backflip. She hit the ground with a sickening crunch. The branch, rotten inside from laying amidst mulch covered ground, shattered on impact. Jason fell upon the would-be High Priestess, momentarily impervious to the impropriety of striking a woman. Erin reacted with the instinct of a coiled viper. Her legs wrapped around him in a scissor motion. Jason lost his balance and toppled sideways. Erin mounted him in a flash, insane glee reflected in a cold steel blade whipped from beneath her robe. She held it aloft above his head, ready for the final plunge.

Louise broke clear of the path as it levelled out. A long grassy mound stood before her; burial site of ages past. She staggered to its summit, then rotated to face across the valley. The desperate, lonely nature of her predicament sent a wobble through tired calf muscles. *What do I do now?*

Oblivious to Jason's interception of the cult leader, Alana burst into the hilltop clearing. Those altered, obsidian eyes locked onto the teenager who swayed from fear and exhaustion atop the long barrow. Alana's voice slurred into a deep, rumbling laugh of jubilation. "Now you're ours." She sprung into the air with sufficient energy to bridge the gap between them.

Fierce, tearing hands dug into Louise's shoulders and knocked her flat against the verdant, historic grave.

Indignant at her treatment, yet unable to resist this creature's physical presence, Louise did the only thing she could. Her lower right arm remained mobile enough to flick inward and take hold of the cross, once buried in the ground upon which she lay. Alana's fiery breath blasted her like brimstone fumes escaping a chasm into hell. Those dark, unfeeling eyes hovered two inches above her face. Louise closed her own. Every ounce of willpower in her spirit vibrated with an insistent intention: *You will not have me.*

Rising waves of determination in her body grew beyond a mere product of emotion. The mound shook as though from seismic shock. For several desperate seconds, the beings infesting Alana's body slackened their host's hands against Louise's restrained shoulders. A power rumbled beneath the grass. It pressed upward into Louise's spine, freezing her fingers to the cross she clutched in a whitening grip.

Louise's eyes flicked open, blazing like twin torches of pure ivory light. Her voice gave utterance to a melodious yet authoritative rebuke. "Leave this place and return no more."

Fear strained Alana's swollen ebony orbs. Her body shook with the uncoordinated spasms of someone undergoing an electric shock.

Mist encircled the barrow. It curled and morphed into a dozen large shapes: semi-translucent white horsemen clad in the battledress of ancient Britons. Each bore a blue and gold shield. They drew swords in unison with a ring like twelve resonating tuning forks. Their snorting, astral mounts pawed at the turf before them.

Jason staggered to the edge of the clearing. Behind him, battered and bruised, Andrew and Nick restrained a raging and weaponless Erin Parsons. Both men held one of her arms in a sturdy grip. No other members of her eclectic spiritual circle followed.

Light poured from the talisman in Louise's hand, almost turning night into day on that curious old hilltop. Alana gaped at the sky. A ray of white brilliance surged beneath the mound, causing each blade of grass to sparkle as though soaked in luminous dew. Its power blasted through Louise and Alana's bodies, shooting skyward from Alana's slack-jawed orifice. A vortex of tiny black fragments whirled aloft, carried high into oblivion. A deafening shriek - the veritable *'wailing and gnashing of teeth'* - accompanied their departure. Both girls shook until the holy fire extinguished and Alana slumped forward onto Louise with an unconscious gasp.

Erin shook herself free of her captors, who'd loosened their hold in stunned disbelief at the scene unfolding before them. One horseman lowered his blade to point in her direction. Luminous blue eyes pulsed beneath his helmet. Erin backed away. "No. No, stay away. What do you want from me?" Her once victorious confidence wobbled into a frantic scream. She ran northwest, stumbling downhill towards the watermill. The horsemen reared their whinnying mounts to give chase. Hooves thundered in a charging gallop, until a terrified, drawn out female wail ended with a splash at the millpond. No further disturbance arose, and the spectral cavalry vanished into the ether.

Andrew crossed himself as Jason and Nick scrabbled up the long barrow.

Alana stirred and moaned. She rubbed her pretty aquamarine eyes, then drew back in shock upon finding herself atop Louise. "Who? Where?"

Nick reached for her. "Easy. This is Louise; the girl I told you about."

Louise awoke. Her body jolted, then relaxed. "What happened?"

Jason knelt beside her as Nick helped Alana dismount the pinned teenager. "The fulfilment of those writings Andrew read to us. Are you okay?"

Louise sat up and threw her arms around him. "It worked?"

"Uh-Huh."

Nick shambled down from the mound, supporting his wife's wobbling pins. "How much do you remember?"

Alana touched her forehead. "Most of it is a blur. I awoke and saw Grant in the bedroom doorway. Everything feels like a dream after that; or rather, a nightmare. One where you're watching something awful but can't intervene."

Nick rubbed her loose limbs. "That makes more sense than you realise. This is Andrew Stallard."

"The vicar?"

"That's me," Andrew replied.

Alana's mouth dropped open. She stared across

Andrew's shoulder and pointed. "What on earth? Would you look at that?"

Andrew spun, then stepped back, face awash with wonder.

A line of figures, some astride horses, and others on foot ascended the path they'd all climbed to Julliberrie Down during the pursuit. Knights, monks, merchants, millers, peasant farmers and other ordinary folk of yore processed over the rise at a sedate pace to round a corner at the barrow.

Andrew clasped both hands before his face, muffling words of awe. "Bless my soul. The Canterbury Pilgrims of old, as though they'd stepped straight from the pages of Chaucer himself."

A man on horseback at the head of the line, tipped his cap at the flabbergasted observers as he rode by.

Alana dug fingernails into her husband's arm. "Nick. Look!"

Midway along the group of travellers on their holy quest, a ginger-haired boy around six years old stepped out of the throng.

Nick frowned at Andrew. "Is this another deception? I thought we'd dealt with all of that?"

Andrew's eyes glittered. "No deception. A gift, I think. An honorarium. A glimpse of something you both long to see."

Grant Preston ran, arms outstretched towards his parents. Alana knelt and swept him into her tearful embrace. Nick hugged his boy from the other side.

Louise and Jason descended the mound to stand beside Andrew. Two other faces in the crowd caught their attention. Barry Wallis strolled beside his father amidst the pilgrims. Both smiled and nodded at the teenage couple as they passed.

Louise lifted the cross from her neck. She handed it to the minister, face aghast at the spiritual procession. "I believe this is yours."

Andrew lowered it over his head. "Thank you. You summoned the faith to save us all, here in the place Nothhelm described."

Louise frowned and fidgeted. "I'm not a religious girl."

Andrew touched her beneath the chin. "Who said anything about religion? Faith is will and belief in something put into action."

Alana and Nick continued hugging Grant. No words came. It wasn't a time for speech. When Nick opened his eyes, he found himself embracing Alana alone. The pair twisted to gaze after the pilgrims. At the rear of the line, Grant turned his head and waved. The last stragglers rounded the corner, fading into nothing. They passed from sight to be replaced by the distant, floodlit cathedral on the horizon.

Nick and Alana rose.

Nick whispered to his wife as they cuddled. "It's over, now."

17

The Path

EXCERPTS FROM 'THE STOUR CHRONICLE' NEWSPAPER.

'A couple out for a stroll beside Bingley's Island in the Whitehall Meadows Nature Reserve, made a shocking discovery last week. They stumbled upon a woman's corpse snagged by a patch of river weeds at the popular spot near the outskirts of Canterbury. Authorities later identified the body as belonging to forty-three-year-old Erin Parsons, a self-described 'Light Worker' from Mystole near Chartham. It is believed she drifted some miles downriver from the point of entry. A post-mortem revealed Ms Parsons suffered a fatal heart-attack prior to falling in the water. Foul play is not suspected, but Kent Police would like to speak with anyone who has knowledge regarding her movements over the past week.'

'In other news, complaints were received from Old Wives Lees and Chilham concerning an incident of light pollution. The nighttime disturbance occurred atop the historic site of Julliberrie Down. A vertical beam, brighter than the lumen level of professional concert lighting, awoke residents of the

two villages. Initial investigations into an illegal rave were dropped, due to a lack of supporting evidence. No further incidents have been reported.'

* * *

"All packed?" Alana lingered in the bedroom doorway at Stour Cottage.

Nick finished zipping a case on the bed. "Almost. In a strange way, I'll miss this place. Not only the cottage; Chilham itself." He ran a slow hand down one of the timber-framed walls. "I must be mad, considering everything that's happened."

Alana took a step inside the room. "Oh, I don't know. Some good came of it. You got what you'd hoped for, if not in the way you'd expected."

Nick sighed, still staring at the wall. "I did, didn't I? Resolution, peace, closure. Call it what you will."

Alana crossed to the window, now fitted with a fresh pane of glass by their landlords. "Hey, it's Louise and Jason."

Nick joined her, seizing the opportunity for a sneaky cuddle.

The teenage couple strolled hand in hand from the bend where Mountain Street turned upward into School Hill.

Alana smiled. "Do you remember when we were their age? The day you went off to university, I thought I'd lost you." She coughed. "The same worry haunted me after you left Midhurst in January."

Nick kissed her face. "Do I remember when we were

their age? How could I forget? All those hormones in play and few safe, undisturbed places to indulge them."

Alana pinched his waist. "Trust you to make everything about sex." She sighed and melted into his arms. "Louise really loves him. I like her, Nick."

"Yeah. You look at some kids and think: *that will never last; it's an experiment*. I've a good feeling about those two."

"If they ever tie the knot, I hope they send us an invitation."

"With Andrew to conduct the ceremony?" Nick stroked her hair. "I can't get over how we all came together at the right time. Unique pieces of the same odd puzzle. Was it the hand of God or providence?"

Alana bit her lip. "Something bigger and older than any of us, either way. Thank goodness. Did you catch that article in the paper about light pollution? I meant to point it out."

"I did. When I bumped into Andrew yesterday, he said he'd found Larry arguing in the shop with May, the owner. Larry is an old boy who loves weird stories. He kept insisting the light pollution was supernatural."

Alana sniffed. "He was right."

"True, but May would have none of it. Much to Andrew's quiet amusement, if I read him right."

"We should say goodbye to Andrew."

"Of course. I wasn't planning to leave without."

Louise and Jason knocked on the cottage door.

Alana released Nick. "I'll let them in."

The teenagers waited in the dining room with Alana as Nick hauled his case through to the kitchen. "How are you two this morning?"

"We're great," Louise replied. "Still dumbstruck, but great. We came to see you off."

"Have you bid Andrew farewell?" Jason asked.

"We were talking about that when you arrived," Alana said.

Nick glanced at a wall clock. "Sunday service should be over by now. Why don't we take a stroll up to the church?"

Azure skies greeted the quartet during their ascent to the village square. They passed the primary school on their right, then further up the main castle gates on the opposite side. Chilham's black and white, timber-framed chocolate box splendour shone as though reborn. Kent's traditional rustic roof tiles almost glowed in the wash of life-giving, uplifting rays slanting down from the heavens.

A final handful of attendees exited St Mary's, passing beside The White Horse on their way home.

Nick, Alana, Louise and Jason let them through, before taking that pretty path next to the lovely old pub in the opposite direction.

Inside the church, Andrew collected errant hymn books several parishioners had left in their pews. This regular task formed part of the simple life rhythm he enjoyed each Sunday. An informal way to mark the closure of another week passing into history. He stacked the books on a table, until movement from the open, sunlit doorway caused him to look up.

"Good morning to the four of you." Andrew abandoned his task and crossed the aisle to greet them.

Nick couldn't disguise deep emotion on his ordinarily unreadable face today. "We've come to say goodbye, Andrew."

Andrew hesitated, as though allowing Nick's statement time to breathe or percolate. "Back to West Sussex then, is it?"

"Midhurst or bust," Nick nodded.

Andrew's eyes twinkled. "I would say it's going to feel quiet around here without you. But, given everything that transpired…"

"That may not be a bad thing?" Alana finished with an inquisitive grin.

Andrew laughed. "I suppose. What happened was going to happen, regardless of whether you came here. The outcome could have been devastating, under other circumstances."

Nick nudged his wife. "Alana and I commented how everything and everyone came together at the right moment. It's too bizarre for mere chance."

Andrew coughed. "*And we know that all things work together for good to those who love God, to those who are the called according to His purpose*. That's Romans 8:28, by the way."

Nick fidgeted. "Yourself excepted; I don't know that

we'd describe ourselves as *'those who love God.'* As far as I'm aware, none of us were believers prior to those events."

"And now?" Andrew raised an eyebrow.

"I can't speak for the rest, but I believe someone or something watched over us. That much is certain. What we experienced on Julliberrie Down blows my mind."

Andrew studied him with a gentle smile. "You'll find your own way from there. Whatever we believe about God or ourselves, I'd say the second half of that scripture rings true."

"Those who are the called according to His purpose?" Jason asked.

"Indeed. You, your lovely young girlfriend, Alana, Nick and this battered old historian cum man of the cloth," he thumped his own chest. "We were *'the called'* for one special moment in time. I have no doubt about it."

Nick snorted. "Battered and old? You're only fifteen years my senior." He smirked. "Still, I wouldn't square up to you in a fight." He feigned a jab in the air towards Andrew with a light fist.

Louise's eyes softened. "Will the disturbances on White Hill cease now, Andrew?"

Andrew rested against the back of a pew, arms folded. "Who can say? The Circle is broken. They're leaderless, opportunistic seekers, lacking the now banished spiritual principalities and powers who once seduced them. I imagine they'll fade back into their own, ordinary lives. A good thing for any future nocturnal visitors to King's Wood. It'll be a safer place." He sighed. "That the nefarious forces seeking a bride to possess at White Hill have been vanquished, appears without question. As to any ongoing ability of the hill to draw in spiritual energies? Nothhelm never reached the other side of his suppositions regarding the place, because The Vessel hadn't come forth. He remained unable to comment further, speculating over myths, legends, folktales and personal insights."

"Perhaps you'll continue his scholarly work?" Nick suggested.

Andrew thought for a moment. "You mean: someday a future historian or minister will blow dust from a long forgotten volume by Andrew Stallard; onetime vicar of St Mary's, Chilham?" He licked his lips. "I must confess, the idea of recording what happened for posterity appeals to my nature. Not that anyone - and especially not my superiors - should ever read it in my lifetime. It's too fantastic." He pushed away from the pew. "I'm glad you've all come. I was hoping to take a group photograph."

"Is photography another hobby?" Nick asked.

"I like to record and collate mundane features of daily life as a 21st Century vicar. That which seems ordinary to us, will be extraordinary to future generations with no frame of reference to our time. Taking pictures is part and parcel. If I ever tell our tale, a group image should accompany it."

"Where's your camera?" Alana asked.

"This way." Andrew walked out of the church.

The elegant facade of St Mary's vicarage provided a suitable backdrop for a posed shot. Andrew setup his camera on a tripod, then started its timer function.

"Do we say 'cheese,' or something else?" Nick stood in a casual pose, holding Alana close.

"How about 'Nothhelm?' That seems appropriate," Louise suggested.

Andrew hurried into the frame between both couples. "You remembered his name."

Louise cuddled into Jason's side and stared at the camera lens. "I'll never forget it again."

Camera countdown warning tones quickened. All five companions uttered the word, 'Nothhelm,' in unison, and the shutter fired.

Louise, Jason, Alana and Nick strolled back down School Hill to Stour Cottage. Andrew had said goodbye at the vicarage gate and promised to send them each a copy of the photograph.

Nick stopped at the side driveway entrance. "I'll load my car and drop the house keys off with Brian and Doreen."

"Say goodbye for me," Alana called after him. She clasped Louise's hands. "I can't thank you enough for what you did; either of you." She glanced between the pair. "But you most of all, Louise. I'm sorry for what happened. I might not be alive today if…"

Louise squeezed her fingers, sharing a knowing moment.

Alana's sombre tone brightened. "What's next for you two?"

Louise smiled. "Today? Back to Jason's house for Sunday lunch with his parents."

"And whoever else Dad has invited." Jason rolled his eyes.

"How's that?" Alana cocked her head.

"Ever since Lou and I became an item, he's brought business clients round to show her off to them. Sort of: *'This is my son's girlfriend. Hasn't he done well?'* All the while his chest swells with pride." Jason snorted. "You'd think I'd won the Nobel Peace Prize or something."

Louise poked him with a finger and giggled. "I hope I'm better than any old trophy."

Jason groaned. "Of course."

Alana laughed. "And so it starts. Welcome to the wonderful world of relationships, Jason."

Nick returned clutching a glass jar. He handed it to his wife. "Doreen gave me some homemade marmalade."

Alana examined its decorative label. "I'd best not drop this. I've nothing in for dinner once we get home. Shame she didn't have a spare loaf handy."

Nick kissed Louise on the cheek. "I needn't say this, but take care of the lad for me."

Louise flushed. "I will. I hope everything works out for you and Alana."

Alana exchanged glances with her husband. "We'll be fine, now."

Nick offered a hand to Jason, who struggled to

contain tears brimming over his ducts. They clamped arms around each other in a masculine embrace with much backslapping. Nick pulled away to stare at his face. "Never let anyone suggest you're less than a man. A fiercer, more courageous and loyal friend I've never known. People measure that in deeds when it counts, not years or assertiveness."

Jason blinked back his tears and nodded. "Thanks, Nick."

Nick released him and took Alana's hand. "We'd best be on our way."

Two minutes later, Louise and Jason paused at the bend. Nick's silver Honda CR-V followed by Alana's red Ford Fiesta, tooted horns, and then drove off along Hambrook Lane. The teenage couple waved. Hand in swaying hand they wended their way up the no through road of Mountain Street. Sparrows chirped among the hedgerows, while a cow lowed from a nearby field. Nature's unrehearsed bucolic symphony accompanied young love on its heady way towards whatever fresh adventures awaited.

* * *

"I never thought this would be easy, but it's the right thing to do." Alana lowered a plastic storage tray of Grant's toys into a large cardboard box beside their deceased son's bed.

Nick passed her a wide roll of brown packing tape.

"The toys aren't going anywhere; they'll be safe upstairs. I can fetch them from the attic whenever we feel the urge to connect with their memories."

Alana touched the room's blue, racing car wallpaper as though it were a priceless heirloom. "Redecorating in here will prove hardest of all. Do you remember how excited he was when you put this paper up?"

Nick lifted the football he and Grant had played with the morning of his death. "Once upon a time, I couldn't imagine touching this again without suffering a full-blown breakdown." He popped it inside the box next to the tray.

Alana pulled him close. "I'm glad you're home, Nick."

"Me too. Three whole weeks since we got back. Do you realise we haven't argued once?"

Alana grimaced. "That can't last." Her face softened. "But it won't be like before."

"No, it won't." Nick kissed her.

* * *

On the anniversary of Grant's death, the couple took another trip to the churchyard of St Mary Magdalene & St Denys, Midhurst. The mood differed from before. This time the bond between man and wife had never been stronger. They cleaned their son's headstone and laid fresh flowers before it.

Nick stood back to read the inscription aloud. "*Grant Preston - who departed this life, aged six. Suffer little children, and forbid them not, to come unto me: for of such is the kingdom of heaven."*

Alana lifted her gaze to the firmament, pockmarked with cotton wool clouds like a child's painting. "We know that's true first-hand, after Chilham." She switched to focus on her husband. "Though, I don't understand what it all meant."

Nick thought back to that night on Julliberrie Down. "I believe it was a visual metaphor to illustrate the soul's journey."

"In what way?" Alana looked deep into his eyes.

Nick stroked her face, his expression calm. "We never lose those we love, inside. Not even after they're gone. But it's important to still connect with and love those who remain. I forgot that, for a time." He pressed their foreheads together. "Love is the path, Alana. That's what they were trying to show us. Regardless of religious faith and irrespective of personal belief, we're all spiritual travellers on our way to Canterbury."

ABOUT THE AUTHOR

Devon De'Ath was born in the county of Kent, 'The Garden of England.' Raised a Roman Catholic in a small, ancient country market community famously documented as 'the most haunted TOWN in England,' he grew up in an atmosphere replete with spiritual, psychic, and supernatural energy. Hauntings were commonplace and you couldn't swing a cat without hitting three spectres, to the extent that he never needed question the validity of such manifestations. As to the explanations behind them?

At the age of twenty, his earnest search for spiritual truth led the young man to leave Catholicism and become heavily involved in Charismatic Evangelicalism. After serving as a part-time youth pastor while working in the corporate world, he eventually took voluntary redundancy to study at a Bible College in the USA. Missions in the Caribbean and sub-Saharan Africa followed, but a growing dissatisfaction with aspects of the theology and ministerial abuse by church leadership eventually caused him to break with organised religion and pursue a Post-Evangelical existence. One open to all manner of spiritual and human experiences his 'holy' life would never have allowed.

After church life, De'Ath served fifteen years with the police, lectured at colleges and universities, and acted as a consultant to public safety agencies both foreign and domestic.

A writer since he first learned the alphabet, Devon De'Ath has authored works in many genres under various names, from Children's literature to self-help books, through screenplays for video production and all manner of articles.

Manufactured by Amazon.ca
Acheson, AB